Arabesque is excited to p[...] **Winning Hearts** summer [...] featuring four heroines involved in the world of sports—both as athletes and in relationships with professional sports figures. It is a first for Arabesque, and we hope you enjoy these stories about strong, confident women who find romance and happiness by believing in themselves and trusting their hearts.

In Donna Hill's *Long Distance Lover,* world-class runner Kelly Maxwell finds herself at the center of a doping scandal *and* a love triangle. How she resolves her romantic dilemma could ultimately determine the outcome of her career.

When sexy pro quarterback Quentin Williams makes a pass at LA assistant DA Sydney Holloway, only to be rebuffed—it's more than just his ego that gets bruised. In *The Game of Love* by Doreen Rainey, fame and fortune can sometimes mean paying a high price for love.

The world of Major League Baseball is tough. But so is Roshawn Bradsher, a feisty divorced single mom with a teenage daughter, in Deborah Fletcher Mello's *Love in the Lineup.* So when young hotshot Latin baseball player Angel Rios—who was recruited by Roshawn's ex—suddenly takes an interest in her, it's only the first inning in this home-run romance.

The summer series ends with Gwynne Forster's *McNeil's Match.* After a bitter divorce, Lynne Thurston is faced with the prospect of not knowing what to do with the rest of her life, having given up a successful tennis career six years ago when she got married. But when she meets Sloan McNeil, all of that changes as he tries to convince her that she still has what it takes to compete—on and off the court.

With bestselling and award-winning authors **Donna Hill, Doreen Rainey, Deborah Fletcher Mello** and **Gwynne Forster** contributing to this series, we know you'll enjoy the passion and romance of these vibrant and compelling characters.

We welcome your comments and feedback, and invite you to send us an e-mail at www.kimanipress.com.

Enjoy,

Evette Porter
Editor, Arabesque/Kimani Press

DEBORAH FLETCHER MELLO

Love in the Lineup

ARABESQUE®

If you purchased this book without a cover you should be aware that this book is stolen property. It was reported as "unsold and destroyed" to the publisher, and neither the author nor the publisher has received any payment for this "stripped book."

ISBN-13: 978-1-58314-698-9
ISBN-10: 1-58314-698-9

LOVE IN THE LINEUP

Copyright © 2006 by Deborah Fletcher Mello

Love in the Lineup is a work of fiction, and is not intended to provide an exact representation of life, or any known persons in amateur or professional baseball. The author has taken creative license in development of the characters and plot of the story, although Major League Baseball teams, games and sites referenced may be real. Arabesque/Kimani Press develops contemporary works of romance fiction for entertainment purposes only.

All rights reserved. The reproduction, transmission or utilization of this work in whole or in part in any form by any electronic, mechanical or other means, now known or hereafter invented, including xerography, photocopying and recording, or in any information storage or retrieval system, is forbidden without written permission. For permission please contact Kimani Press, Editorial Office, 233 Broadway, New York, NY 10279 U.S.A.

All characters in this book have no existence outside the imagination of the author and have no relation whatsoever to anyone bearing the same name or names. They are not even distantly inspired by any individual known or unknown to the author, and all incidents are pure invention. Any resemblance to actual persons, living or dead, is entirely coincidental.

® and TM are trademarks. Trademarks indicated with ® are registered in the United States Patent and Trademark Office, the Canadian Trade Marks Office and/or other countries.

www.kimanipress.com

Printed in U.S.A.

For my very best friend, Angela Thomas,

May your own glorious love story
continue to bring you the joy and happiness
that you deserve.

ACKNOWLEDGMENTS

As always, I must first give thanks to a loving and powerful God for His many blessings. It is only because of Him that all of this has been possible.

Many thanks to my agent, Pattie Steele-Perkins, of the Steele-Perkins Literary Agency. This one had me stressed and you kept it real, and me sane. I can't begin to tell you how much I appreciate your efforts.

Thanks to my husband, Allan, and my son, Matthew, for understanding why the microwave had to work more than the oven did, and the laundry didn't get done until the last sock was taken out of the drawer.

And most especially, I want to thank each and every one of my fans who have inspired me to keep doing this, who keep me and my characters in check, and who continually campaign for the personalities that touched their hearts. I would surely not be here if it weren't for you and your magnanimous outpouring of support. Thank you, again and again. Your love has been overwhelming.

Chapter 1

Roshawn Bradsher couldn't help but think that slamming doors had become more the norm than not in their home since her daughter, Ming, had celebrated her seventeenth birthday. She stared up the short flight of stairs to the second floor as her daughter's bedroom door still vibrated from the violation.

"We're not done discussing this, Ming!" she yelled, her voice rising another octave to ensure the young woman heard her. "I have had just about enough of your nonsense!"

Roshawn winced as the door to the girl's adjacent bathroom slammed in response. Roshawn swore under her breath, her body quivering with anger. With her hands gripping the lean line of her thin hips, she glanced toward the grandfather clock against her dining room wall. It was half past three o'clock in the morning and Ming was just now coming home from hanging out with her friends. The child was out of control, Roshawn thought as she headed into the living room and reached for the portable telephone resting on the coffee table. She dialed quickly, the ten digits to her ex-husband permanently engraved in her memory.

When the man's answering machine picked up the call, Roshawn became even more irritated as she waited for the annoying beep to sound so that she could leave a message. "Chen, it's me. If you're there, pick up. It's about Ming." Roshawn waited. Getting no answer she continued. "Your daughter went out tonight and didn't bother to come home until just now. It's three o'clock in the morning, John Chen. I have had enough of this girl. I'm telling you right now, she might not live to see sunrise! You need to call me before I knock the pee water right out of her! Since you moved to Arizona she's just been impossible to deal with. Call me, Chen!"

Roshawn slammed the receiver down, her head waving from side to side. She was too through, she thought as she stood with her eyes closed and her chin hanging against her chest. Too through dealing with her daughter and the weekly antics that had begun to turn too many strands of her blue-black, shoulder-length bob a vibrant shade of silver gray. She had not a clue how one child could cause a parent as much angst as Ming had begun to cause her. Things had been better when Ming's father, John Chen, had lived two blocks away. Whenever Ming got out of hand all Roshawn had to do was drop her off on the man's doorstep to be disciplined. But last year Chen up and moved from his home in Seattle, Washington to Phoenix, Arizona. Roshawn had been certain such had been the brainchild of her ex-husband's new wife, a mousy brunette with a tiny face and big, brown eyes that constantly made her look like a deer caught in headlights. Roshawn skewed her face with displeasure. And now, with her father gone, Ming was hell-bent on testing every nerve in Roshawn's body.

Roshawn tossed her hands up in frustration as she screamed out her daughter's name. "Ming Louise Chen! Get your butt down here. Now!"

When she received no response, Roshawn hurled herself up the stairs and into her daughter's room. Ming sat cross-legged on the bed, her new iPod and headset against her ears. Her head bobbed in time to whatever music was playing on the sound system. Roshawn gestured for the girl to remove the appliance and in response Ming rolled her eyes, slowly dropping the instrument onto the bedspread.

"What?"

"Don't take that tone with me, young lady. You know what. Where were you?"

Ming sighed, tossing the length of her black hair down her back, the strands falling to the line of her paper-thin waist. "We were just hanging out. It's no big deal."

"No big deal? You stay out until sunrise and I'm not supposed to get upset about this?"

"Why can't you leave me alone? You're always on my back!" the girl shouted, moving to ease the earphones to the iPod back onto her head.

Ire raced across Roshawn's face as she snatched the iPod from Ming's hand and flung it out the door, listening as it slammed against the wall and rolled down the length of stairway. Both jumped when it landed with a hard bang on the hardwood floors below, the harshness of it a surprise to the two of them. Roshawn turned back to her daughter. "Ming, when I get on your back you're going to know it," she hissed, leaning down to stare her child in the eye.

Ming's eyes widened in surprise, words caught in the back of her throat. It had been a good while since she'd seen her mother this angry.

Roshawn continued, her tone harsh but controlled. "Now, I want you in that bed. When you get up in the morning don't turn on a thing. No television, no stereo, no nothing. In fact, don't even open your mouth to speak unless I give you permission to. Not one word. And don't even think about leaving this room. You're grounded until I feel like letting you out. Do you understand me?"

Ming nodded, slowly still eyeing her mother cautiously. Roshawn spun around on her heels and headed for the entrance. As she reached the door, Ming ventured to utter one last comment.

"I want to go live with Daddy."

Glancing over her shoulder, Roshawn gave her child one last glare, the final threads of her anger spinning from her eyes. Ming was the perfect melding of the best genetic material her parents had to offer. Roshawn marveled at just how beautiful her child was with her father's Asian eyes and thin lips, and her petite frame, dimpled cheeks, and mahogany complexion. From the moment she'd been born, Ming had been her mother's chocolate China doll. At that moment, with her jaw tightened, tears beginning to drip down her face, she looked like a China doll with a serious attitude problem. Heaving a deep sigh, Roshawn said nothing, the door slamming closed behind her the only response.

Roshawn dropped fully clothed onto her queen-size bed, curling up into a fetal position as she pulled a heavy quilt up over her body. The start of a migraine pressed angrily against the front of her skull, an initial rise of pain shooting current from one end of her body to the other. For a brief moment she thought about heading back downstairs to grab two Tylenol pain pills and a glass of water, but changed her mind. She had no desire to move herself from where she rested, comfort coming from the warmth of the hand-sewn quilt she'd inherited from her grandmother.

She couldn't begin to fathom why every aspect of her life was suddenly out of control. Ming's sudden defiance was just one of many aspects of Roshawn's existence that seemed to be spinning in a quandary. For the last year it seemed as if one thing after another had gone wrong. John Chen had started the vicious cycle and although common sense told her it really wasn't her ex-husband's fault it made her feel better to drop the blame smack-dab into the man's lap.

She and Chen had been divorced for over a decade, having severed their legal alliance just after Ming's fourth birthday. Their separation had been amicable, the divorce more of a technical notation than anything else. Despite having just divided up their assets and claiming joint custody of their only child, she and Chen had left the Seattle Justice Center hand-in-hand, stopping for a quick sandwich, and a lunch-time quickie immediately afterwards.

Her friends and family had never understood why they hadn't just stayed married. It had become an ongoing joke amongst their mutual acquaintances that they did more together divorced than they ever did while they'd been married. Only the two of them had known how different their home was once the doors were closed and the outside world couldn't see inside. John Chen had very traditional views about marriage, wanting a barefoot, and pregnant, stay-at-home wife. Roshawn's spirited personality had never really fit the job description and the formal union between them had become more battle than pleasure. Roshawn had insisted on the separation and the divorce, but the friendship that had initially drawn them to each other had remained intact. It hadn't hurt that their sexual relationship had been off the charts and neither had seen any reason to stop doing what obviously worked for them. Why fix what wasn't broke?

That was until Chen met and married the mousy flight attendant who'd become an instant thorn in Roshawn's side. Despite the relationship putting an end to their extracurricular activities, she had been happy for Chen because Chen had clearly been happy. Although both had dated other people off and on over the last ten years, Roshawn hadn't met one man worth giving a second thought to. But she had been glad that Chen had found a woman who managed to hold his attention longer than a minute. So maybe she had been a little bitter, and a touch jealous, she thought as she rolled from one side of the bed to the other. It had passed. Just as she and Ming had been adjusting to his new relationship, Chen announced that he'd taken a new job in a new city and was moving his new family away from them. And then all hell broke loose.

On the heels of Chen's departure, Roshawn's business partner decided he no longer had any interest in working the beauty salon the two had spent over eight years building into an emporium for their upscale clientele. His insistence on Roshawn buying out his interests, and his threat to sell it to a third party had just upped the mountain of debt Roshawn already owed, sending her credit score into the abyss. Struggling to keep the ends meeting now required sixteen-hour workdays with no benefits and Roshawn was beyond tired. Exhaustion had become her middle name and the collection agents her new best friends. Sending her clients out with the newest hairstyles no longer thrilled her, each new hairdo now a required commodity instead of the output of creative energy it had once been.

Roshawn heaved a deep sigh as she extended her legs and then pulled them back into her chest. She wished she could call one of her best friends. There was a time she could have awakened her friend Jeneva Tolliver at any hour of the night, but Jeneva now had a new husband and a toddler and was no longer available twenty-four seven.

She would call her friend Bridget Hinton, but she and Bridget hadn't spoken in weeks. Roshawn stalled the memory, letting it drop like dead weight from her mind. There was no point in upsetting herself any more than she already was, she thought, the fringes of depression beginning to take control.

Footsteps creaking against the wood floors suddenly pulled her from her reflections. She didn't bother to open her eyes knowing it was Ming who stood in the doorway of her bedroom, peering inside.

"What is it, Ming?" Roshawn asked, still not moving from where she lay. "I thought I told you not to leave that room."

The young woman came closer to the bed, her low sobs tainting the air. Roshawn lay listening, allowing the soft inhale and exhale of her daughter's tears to fill the four walls of the room. When the hurt of it became too much to bear, coating the pale blue walls a deep shade of unhappy, Roshawn wiped her own tears against the back of her hands. Sliding to the center of the bed, she lifted the edge of the blanket and beckoned toward the girl to crawl in beside her.

As Ming settled down against her mother, tears still falling, Roshawn wrapped her arms tightly around her daughter's shoulders. Roshawn said nothing, allowing Ming to calm herself, sobs eventually giving way to intermittent hiccups.

"Are you ready to talk to me?" Roshawn finally asked, the digital clock on the nightstand reading ten minutes past four o'clock.

There was a moment's pause before Ming responded. "I'm sorry, Mommy. I'm really sorry."

Roshawn sighed, air blowing in a quick gust past her full lips. "Girl, that seems to be your theme song lately. I was tired of Ruben Studdard singing it a year ago, so you know I'm tired of hearing it from you." Silence filled the space between them. When Roshawn spoke again there was no mistaking the fact she intended to get some straight answers from her child. "Where were you tonight, Ming?"

"Evergreen Cemetery."

Roshawn rose up on her elbows, tossing her daughter an incredulous look. "The cemetery?"

Ming nodded. "A group of us just hang out there sometimes. As long as we don't make a lot of noise no one bothers us."

Roshawn shook her head. "Were you drinking?"

The girl hesitated.

"Don't lie to me, Ming. I will find out the truth if you lie."

"I had one beer."

"Who were you with?"

"It was just me, Kara, Leslie, Stephanie and a few of the guys from the baseball team."

"What guys?"

"David, John Peters and that crew."

"Were you having sex tonight, Ming?" Roshawn asked, dread coating her words as she imagined what Ming and her boyfriend David could have been doing until three o'clock in the morning.

Ming didn't answer, shifting her body to lie flat on her back.

"Did you?" Roshawn persisted.

"In the cemetery? No, that's gross!" she exclaimed, her face twisted in disgust at the thought.

"Please, do not lie to me, Ming."

"I'm not, Mommy. I swear I didn't do anything. I told you I'm still a virgin. David and I just kissed, but that's all. Who'd want to do that in the cemetery anyway?"

Roshawn blew another loud sigh. It was moments like this that made her regret her decision to give up smoking. Even though she'd not had a cigarette since before Ming was born, she couldn't help but think that one would really calm her nerves right about now. This was clearly her mother's fault, Roshawn thought. That blasted curse old folks always put on you when you're young and enjoying life without thought to the repercussions. *One day you'll have a daughter just like—* the woman had crooned more times than anyone cared to count. *Just like you.*

Roshawn allowed the silence to regroup, the quiet doing battle with the patter of rain that had begun to fall outside her window. Ming rolled back toward her and apologized for the third time.

"Go to sleep, Ming. It's late and we're both tired. We'll finish this conversation tomorrow." She brushed her fingers down her daughter's cheek. "And you're still grounded, Ming."

The girl nodded her understanding, her eyes fluttering open and then closed, sleep beginning to consume her. Minutes later Roshawn was snoring soundly by her child's side.

Chapter 2

John Chen sat at a corner table in McArthur's Restaurant, the eclectic dining room of the Dallas Crowne Plaza Hotel. He sat with his cell phone propped between his ear and his shoulder as he searched his briefcase for a specific folder from the dozens that filled the embossed leather cavity. As he finally found the file he was looking for, tossing it onto the table before him, the line connected to the telephone in his home office. He pulled the cell phone back into his hand and quickly pushed the two digits that would allow him to retrieve any messages. There were two of them.

The first was from his wife, reminding him that she would be filling in for one of the other stewardesses who was out ill, she wouldn't be home until the weekend, and that she loved and missed him very much. The other was from his ex-wife. As he listened, his jaw suddenly tightened, his eyes widening with annoyance. He depressed the off button and glanced down to the watch on his wrist. He had barely a minute before his next interview. Definitely not enough time to deal with Roshawn and their daughter, and with the time difference, it was still too early to be calling Seattle. He had no doubts that if they'd been up doing battle at three in the morning, then both were more than likely still sleeping soundly.

He heaved a deep sigh. His baby girl was becoming difficult and he knew that it was long overdue to put the brakes on her behavior. Roshawn had sounded on the verge of hysteria and he knew things weren't well between mother and daughter. He sensed it was well past time for him to intercede before the duo waged all-out war against each other.

John's attention was distracted by the rush of noise at the restaurant entrance. The chatter had risen tenfold and some of the restaurant's patrons had risen from their seats to stare where a small crowd had begun to gather. John leaned back in his seat, a wry grin pulling at the lines of his mouth as he observed the man who was trying to politely extricate himself from the throng of fans who'd formed a wall around him.

An expensive gray suit fit his athletic frame nicely, the ensemble complemented by a crisp white shirt and red print tie. His leather shoes were polished to a high shine and he sported a fresh haircut, his oversize Afro cropped neatly. John took note of the women who clamored for the man's attention, one or two brazenly stroking his arm and back muscles. Glancing from the spectacle before him and down to the press photo that lay on top of the folder he'd extracted earlier, John noted that the man was exceptionally photogenic, his warm coloration complemented by brilliant white teeth and eyes that gleamed with energy. It would make for some great promotional opportunities, John reasoned. And from the man's polite, yet firm manner with his fans it was clear he knew how to handle himself well. That would surely be an advantage if he were hired, John found himself thinking.

John glanced down to his watch a second time, noting that his interview was right on time. As the man finally shook off the last admirer, making his way to John's side, he was just a tad flustered and maybe a touch embarrassed by all the attention. He extended his hand politely.

"Mr. Chen, it's a pleasure to see you again," he said, his thick Spanish accent spilling past his full lips.

John rose from his seat as he shook hands. "Angel, it's good to see you again as well. And, please, call me John."

Angel Rios nodded as he dropped into the cushioned seat across from John. John gestured toward a waitress who appeared almost instantly at their side.

"Are you gentlemen ready to order?" the young woman asked, looking from one to the other, her smile widening to a full grin as her gaze rested on Angel.

John shook his head. "Not just yet, but if I can please have a second cup of coffee. How about you, Angel?"

"An orange juice, please."

The young lady paused. "Right away, Mr. Rios. And I just want to say that was a great exhibition game you played last night."

Angel smiled politely. "Thank you."

The woman continued to gush compliments. "I can't believe you hit two grand slams. It was awesome!" she exclaimed, her auburn ponytail swaying against the back of her head. "Do you think I could have your autograph?"

Angel reached for a napkin, pulled a pen from his pocket,

then looked up at the girl with a shy smile. "What's your name?"

"Lisa."

With a quick sweep of his pen, he wrote a quick message wishing Lisa well, then signed his name and passed it to her. "I really appreciate your support, Lisa. And I don't want to be rude, but if I don't finish this meeting my baseball career may be over before it gets started good. I'm sure you understand," he said, his fingers squeezing hers as he pressed the signed napkin into her palm.

Lisa nodded. "Of course. I'll bring your drinks right back and be right out of your way." She turned to give John just a hint of the smile she'd given Angel, then spun around on her heels toward the rear of the restaurant and the kitchen to get their beverages.

"I'm glad you could make it," John said, directing his attention back to Angel.

"I appreciate you coming all the way to Dallas to see me. Were you able to catch any of the game last night?"

John nodded. "I did. Very impressive."

Angel smiled shyly. "Thank you."

"So," John said, "how do you feel about playing in the major leagues?"

Angel's head bobbed up and down against his thick neck. "That's my dream. I've wanted that since I was a boy. And I would love to play for the Titans. I have much respect for Coach Daves and Coach Henry."

John leaned his elbows against the table, his chin resting against the backs of his hands. "Daves and Henry spoke very highly of you. They liked what they saw back in Phoenix. Henry can't wait to get you swinging a bat for him."

Angel grinned widely.

"Tell me, Angel, are you married? Any children?"

Both men paused as Lisa glided up to the table and placed a large orange juice down in front of Angel. From a carafe in her other hand she refilled John's cup with hot coffee.

"Are you two ready to order?" she asked looking from one to the other.

John nodded. "Just a toasted bagel with cream cheese for me, please, and a bowl of your fresh fruit salad."

The woman nodded then smiled down at Angel.

"I'll take toast, a side of bacon, a side of sausage, hash browns and three eggs over easy."

"Coming right up," Lisa said.

The two men waited until she had disappeared back through the kitchen's swinging door. Then Angel responded to the question that John had posed before they'd been interrupted. "I'm still single. I don't have time for a wife and children right now. All I want to do is play ball."

"Do you have any family here?'

"Just my father. The rest of my family is back in the Dominican Republic. But my father, he is here in the States with me. He's my biggest fan and whatever I do, he's always a part of it."

John nodded. "As you well know, the Titans believe in family and we fully support each other through everything." A pained expression suddenly crossed John's face.

Angel stared at him curiously. "Is something wrong?"

John shrugged. "I was just thinking about my daughter. She's seventeen and is giving her mother some trouble lately. As soon as you and I are finished I need to go be Daddy and get her in check." He smiled widely, fanning his hand dismissively in the air before him. "Children are something else. But I'm sure you'll get to find out yourself one day."

Angel nodded, smiling back. "You sound like my father," he said, chuckling lightly.

As their breakfast was served, the duo continued chatting easily together. There was only one other interruption, an eight-year-old with his father wanting an autograph. John watched quietly as Angel interacted with the youngster, the two conversing like best friends. The boy's father was thrilled, shaking Angel's hand before excusing them both and returning to their own table. John leaned back in his seat and stared at the man for a quick moment. Angel Rios had a confident air about him, but he was also reserved, almost shy, John thought. Clearly, the fans adored him, which was a positive attribute for any player that might represent their team. And he seemed to handle himself well under pressure. John nodded slowly. There was something about Angel that he liked and he could sense that the man would be a good fit for the organization.

"Angel, if you're interested in moving to Arizona and playing for the Titans, we'd like to make you an offer. I can fax the specifics and preliminary contract over to your agent this afternoon."

Angel beamed as he shook John's hand. "Thank you," Angel exclaimed excitedly. "I'm very interested. All I want to do is play is major league baseball!"

It was Ming who reached for the ringing telephone, pushing past her mother's digital clock, a box of tissues and a copy of Zane's newest book to find the receiver. Roshawn lay on the opposite side of the bed, still held hostage by her need for another hour of sleep.

"Hello?"

Roshawn yawned, fighting to wake herself up, her eyes still as heavy as the rest of her body.

"Hi, Daddy!"

Rolling onto her back, Roshawn stretched her body lengthwise, her back arching ever so slightly off the padded mattress.

"But I didn't do anything!" Ming whined into the receiver.

Roshawn reached out for the telephone. "Let me speak to your father," she commanded, pulling the instrument from the girl's hand.

John Chen's deep baritone voice echoed into her ear. "What happened?" the man asked after giving her a quick greeting.

"She stayed out past her curfew. She was hanging out in some cemetery with her friends and didn't come home until after three this morning. I swear, Chen, if it's not one thing it's another with this girl."

"Is she doing drugs?"

"I don't think so. She was drinking though. Said she only had one beer and there were boys there."

Roshawn could feel her ex-husband bristle at the thought of his baby girl lost in the arms of some hormone raging male.

"Put Ming back on the telephone," the man commanded, his tone stern.

Roshawn passed the receiver back to her daughter. As the girl pleaded her case to her father, Roshawn lifted her body from the bed and headed into the adjoining bathroom. Catching a quick glimpse of herself in the ornate mirror, Roshawn jumped. Her reflection was frightening, she thought as she leaned closer to the glass, her fingers brushing the residue of sleep from beneath her eyes. She shook her head. She had fallen to sleep without wrapping a satin scarf around the length of her hair and the length of baby-fine silk now stood all over her head, reminiscent of a bad Medusa impersonation. Roshawn shuddered.

Back in her bedroom, Ming was still pleading over the telephone. Roshawn chuckled ever so slightly, shaking her head as her daughter pulled out the big guns, sobbing her apology in her father's native Cantonese, the words rolling effortlessly off her tongue. When she'd been born Chen had insisted their baby girl learn the language, as well as English, wanting her to be able to communicate with her paternal grandparents on those rare occasions when one or the other made the trip between Hong Kong and the United States. She could see from the expression on her daughter's face that she was losing her battle, unable to manipulate her father who couldn't see her batting her dark eyelashes for sympathy. The dialogue ended when Ming muttered what sounded like "woe eye knee" into the receiver, closing the conversation with "I love you" in Cantonese. She passed the phone back to her mother.

Roshawn dropped to the edge of the bed, pulling the appliance to her ear. "Yes, Chen?"

"I told her she's grounded for the next two weeks. She's only allowed to go to school and come home. Nothing else."

Roshawn shook her head. "You were kind. I had planned on locking her away until she turned twenty-one."

"How are you doing?"

"I'm still standing if that's what you want to know."

The man nodded into the receiver. "You sound tired."

"Well, it's not like I got much sleep last night," she answered facetiously.

"No, you sound like there's more bothering you than just Ming."

Roshawn shrugged. "It'll get better. Some problems with the salon, nothing major."

"I'm going to put a check into the mail. Something to help you out a little."

"I already got your support check this month."

"This is for you, not Ming."

"I don't need your money, Chen. I'm doing just fine."

"It's a gift. Stop being so stubborn and just say thank-you."

"So, how's that woman?" Roshawn asked, not wanting to argue as she changed the subject.

"My wife is well. Thank you for asking."

"Tell her we said hello."

Chen smiled. "So, are you seeing anyone special? Ming said you had dinner with a new friend last week."

Roshawn cut her eye toward her daughter who lay sprawled across the bed watching cartoons on Roshawn's small television, the volume barely audible. "It was just dinner, nothing else."

"You need someone in your life, Roshawn. You know how you get when you go without pleasure too long," the man said softly, just a hint of seductive overtone in his voice.

Roshawn rolled her eyes. "That's not any of your business anymore, John Chen. You have a wife now."

He laughed softly into the receiver. Silence wafted over the telephone line as Roshawn refused to acknowledge the innuendo in his tone. Whether he knew her that well or not, she had no intentions of giving him the pleasure of thinking he was anywhere close to being right.

She changed the subject for a second time. "Where are you, anyway?"

He chuckled. "Dallas. I'm on the tail end of my recruiting tour. Just picked up a new player as a matter of fact. Maybe I'll get to introduce you one day. He's single, too."

Roshawn moved the receiver from one ear to the other. "Thanks, but I'm not interested. If you like him, then I'm sure he's not my type."

"Why would you say that?"

"Because he's probably like you—demanding, overbearing, chauvinistic…should I go on?"

John shook his head as he laughed again. "I thought those were the traits you loved most about me," he said.

Roshawn laughed with him, finally breaking into a deep smile. "You were wrong," she chimed, beginning to feel better.

They both fell into the warmth of the moment, silence once again filtering over the telephone line between them.

"Did Ming say anything to you about wanting to come live with me?" John finally asked, the moment turning serious.

Roshawn eyed the girl for a second time. "I know I'm not in the mood to discuss that right now, Chen," she said, her tone emphatic.

"Give it some thought, Roshawn. We can talk about it when I come to visit next month. It's not a decision we need to make right now."

"I don't remember saying it was even an option."

The man laughed again. "Call me if you need me. Anytime. Okay?"

"Thanks. I'll talk to you later. Bye, Chen."

"Goodbye, Roshawn. *Wo ai ni.*"

Hanging up the telephone Roshawn smiled. John Chen had proven early in their relationship that he was her friend first, before all else, and despite the history between them he would always be a friend. Lifting her body off the bed, she headed back into the bathroom, stopping to grab a clean change of underclothes from the top drawer of her bureau.

As she eased her way toward the shower, closing the bathroom door behind her, she snapped at Ming one last time. "Cut that television off and go get dressed. Grounded means no TV,

Ming. No TV, no telephone, no radio, no computer, no nothing.
Now, move it. We're going to go see your aunt Jeneva."

The trip to San Juan Island had taken longer than Roshawn
would have liked and as she and Ming pulled into the driveway of her best friend's new home, her only child had suffi-
ciently worked her last nerve. Roshawn glared in the girl's
direction, annoyed by the defiant body language as she
leaned against the car door. Ming's arms were crossed against
her chest as a full pout pulled at her thin lips. Her eyes were
narrowed, almost closed, hostility gracing her warm mocha
complexion. It had taken over an hour of nagging and
eventual screaming before they'd been able to leave their own
house, Ming intent on staying home alone, not wanting to
waste her Sunday afternoon with her mother.

As the duo approached the entrance of the exquisite wa-
terfront property, Roshawn could feel the fine threads of a
new headache begin to weave a pattern across her brow.
Ming leaned on the doorbell, peering through the sidelights
as she heard the patter of excited feet skipping on the other
side. Mecan Tolliver pulled open the large, double door with
one hand and reached down to scoop his baby daughter up
into his arms with the other.

"Come on in!" the large black man chimed, leaning to kiss
both their cheeks hello.

"Hi, Mac," Roshawn said, stepping into the large foyer
behind her daughter.

"Hi, Uncle Mac! Can I hold Alexa?"

Mecan grinned as he play-tossed the giggling two-year-
old into the teenager's outstretched arms. Alexa Tolliver
squealed with delight as she wrapped her arms around Ming's
neck. Roshawn grinned widely, her eyes widening in awe at

how much the little girl had grown since they'd last seen her. The spitting image of her father, there could be no denial of the child's paternity with her deep, blue-black complexion and wide eyes. Her chubby legs kicked excitedly as she spun around to stare at Roshawn, offering the woman a quick kiss when Roshawn asked where her sugar was.

Ming made a sour face, pulling the child out of Roshawn's reach. "That's yuck," she chimed as Alexa broke out into a fit of giggles.

Roshawn shook her head. "I'll trade you," she said, looking toward Mecan before rolling her eyes skyward.

Mecan laughed, wrapping his arms around her shoulders. "Oh, it's not all that bad."

"That's what you think. Where's my girl?"

The man gestured toward the back of the house. "In the kitchen with Bridget."

Roshawn stopped short, a look of pain skewing her face. She dropped her head into her hands, the appendage waving in frustration from side to side.

"Why didn't Jeneva tell me Bridget was going to be here?"

"Because she knew you wouldn't come. Now, go on inside. They're waiting for you."

Roshawn sighed.

Easing past her, Mecan chuckled lightly. "Come on, kiddo," he said to Ming, gesturing for her to follow him. "Alexa and I were watching *Dora the Explorer* on the big screen in the den."

Roshawn watched as Ming followed behind him, chatting a mile a minute to the little girl in her arms. She stood frozen in place as she struggled to contain the wave of anxiety that had suddenly consumed her. Taking long, deep breaths she fought to focus on anything except the confrontation she expected was waiting for her in the other room. Jeneva calling her name interrupted the moment.

Jeneva Tolliver rushed forward, wiping her hands against a cotton dishrag. "Roshawn, what are you doing? Come on in here," she said leaning to give her friend a quick hug and kiss.

"Hi. Mac said Bridget was with you and I didn't know…" She paused, her eyes skating about anxiously.

"You two need to get past this. You've been friends too long for this to keep on. Come talk to her," Jeneva said, pulling the woman's arm as she led her down the hall.

The end of the corridor opened to an expansive gourmet kitchen with a large center island and top-of-the-line, stainless-steel appliances. Corian countertops and custom cherry cabinets set the tone for a comfortable gathering space and the aroma of something decadent and sinful billowed from the double oven out into the room.

Roshawn smiled. "I smell chocolate."

Bridget Hinton sat at the counter, her lean legs swinging from side to side from her perch on the high bar stool. "Jeneva made our favorite, Death By Chocolate cake," the woman said, nodding in Roshawn's direction.

The two stood staring at each other until Jeneva pushed her friend farther into the room. Roshawn chuckled ever so softly, then strode to Bridget's side, extending her arms in an offering of peace. Bridget eyed her friend with a hint of reservation before slipping from her seat to give the woman a hug.

"If it wasn't for the fact that you have my blue silk suit in your closet, I would still be mad at you. "

Roshawn gave the woman another quick squeeze. "I love you, too," she whispered, tears spilling out of her eyes.

Bridget stepped back, gripping her by the shoulders. "Hey, what's all this?" she asked, concern shadowing her expression. "We've had worse fights before, Roshawn. Why are you crying?"

Roshawn's tears had transformed into a low sob. Bridget and Jeneva stood eyeing her, both disturbed by her obvious distress. The moment was circumvented by Ming and Alexa bursting into the room. Roshawn quickly wiped her eyes, then slipped out the French doors onto the screened porch. She stood staring out toward the Olympic Mountains and the large body of oceanic water that lay between it and the shoreline just a few lengthy feet away. Inside the living space, Ming greeted each of her godmothers, her youthful exuberance only outdone by the toddler's boisterous energy.

Wrapping her arms tightly around her body, Roshawn struggled to regain her composure. What in the world was going on with her? she thought. Why was she suddenly feeling so completely out of control? As she stood reflecting on all her issues: her daughter, the salon, their finances, her ex-husband and her best friends, she couldn't help but reflect back on the disagreement between her and Bridget. The bad behavior that had put a blemish on their lifelong friendship, weighed heavy against her heart.

It had been New Year's Day, a brisk afternoon much like the day's weather. A cold breeze had been blowing rapid gusts across the bay and like today they had all been gathered in the Tolliver home in celebration. The women had been in the kitchen giggling, and gossiping, and carrying on like they always did when the three of them were together. Bridget had been giddy. Giddy over the anticipated arrival of Darwin Tolliver who was returning from a trip to Louisiana to spend the week with his twin brother and sister-in-law. Bridget's giddiness had been infectious.

"Look at her, Jeneva!" Roshawn had exclaimed, laughter pulling at her lips.

Jeneva shook the length of her natural hairstyle from side to side. "I don't know why she's acting like that. When he gets here Bridget won't say ten words to the man."

The two women laughed.

"I'll speak to him," Bridget said, flipping her hand at the two of them.

"I think she's afraid of him," Roshawn said, her eyebrows raised.

"Do you think?" Jeneva answered as if Bridget wasn't sitting there beside them.

Roshawn nodded, a wide grin spreading across her face. "Either that or she's got some deep-seated attachment to that vibrator of hers!"

"Look, heifer," Bridget gushed, spinning around in her seat to give her friend a playful push.

The trio fell out laughing, then the moment turned reflective as Bridget fell back against her seat, leaning her head on Roshawn's shoulder.

"Darwin's not interested in me. I've been batting my eyelashes at the man for a year now and he treats me like he treats Jeneva."

"That's your problem. You need to be batting something other than your eyelashes at him."

Jeneva rolled her eyes, jumping to her feet to check a pot of chili simmering on the stove. "Lord, please don't get her started."

Roshawn chuckled. "You need to take some of my advice.

I know these things. Look at what I did for Jeneva and Mecan," she said, her head waving up and down against her shoulders.

Jeneva tossed her a look that said, *You wish you'd done something for Jeneva and Mecan.*

Bridget swatted at her again. "What things? The only man you have ever given any serious time to is your ex-husband. What's to know about that?"

Returning to the seat opposite the two women, Jeneva shrugged. "Roshawn may actually have something, Bridget. How many divorced women have slept with their ex-husbands as long as Roshawn did? If the man hadn't gone and gotten married on her, she'd still be enjoying it!"

Roshawn snapped a finger. "That's right. Girlfriend had it like that. And you wish you did too!" she said smugly.

Bridget shook her head. "What I wish is that I had more of your confidence, Roshawn. Even when we were in school, you were like a man magnet. They all loved you."

"That's only because she was putting out," Jeneva said matter-of-factly.

"Says you!" Roshawn exclaimed.

"Said half the football team," Jeneva said with a laugh.

Bridget nodded. "And the basketball team, the band and the chess club."

Roshawn gestured toward the two of them with her pinkie finger.

"What's that for?" Jeneva asked.

"You little people who aren't worth the full thing," she said as she extended her middle finger in another crude gesture. "And, I never did anyone in the chess club."

Again, laughter rang through the room.

Bridget heaved a deep sigh.

"I'll tell you what," Roshawn said, leaning forward in her seat. "When Darwin gets here I'll show you how to work a man the right way."

Bridget winced. "Don't you dare, Roshawn. Leave the man alone."

Jeneva nodded. "She means leave *her* man alone."

Roshawn grinned.

"I mean it, Roshawn. Please don't flirt with Darwin. I really like him and if you start acting up and he goes for it I'll never forgive you. I don't want a man who's wanted you first."

Roshawn sat back in her seat and shrugged. "Whatever. You just need to stop hating on a sister. I'm only trying to help you out."

Roshawn closed her eyes, shaking her head as she willed away the memory. The evening had ended badly, Bridget driving off in haste, disappointment spilling from her eyes. Roshawn hadn't been thinking anything of it when she and Darwin had stood like co-conspirators in the corner of Jeneva's family room, bodies hovering too close together for anyone's comfort. An off-color joke had incited the moment, the two laughing coyly as if they shared a personal secret. For Roshawn, flirting was a natural state of affairs when in the company of a good-looking man, and Darwin Tolliver was one good-looking, black man. Tall, like his brother, with the same blue-black complexion, brilliant white smile, and dimpled cheeks, Darwin had a majestic presence, and what woman could resist a man who carried himself like the emperor of his own private kingdom?

Bridget had not been at all amused, her feelings clearly hurt after she had asked her friend to not muddy the playing field where she wanted to navigate her own game plays. As innocent as the moment was, Roshawn had overstepped the boundary of their friendship by not abiding by the one request that had been made of her. Bridget hadn't spoken to her since. Not until today. Both had been too stubborn to reach out and make the first gestures of apology and forgiveness. Like always, Jeneva had been the catalyst to bring them back to the folds of their lifelong friendship.

The doors behind her slid open and Bridget stepped out onto the porch by her side. Her friend wrapped her arms around Roshawn's shoulders and hugged her tightly. Roshawn fought the urge to start crying all over again.

"I'm sorry, Bridget. I really didn't—"

"Stop," Bridget interrupted. "I know you didn't mean anything by it. I was just jealous. You always get along so easily with men and I can't seem to stop shaking when I'm around a man I like. I deal with dozens of men every day of the week but let me be around a man I'm interested in and I can't function." She paused. "But did you have to kiss him, Roshawn?"

Roshawn winced. "It wasn't like that, Bridget. I swear it wasn't. We'd just been talking and joking and teasing and when I kissed him I wasn't trying to come on to him. It was just a light peck, Bridget. Nothing else. The man didn't even give it a second thought and neither did I." Contrition punctuated the lines of her expression as her gaze met Bridget's.

Bridget heaved a deep sigh before continuing. "I know you wouldn't do that to me on purpose," she said, her voice coming in a loud whisper. "I was just frustrated, that's all, and you two had looked so comfortable together. I guess I just jumped to the wrong conclusions."

"You raced out so fast you didn't give me a chance to explain. Darwin is a friend, but he's really interested in you,

Bridget. I think he's just a bit nervous, too. I caught him looking at you a few times. Boyfriend was all glassy-eyed and drooling. He was a mess and I was giving him a hard time about it."

Bridget giggled softly. "Well, he's back in Shreveport so we can forget anything happening there."

The two stood quietly together for a brief moment before Bridget spoke again.

"What's wrong, Roshawn? We know you, and you aren't yourself. You haven't been yourself for a long while now. What's going on?"

Roshawn shrugged. "I don't know. I just can't seem to pull myself together. Ming's out of control. My business is falling apart. My life just feels so empty all of a sudden. I'm not having fun anymore. And, I'm just tired, Bridget. Just too tired for words."

"Sounds like depression to me. That's not good, Roshawn. We've got to fix that."

Roshawn shrugged, allowing her body to lean heavy against her friend's shoulder. Jeneva eased out onto the porch to join them, catching Bridget's last comment. She joined in the embrace, hugging both of the women warmly.

"I think you need a change, Roshawn," Jeneva said softly. "I think you need to step out of your comfort zone and stir things up a bit. The Roshawn we know would never let herself stagnate and you've been stagnating."

Roshawn's gaze met Jeneva's, the statement wrapping itself firmly around her attention. She mulled it slowly, allowing it to seep deep into the recesses of her thoughts. The truth of it was suddenly disconcerting and it was in that instant Roshawn knew she needed to do something, but what that something was, she didn't have a clue about.

She nodded her head slowly, an easy smile rising to her lips. "You both may be right," she said. "I know I need to get myself together. Maybe a change would do that for me."

Jeneva gave her a smile back. "Why don't we discuss it over chocolate cake?"

"You've got ice cream, too, right?" Bridget asked.

"Edy's Toffee Bar Crunch."

Roshawn giggled. "Now, that's what I'm talking about!"

Chapter 3

Back inside the house the three women settled themselves around the kitchen counter as Jeneva sliced oven-warm cake into deep bowls, topping each off with huge scoops of melting ice cream. Roshawn hummed as she savored the first bite, allowing the warmth of the fudge dessert to meld with the creamy texture of caramel, and the delicate crunch of toffee candy.

Bridget nodded her agreement. "If this doesn't cure what ails you, girlfriend, I don't know what will."

Roshawn grinned. "It may not cure it but it is sure making it feel a whole lot better."

Jeneva laughed as she sat down and took her own bite. "So, what's up with our godchild? She said you were mad at her. And, you threw her iPod down the stairs and broke it? Didn't that thing cost like three hundred dollars?"

Roshawn laid her spoon down in the bowl and shook her

head. "Ming didn't come home until three o'clock this morning. She was hanging out in the cemetery with that boyfriend of hers and his gang, drinking and doing God only knows what else."

Jeneva groaned. Bridget chuckled.

"That's not funny, Bridget," Roshawn said.

"Yes, it is. She's just like you, Roshawn. Remember that night in the Recovery Room?" the woman asked, referring to the defunct dance club that should have been off-limits to them when they'd been Ming's age.

Jeneva burst out laughing, drawing her hand to her mouth. "I'd forgotten all about that."

Roshawn tossed a quick glance over her shoulder toward the doorway. "I can't believe you remembered that," she whispered.

"How long did we stand in that bathroom?" Bridget asked, looking from one to the other. "Hours," she said, answering for them. "And, your father knew we were there. That man sat at that bar until closing time trying to catch us."

The three of them giggled.

"We got in so much trouble," Jeneva exclaimed, catching her breath. "My folks wouldn't let me out of the house for almost a month."

Bridget nodded. "Same here. The sun was coming up by the time we made it home and we couldn't tell them where we'd been. Can you imagine what they would have done to us if they had known we'd crawled under the tables to go hide in the bathroom when we saw Mr. Douglas come in?"

The trio shook their heads at the thought.

Bridget continued. "We stayed in trouble hanging out with you, Roshawn. You were always getting us into some kind of mess."

"I was not!" Roshawn exclaimed, a wide smile filling her face.

Jeneva's head bobbed up and down. "Yes, you were. How about the time we met those guys at the club and one of them convinced you to go to that private party?"

Bridget burst out laughing, clasping her hand over her mouth to silence the outburst. "It was a private party all right. You made us go with you and we followed them to the dredges of town. All they wanted was to get us into that nasty-looking apartment for some one-on-one fun."

"I cannot believe we were that naive," Jeneva chimed. "Anything could have happened to us."

"And don't forget," Bridget added. "We only got out of that mess when Roshawn ran over that fool's foot."

The three women laughed hysterically at the memory, reflecting back on the young man who had jumped up and down in the middle of the darkened street drawing attention to the fact that his right foot had just been mauled by the Chevy Impala's front tire.

Roshawn wiped the damp tears from her face. "But we had a lot of fun. You have to admit, we always had a great time."

Her two friends nodded, wiping at their own faces.

Jeneva reached to stroke Roshawn's forearm with the flat of her palm. "That's what you need to get back, Roshawn. That feeling you have when you're enjoying life."

Bridget dropped her hand beside Jeneva's. "You've forgotten how much fun you have when you're *living* life in that special way only you know how to do, Roshawn. And, that's what Ming's doing now, living her life and enjoying every minute of it. Just like you taught her."

Jeneva laughed again. "Baby girl got it honest, Roshawn. That apple didn't fall far from your tree."

Roshawn heaved a deep sigh. "I'm doomed," she said jokingly. "I've got to put the brakes on her. I don't want her married with a baby before she's twenty. I know I got lucky. Chen was a good man and he's been a great father. But there is no guarantee that Ming will be as blessed. And, if that boy she's hot after now is any indication, then I surely don't want her following in my footsteps."

The three women pulled their spoons into their mouths at the same time, silenced by the decadent pleasure dancing against their tongues.

"How's Quincy doing, Jeneva?" Roshawn asked, changing the subject.

Jeneva smiled. "My son is doing very well. Next month they start him on life skills training. Mac is going to open a checking account for him and they're going to teach him how to manage his money, make a budget, grocery shop and do those kinds of things."

As if hearing his name, Mecan Tolliver entered the room. "What's this? Dessert before dinner?" he asked, leaning to steal a taste of his wife's cake.

"Comfort food. We needed it," the woman answered as he reached to kiss the chocolate from her lips.

Mecan gave her a light squeeze as he winked at her two friends. "You two need to talk to Jeneva. Quincy's going to get an apartment next year with two other boys who are also challenged. She's not happy about it."

"He needs to come home, Mac, so we can help him. He's not ready to be living on his own."

"Yes, he is. He'll still be going to school at Hewitt and learning how to function independently. It's necessary and he's excited about it."

Jeneva rolled her eyes.

Roshawn grinned. "I thought you broke him of that bad habit?" she asked teasingly.

Jeneva shrugged. "I keep trying but telling me what he thinks is best for our son seems to be his mission in life."

Bridget nodded. "That's why you keep him around."

Jeneva grinned. "That and the tricks he can do in that car of his," she giggled.

Mac blushed, the rush of color heating his dark complexion. "You women are vicious," he stammered, visibly embarrassed. "I'm going back to play with the girls." He leaned to kiss his wife one last time before easing his way out of the room, laughter following behind him.

The ride home was not nearly as tense. Ming was animated, actually speaking to her mother without her usual annoyed tone of voice. As they stood at the rail of the ferry looking out to the waves of water that rolled beneath the vessel, Roshawn thought back to her conversation with her friends.

"Mom, did you hear me?" Ming asked, her high-pitched voice pulling her back to the moment.

Roshawn took a deep breath, filling her lungs with the cool evening air before turning toward her daughter. "I'm sorry, Ming. What did you say?"

"I wanted to know what you thought about me…maybe…going to live with Daddy?"

The two studied each other momentarily before Roshawn answered. "Why do you think you should go live with your father, Ming?"

The young woman shrugged, unable to voice the answer that was shining in the bright depths of her eyes. Roshawn nodded her understanding, instinctively knowing that it wasn't about Ming being unhappy in her current situation, but about the girl needing something there with her dad that she couldn't find with Roshawn.

"What about school? Do you really want to change schools your senior year?"

"Except for senior English, I already have enough credits to graduate. I can take that this summer and fulfill all my requirements. I wouldn't need to stay for senior year."

"And what would you do next year?"

"Start college early. I can live with Daddy and go to the University of Phoenix."

Roshawn nodded. "Won't you miss your friends?"

"We can always talk on the telephone, and I'll make new friends."

"What about that boy David?"

Ming shrugged. "What about him?"

Roshawn laughed, turning her gaze back to the landscape. She allowed a moment of silence to fill her, closing her eyes as she focused on the slow inhale and exhale of her breathing. "I would miss you, baby girl," she said finally. "I don't know that I'm ready to miss you yet."

Ming looped her arm through her mother's arm, leaning her head against Roshawn's shoulder. Side by side they stood watching the crest of oceanic waves rolling behind the ferry. In the distance, the last remnants of the day's sun slipped down into the water, pulling a blanket of darkness down behind it. The two stood quiet as the ferry pulled into the harbor, and the other passengers prepared to disembark.

Hand-in-hand they headed toward their car and the other side of the ferry. Roshawn squeezed her child's hand. "We'll call your father when we get home. We don't know yet if he even wants your rude behind."

Ming giggled. "My daddy loves me. Rude and all!"

Chapter 4

Roshawn stood in the doorway of her home as John Chen pulled his rental car into the driveway. As he stepped out of the black Lincoln Navigator, Ming jumped into his arms, her excitement over her father's arrival spilling out into the late morning air. Roshawn smiled, stifling her own excitement as the man gestured in her direction and winked his eye in greeting.

Roshawn took a deep breath and held it, willing away the sudden rush of tingle that filled her stomach whenever she saw John Chen after a brief absence. The man had been giving her butterflies since she'd been fifteen years old and a sophomore in high school. He'd been a senior, and on the verge of graduation, when the two had fallen head over heels in love. Even after their divorce and his remarriage, it was a comfortable feeling that Roshawn had no desire to relinquish hold of, knowing where to put it when it was most inappropriate.

John Chen was the embodiment of male perfection, dispelling every stereotype that portrayed Asian men as weak and effeminate. With his tall, muscular build, wavy, black hair, almond-shaped eyes, and butter-toned complexion, he was breathtakingly handsome. The white dress shirt opened at the collar, black leather shoes, and gray slacks that fit his body to perfection only added to the attraction. His gaze met hers and he smiled broadly, a row of pearl-white teeth shimmering in the sunlight.

Roshawn stood with her arms folded across her chest, leaning against the door frame as the two strode in her direction. Chen greeted her warmly, leaning to kiss her cheek as he said hello.

"Hello, Roshawn."

"Hi, Chen. How was your flight?"

"It was good. We made great time."

"You didn't bring the wife?"

He smiled. "She worked the flight I came in on but she had to fly right back to Phoenix. She sends you her regards."

Roshawn smiled. "Send her mine back," she said as she turned to go back into the house, Ming and her father following close on her heels.

"My stuff is all packed up, Daddy," Ming said, dropping down to the living room sofa.

Her father nodded. "I can see," he said, his eyes roaming over the packed boxes that littered the living room floor. "Are you moving the whole house, Ming?"

The girl giggled. "That's what Mommy said. I just have a lot of stuff."

The man raised his eyebrows questioningly, his gaze moving toward Roshawn.

She shrugged her shoulders. "Stuff. What do I know?"

Ming jumped from her seat. "I need to go meet Leslie and Tara. We're having lunch together before I leave. Mommy said it would be okay."

Chen looked down to the gold wristwatch on his arm. "We have plenty of time. Our flight doesn't leave until tonight. We need to be back at the airport by seven o'clock."

"That doesn't mean you can be gone all afternoon, Ming. I want you back here by two. You need to help your father get this mess into his car so we can get it over to the shipping company."

"Yeah, yeah, yeah," the girl chimed as she headed for the door.

Chen called her back, his tone firm. "How do you speak to your mother?" he asked, his finger waving in her face. He spoke in Cantonese, the stern reprimand wafting through the room.

Ming apologized. "I'm sorry, Mommy. I'll be back by one-thirty."

Roshawn nodded as Ming kissed her cheek, and then her father's, heading out the front door.

"You let her get away with too much," Chen said, following Roshawn into the kitchen.

"And, you won't let her get away with anything," Roshawn responded. "We're a good balance."

She pulled a bottle of cream soda, his favorite, from the refrigerator, popped the top and passed it to him. She watched as he pulled the cold fluid to his lips, leaning his head back to allow the chilling flow to fill his mouth and trickle down his throat. A perverse thought suddenly crossed her mind and she turned quickly, kneeling back into the refrigerator to hide the rush of color that had crossed her face. *It's been too long,* Roshawn thought, remembering what the man's lips had felt like against her own mouth. Chen called her name and she released the wealth of breath that she had been holding.

"What?"

"You didn't answer. I was asking why you won't come to Arizona for a few weeks to help Ming get settled? She's going to have a lot to adjust to and you being close will make it easier for everyone."

Roshawn spun back around to face him. "What will Ming have to adjust to? She and your wife seem to get along fine and she's always happy wherever you are."

The man licked his thin lips and leaned over the countertop toward her. Roshawn cut her eyes toward the kitchen cabinets behind his head, heat wafting through her body.

"The season is about to get started so I'll be busy with work. Allison is still flying a regular schedule so she won't be home much. I want Ming to get settled, but I think her being alone during the summer before school starts could be an issue."

"So I should just pack up and come to Arizona? What about my business? I have responsibilities here."

The man nodded. "Our child is your first responsibility," he stated matter-of-factly.

"Ming is seventeen years old. She doesn't need me there to babysit her, John."

"No, she doesn't. But she needs you there to give her guidance. She needs both of us and this past year hasn't been easy. I think that's why you've been having a difficult time."

"You moved away, John. That was your choice. Now you're saying I should let you and Ming dictate what I need to do?"

The man came to his feet, strolling to her side. "I'm saying that with you close, Ming will better be able to make this transition. Once she's comfortable you can come back here or go whereever you want. But right now, I want you to think about Ming and what she needs."

Roshawn took a step back from him, the nearness of his body to hers causing her temperature to rise.

"And where am I supposed to live? What about work?"

"You can stay in my old house. It's vacant. It's furnished. All you would need to do is pack a suitcase and come. And if you want to work, I can give you a job. I need a temp for the summer. My assistant will be leaving on maternity leave in a few weeks. You can fill in until she gets back. It pays extremely well, plus you'll have the freedom to set your own schedule. Ming will live with me, visit you when she misses you, and by the time school starts both of you will be ready to let go."

Roshawn met the man's intense gaze, understanding washing over her. "Is it that obvious?"

He smiled, stepping back toward her as he pulled her hand into his. He leaned to kiss the back of her fingers, his palm brushing against her cheek.

"I just know you that well. And I knew when you started calling me John that you were having a hard time with this."

"Your name is John."

"But you have always called me Chen. Since the day we met you've never called me anything else, unless something was causing you much unhappiness. The day you asked me for a divorce was the only other time you've called me John more than once in a conversation."

The two stared at each other for a long minute. Chen gave her hand a quick squeeze. "Let's get out of here. We can go get some lunch or something," he said, his voice a loud whisper. "Before we do something we'll both regret."

Roshawn laughed. "You're so full of yourself, Chen. I don't sleep with married men."

"And I don't plan on being unfaithful to my wife, but being alone with you always causes me to lose my mind. It's been that way since high school."

Roshawn laughed again as she reached for her purse and headed for the door, putting much distance between them. "It's that sweet tooth of yours. You never could resist a sweet piece of chocolate!"

Bridget answered her phone line on the second ring.

"Hold on, Bridget," Roshawn said, depressing the button labeled Flash to connect the third line. "Jeneva? You there?"

"Yeah."

"Bridget?"

"Right here. Hi, Jay."

"Hi. What's up?"

"Chen wants me to move to Arizona," Roshawn said, the rush of words coming in one quick breath.

"What about his wife?" Jeneva asked.

"That's just freaky!" Bridget said.

"Not to be with him, fool! To make things easier for Ming, and me. I would have my own place and it would only be temporary. Just for the summer."

There was a brief moment of silence and Roshawn could hear her two friends contemplating her statement.

"So," Bridget finally said, "when do you leave, 'cause we have to have a going-away party."

"Definitely," Jeneva added, "at least one more girl's night."

"So you two think I should go?"

"Personally, I think you should have gotten on the airplane with them tonight."

"I agree," Jeneva said. "I think it's exactly the change you need. And, you'll love Arizona. Mac and I had a great time when we were there."

"Did you get to see anything besides the backseat of your car?" Bridget asked with a wry laugh.

The other two women laughed with her.

"Leave it alone, Bridget," Jeneva said with a chuckle. "Just leave it alone."

"What about the salon, my house, my bills?" Roshawn exclaimed. "I can't do this!"

"Jay, there's something wrong. Roshawn has been possessed. Some alien just said she 'can't.'"

"Don't be cute, Bridget. I'm serious."

"So are we."

"So, what do I do?"

"Go. Personally, I think you need to sell the salon. It's an albatross around your neck right now. You're headed for bankruptcy if you don't let it go. That so-called ex-partner of yours mortgaged you and that building to the hilt. As your attorney, I would have to advise you to sell it and pay off your debts. As for your house, I'll take care of your house. You just pack your bags and call us once or twice a week to say hello. But go, Roshawn. Go have some fun. Go make yourself happy. Go. You're not getting any younger so you need to do it now while you still can."

Jeneva nodded into the receiver. "It's not like you have plants or a dog, Roshawn, that you need to worry about. Lock the house up and we'll keep an eye on it until you get back in the fall."

"What about my Shrek and Donkey Chia Pets? Shrek is still green."

Jeneva laughed. "Really?"

"Well, half of it is."

Bridget giggled. "I'll water the Chia thing, Roshawn."

Roshawn smiled. "I love you guys."

"Don't get sentimental on me, heifer! Jeneva does enough of that for the both of us."

Chapter 5

The flight from Seattle to Phoenix was cathartic. Roshawn felt as if her spirit was slowly being revived as the Boeing 737 jet ascended sky-high, settling its massive wings against a cushion of clouds. From her first-class seat, courtesy of John Chen, she stared out the window, calm washing over her as she contemplated how quickly, with a little help from her friends, everything had fallen into place.

Less than two months ago, she had been in a constant state of angst, depression raining control over her day-to-day activities. Since that time, her only child appeared to be back on track thanks to her ex-husband. Her pariah of an ex-partner had secured a buyer for the business and it had changed hands with minimal negotiation and her quick signature across a stack of legal documents drawn up by Bridget. Each of her creditors had received financial compensation to deem her accounts paid in full and the weight of the world was suddenly off her shoulders. Roshawn smiled, lifting a requi-site glass of airline champagne to her lips.

There was little she would miss about Seattle. Without her daughter, her home was just a shell of brick and mortar. Without her salon, her career was tentatively extinguished, and without the threat of legal bankruptcy looming over her head, she was free to rebuild, to start anew, and make more of this second chance than she had made with the first. Small blessings were one thing, but big ones like that just seemed to fill her whole heart and soul with warmth and light.

As the plane glided toward its final destination, Roshawn thought about Jeneva and Bridget. Those two she would miss. She would miss their antics and the laughter that seemed to flow like water between them. She would miss those necessary words of wisdom that came when she least wanted them. She would miss the day-to-day comforts of their friendship. She shook her head. She would miss everything about the bond between them and she could only imagine what the toll would have on her tele-phone bill once she was settled in her new home.

Running a palm across the top of her head, Roshawn smiled. Gone were the shoulder-length, overprocessed tresses that had been her crowning glory since the last time she'd been bored with her look. Over the years her hair had under-gone a host of transformations. She'd worn it curly, straight, dreadlocked, permed, dyed and fried. It had gone from long to short, blond to black, and everything else in between. But the decision to shed all her hair had not been an easy one. She had contemplated the idea for weeks before finally taking her scissors and then the lowest blade on her electric clippers to task. The style was now shorter than short, barely a blush of fuzz to cover her skull. It spoke volumes about her confi-dence, a style few women could even imagine pulling off and with her oversized earrings and picture-perfect makeup, Roshawn was supermodel stunning.

Roshawn pulled her designer handbag into her lap, the Chanel tote an appealing accessory to her two-piece Tahari suit. Searching the interior, she pulled a small envelope from the confines of a side pocket. Inside, Chen had placed two keys, one for an automobile and the other for the front door of her temporary home. Directions, neatly printed on a white index card, accompanied the keys. Although Chen had offered to pick her up from the airport, she had wanted to do this on her own. She would find her way, enjoying every step of the travel as she rediscovered a sense of independence that didn't involve being a divorced, single mother.

With some assistance from a very young skycap with a head of blond curls and a rash of acne, Roshawn maneuvered her luggage through Phoenix's Sky Harbor airport to the terminal two parking garage. Just as Chen had noted, the vehicle that belonged to the key in her hand was waiting for her in the second row, fifteenth parking spot. Roshawn stood staring at the Chrysler 300C. The color was linen-gold with eighteen-inch, chrome-clad, aluminum wheels. The sleek design reminded her of an exotic Bentley and Roshawn couldn't help but be impressed. Chen had promised her a comfortable stay for the next sixteen weeks, but this was beyond her expectations.

"Nice ride," the young man stated, a wad of chewing gum twisting in his mouth.

Roshawn grinned as she opened the trunk. "Thanks."

After her luggage was settled, Roshawn passed the guy a folded dollar bill. His expression showed he expected more, but the one Roshawn returned clearly let him know more wasn't coming. Chen may well have had it like that with his six-figure salary, but she still didn't have a clue what he intended to pay her to answer telephones in his office for a few hours a day. She intended to stick close to her budget until cash in hand allowed her to do differently. Nodding his thanks, the young man rushed behind a couple struggling with their own luggage, anxiously offering them the services of his cart.

Following the detailed directions from the airport, Roshawn pulled onto Interstate 51 north toward Paradise Valley, and her ex-husband's former residence. "It's way bigger than our house, Mommy, but not nearly as big as Daddy and Allison's," the girl had said. Ming had told her about the house, her excitement spilling over the telephone lines. She and her father had taken the time to give the home a quick cleaning before stocking it with essentials they thought Roshawn would want when she first arrived.

Roshawn was suddenly overcome with emotion and she pulled her car off to the shoulder, shifting it into park. Stepping from the vehicle she spun about to take in the view. Arizona was spectacular. The day was warm, the mild morning temperatures having risen to a comfortable seventy degrees. The sky was clear, the bright blue color shimmering behind the rays of sunlight that beamed down upon her. On either side of the roadway the landscape stretched out, dry desert with a bush of cacti growing here and there. And then the mountains rose magnanimously, stretching skyward as if trying to touch the edge of the galaxy. It was breathtaking.

As Roshawn sat back in the car and pulled back onto the road, she knew that she would surely not miss the Seattle rains if the balance of her summer days were anything like this one. A few quick turns onto Tatum Boulevard and then Las Brisas, put Roshawn just minutes from her new home.

The left turn to Paradise Canyon Road felt as if would take a lifetime to reach and when she did, pulling into the circular drive that led to the split-level Mediterranean-style architecture, she knew instantly that the decision to come to Arizona had been the best suggestion John Chen could have ever had.

The house had been Chen's first home in Arizona the year he'd been hired as a scouting director for the Titans, Arizona's expansion league baseball team. It had been the residence he had commuted back and forth to before finally moving away from Seattle for good. During those first two years, on his numerous flights around the States, and back and forth between Phoenix and Washington, he'd met the woman who'd become his second wife. It had been this second wife who'd determined they needed bigger and better to keep up with Chen's rising status within the Titans' organization. Chen's first home had been abandoned, serving as a guesthouse for his parents' infrequent visits, and periodic rental property for vacationing friends.

Roshawn could only shake her head as she let herself into the home, securing the front door behind her. As she moved from room to room she wasn't sure if she should laugh, cry, or do both. Maybe divorcing John Chen hadn't been such a good idea after all, she mused, laughing out loud at the notion. She couldn't wait to call Bridget and Jeneva to tell them how her little Asian sweetheart had come up in the world.

The four-thousand-square-foot home boasted three luxurious bedrooms, and a fully appointed kitchen with stainless-steel appliances. There was a large game room equipped with a pool table, poker table and Ping-Pong table. Just steps away she entered the media center with a large-screen television set and movie theater chairs that would never have fit into the living room of her Seattle home. A second family room and formal dining area completed one end of the house.

Stepping out onto the patio, Roshawn inhaled the tranquility of the midday air. The home backed up to the mountains and the view was breathtaking. Chen would later explain that the view spanned the southern reach of Mummy Mountain, west across Paradise Valley to Squaw Peak, and north all the way to Desert Mountain. The long, shaded patio was decorated with teak furniture, a built-in gas grill, fire pit and its own cocktail area. The one-acre lot was highlighted by a six-foot-deep swimming pool that lay hidden beneath a specially designed pool cover.

Back inside, Roshawn found her way to the master suite, the Asian accents reminiscent of her own home decor. The connecting bathroom was painted a pale shade of green with the whole back wall a massive glass window that looked outside to the mountains and greenery. What privacy that was offered came from the abundance of plant life that filled the space from floor to ceiling. The doorbell ringing and then Chen and Ming's voices pushing through the entrance drew her back to the front of the house.

"Hi, Mom!" Ming cheered, throwing herself into her mother's arms to be hugged. "When did you get here?" The girl stepped back quickly. "You cut all your hair off!" she exclaimed loudly.

Roshawn smiled. "I just arrived a second ago, and yes, I cut my hair." Roshawn reached to give Chen an embrace, lightly grazing his cheek with her lips.

Ming walked a slow circle around her mother. "I love it. I absolutely love it. You look great!"

Chen nodded. "Takes me back to high school," he said, his wide gaze sending her a quiet message.

Behind them, Allison Chen stood nervously, not quite sure where she fit in the moment. The expression across the woman's face was suddenly anxious. Noticing her for the first time, Roshawn smiled warmly.

"Hello, Allison. How are you?"

Allison nodded, waving ever so slightly. "Hi, Roshawn. How was your flight?"

"Very nice. I looked for you."

Allison smiled, her large brown eyes gleaming widely. "I'm off for the next few days. I don't fly out again until next week."

"Aren't you lucky."

The woman nodded again, pushing a strand of hair behind her ear, a blush of color rising to her alabaster cheeks. "Ming's been so excited about you coming. She couldn't wait to get here."

"Daddy let me drive his Mercedes."

Roshawn cut her eye in Chen's direction. "Isn't Daddy brave."

The adults laughed as Ming tossed her mother one of her infamous teenaged looks.

"Allison thought you might like to take a tour of the city," Chen said. "If you're not too tired we thought we'd take you to lunch and show you around."

"Unless you had other plans?" Allison said, moving to take Chen's arm, the possessive gesture duly noted. Her gaze met Roshawn's and there was just a brief moment when Roshawn sensed that Allison might actually prefer her to have other plans.

Roshawn grinned, mischief gleaming in her eyes. "Not at all, Allison," she said. "I'd love to take the tour."

She reached for her keys and her pocketbook, then

grabbed Allison's hand as she pulled the woman toward the front door. "This will be great," Roshawn exclaimed. "This will give you and me a chance to get to know each other better. We can sit in the backseat and whisper about Chen. He hates that. Ming, give your father the car keys. You're riding shotgun."

"Mom!"

"Don't *mom* me. Your father may trust your driving, but I don't. I taught you, remember?"

Laughing, Chen shook his head. Roshawn was back, and in true form. The state of Arizona didn't have a clue what was about to hit them.

Chapter 6

Angel Rios surveyed the short walk from his car to the players' entrance at Tucson Electric Park. Spring training was well underway and the team was just days away from their first exhibition game against the Chicago White Sox. Today's practice was starting at precisely nine-thirty and even at this early morning hour, the man was amazed by the female fans who stood anxiously in wait hoping to catch a player's eye. Despite the cool morning temperature, there was no shortage of cleavage and thigh pining at the entrance for attention.

He twisted his face in annoyance, having no tolerance for the abrasive overtures that were sure to greet his arrival. He was one of a handful of players who was unmarried, a prime target for the female sex in want of an eligible catch to sink their teeth into. Angel hated the distractions, having no understanding of women who thought aggressively pursuing him and his teammates during the season would actually get them anywhere other than to a hotel room for a one-time cootchie call. Although Angel couldn't speak for anyone but himself, his want of any woman when he was focused on the season and improving his game barely amounted to the requisite time required to bring him to orgasm.

He heaved a deep sigh as he reached into the backseat of his new Cadillac SRX for his gym bag, his hand palming the soft leather seats of the luxury SUV as he felt for the nylon bag. As he moved to step out of the vehicle, the cell phone in the pocket of his Nike tracksuit chimed against his leg. Pulling the handset from his pocket, he pulled it to his ear, depressing the button to answer the call.

"Hello?"

His father's deep voice greeted him on the other end. *"Angel, donde esta, hijo?"* Israel Rios asked.

"Hola, Papí! I'm at the ball field. What's the matter?"

"Nada. Tú necesita—"

Angel interrupted the man. "In English, *Papí.* You need to practice your English."

The man balked but complied, albeit reluctantly. "I speak English just fine," Israel chastised, his heavy accent punctuating each word. "You need to go see Mr. Chen when you are finished. His office, they call here for you to stop by there to see him."

Angel nodded into the receiver as he closed the car door and activated the alarm. "I will. Thank you. Everything else is okay with you?"

"Sí. The pretty lady is here cleaning the hotel room. I am going down to breakfast shortly."

"I don't know what time I'll be back, *Papí.*"

"I will be well. Go do good. Have some fun. Don't worry about this old man."

Angel smiled. "Goodbye, *Papí.*"

"*Adiós, hijo.*"

His name being called pulled at his attention as a young woman no more than eighteen years of age screamed at the top of her lungs. The high-pitched squeal cut through him like fingernails grinding against a chalkboard. Angel forced a smile on his face and waved, making his way toward the entrance.

As he pushed his way through the requests for autographs and pictures, his smile never left his chiseled face. But the minute the door closed securely behind him, shielding him from the unwanted attention, it was game face on. Angel Rios was ready to play.

John Chen reviewed the latest statistical information on Angel Rios that Roshawn had prepared for him earlier that morning. He was impressed with his ex-wife's skills, the woman having settled comfortably in her new position. The front office personnel had taken an instant liking to her zealous demeanor and she was making new friends left and right.

Although her outgoing personality was a quality he most admired about her, it had been the one point of consternation during their marriage. Everyone loved Roshawn; and men, in particular, were drawn to her vivaciousness. The fact that she was an exotic, gorgeous black beauty hadn't helped the situation. Her friendliness had been a sore point for him and the cause of many an argument between them. The sound of her laughter pulled at his attention for a quick moment and Chen struggled to focus back on the paperwork before him, flipping slowly through the detailed spreadsheets.

Twenty-eight years old, Angel Rios was the Titans' newest and most promising acquisition. A native of the Dominican

Republic, Angel's baseball career had moved smoothly up the minor league ranks, making him an ideal candidate for the major leagues. What Angel was most noted for was his skills with a baseball bat. Boasting a .380 batting average, the man was any ball team's dream come true. His skills at center field were also on par, making him a winning advantage for the Titans' growing organization. What Chen admired most about Rios was his focus and dedication to a sport the man loved with his heart and soul.

Roshawn standing in his doorway of his office stole his attention for a second time. "Chen, there's a Nina Tracy here to see you."

Chen nodded. "She's Patrick Tracy's wife."

Roshawn smiled. "The third baseman, right?"

"That's him."

Roshawn gestured to the thin brunette to go on inside, returning to her desk and the long list of telephone calls still awaiting her attention. Barely ten minutes had passed before Nina was making her exit, closing Chen's office door securely behind her.

"Men get right on my nerves," Nina said, her hands falling to her full hips.

Roshawn laughed. "They can't help it. Not enough blood flow to their brains."

The two women laughed knowingly.

"So, how can I help? I take it Chen didn't have a clue?"

The woman smiled, the gesture filling her round face. She pulled her fingers through the length of her brown hair, twirling a stray strand around her finger. "Every year the Titan wives host the Back to School Clothing Drive where we collect socks and underwear for kids in need. I'm this year's committee chair and we want John to be our acting

MC. This year's fund-raiser is scheduled for the fourth and fifth of June. We're holding it on the plaza just before the game against Los Angeles. He promised us last year that he'd do it, now he's not sure he can fit it into his schedule."

Roshawn shook her head, reaching for the large, leather-bound appointment book on her desk. She flipped through the pages quickly, scanned the month of June, then nodded her head. "It's not a problem. He'll be there."

Nina grinned, still pulling and twisting the hair atop her head. "I like how you work. I'm sorry, I didn't catch your name."

"Roshawn. Roshawn Bradsher."

The woman extended her hand. "It's nice to meet you, Roshawn."

"It's nice meeting you. I'm sure we'll see each other again soon."

"Let's plan on it," Nina responded as she headed for the door. "Thanks for your help, Roshawn."

Roshawn watched as the woman headed out the door and down the hall. She wanted to laugh out loud but didn't. She didn't have a clue who had cut that woman's head, but the attempted style should have been a hairdresser's crash course in what not to do to a client. The abrupt styling did absolutely nothing to flatter the woman's pretty face and it had taken everything in Roshawn not to say so.

A quick glance to her wristwatch pulled her from her seat. She met Chen as he was heading in her direction. "Chen, I need to take a quick break. I have to go to the ladies' room."

The man nodded. "No problem. I'm waiting for Angel Rios, then I'm out of here. You can actually take off whenever you're ready. I won't need you any more today."

"Thanks, boss," Roshawn chimed with a quick wink. "I'll see you tomorrow then."

"Have a good night, Roshawn."

"I will. Kiss my baby girl for me and tell her to call me before she goes to bed, please."

"I will."

Clearing off her desk, Roshawn grabbed her tote bag and headed out the door. As she reached the elevator, she paused for a quick minute, then backtracked to the restrooms. As she entered the tastefully decorated lounge, Nina Tracy stood at the well-lit mirror, pulling a wide-toothed comb through the length of her locks.

Roshawn shook her head, unable to resist. "Girl, who in the world cut your hair?"

Nina winced. "Some new place in the mall. I swear if I could sue that damn salon I would. I can't believe what that fool did to my head."

Roshawn laughed. "Here," she said, gesturing toward a plush chair in the center of the room. "Sit down."

Nina looked at her curiously. "Why? What are you going to do?"

"I'm going to fix that mess," Roshawn said, searching in her bag for her favorite pair of scissors.

Nina's expression turned anxious. "You're not serious, are you?"

"As a heart attack. I don't travel with these things for nothing," she grinned, opening and closing the shears in midair. "Trust me. You don't have anything to lose."

Nina paused for a quick minute, then finally conceded, dropping into the chair. "At this point, it sure can't hurt."

Roshawn laughed. "No. This is as bad as it gets."

Fifteen minutes later, Nina was laughing excitedly, tossing her head from side to side in the mirror as she studied her reflection. "I can't believe you just did this. It's great!" she exclaimed, the newly coiffed hairdo falling in a tousled crop against her skull. "It's gorgeous."

"It frames your face better. Before, it didn't have enough layers. It was flat and had no body. This gives you more fullness and you need that."

"Roshawn, I don't care what it costs but you are cutting my hair from now on. Just name your price."

Roshawn shook her head. "I'm out of the business. Let's just say this was one last time for the road."

"Like heck we will! I don't care what it takes, but I plan to keep you in a lot of business. My husband needs his hair cut and I know half a dozen wives who'll pay upwards of a few hundred dollars if you can work this kind of magic on them."

Roshawn's eyes widened at the prospect. "Maybe I'll think about it."

"I'll tell you what, are you doing anything later this evening?"

Roshawn shook her head. "I don't have any plans."

"There's a great dance club in town that a number of the Titans' employees and players frequent. Let's meet for drinks. I owe you one. It'll give us a chance to talk and you'll have a great time."

Roshawn nodded. "I'd like that."

Nina reached into her own purse for a pen and a piece of notepaper. She jotted quickly, then passed the page to Roshawn. "Here's the address. I'll meet you at eight o'clock. And come ready. There's usually some very nice eye candy to keep us entertained."

Roshawn grinned. "Now, that's what I'm talking about!"

Angel Rios stood waiting for the elevators in the lobby of the Titans' corporate offices. He took a quick glance at the

Rolex watch on his wrist, noting that he was still a few minutes early for his appointment with the team's scouting director, the man who had been instrumental in negotiating his transition from the minor leagues.

Pushing the button for a second time, he watched as the building's digital readout navigated the descent of both elevators from the upper floors. When one stopped, so did the other, as if the two were descending hand in hand. Angel stepped to the doors on the right when it appeared that conveyor would open first. When it did, he was greated with a rush of noise as the doors opened and a roar of laughter exited before the passengers did.

The two women standing inside the elevator both stopped speaking abruptly, grinning as if they shared a secret no one else was privy to. Nina nodded politely as she eased her way out of the elevator, Roshawn close behind her.

As Roshawn stepped past the handsome man who stood waiting, a rush of heat swept through her body. The man's gaze was intense, burning hot with appreciation as he appraised her, his stare racing the length of her frame and back again.

"Excuse me," Roshawn said softly, her body brushing against his as Angel moved to step inside. The touch was unexpected and both bristled as energy spun from one to the other.

"I'm sorry," Angel said, a rush of color flooding his cheeks as he inhaled the light floral perfume that billowed in the woman's space. A rush of heat rained in a southern direction as the scent danced up his nostrils.

Roshawn's hand moved to the spot between her breasts, a flutter of something she didn't recognize filling her with a sudden yearning. The good-looking man had taken her breath away. Unable to resist she found herself easing slowly backwards toward the front doors, her gaze lingering with his for just a brief moment before she spun back around toward her friend. Her eyes were wide, excitement painting her expression, and the two women giggled like schoolgirls.

As Angel waited for the elevator doors to close, he couldn't help but take stock of the female form that was exiting toward the building's front door. The black woman was exceptionally thin, an A-line skirt in white linen and a floral print blouse adorning her petite figure. Her hair was closely cropped and long chandelier earrings shimmered from her earlobes. Angel grinned foolishly as he stood watching her watching him and when she turned an about-face, he leaned ever so slightly to get a better view of her backside, admiring the easy side-to-side shimmy of her hips and rear end, and the nicely toned length of leg that peeked from beneath her hem. As he stood peering intently, one finger depressing the button that held the elevator door open, the woman turned to look back over her shoulder one last time.

Roshawn could still feel him staring, his eyes burning curiously over her body and she couldn't help tossing one more look in his direction. He was dressed nicely, tan slacks and a white polo shirt complementing the warm bronze tones of his complexion. His expression had been a mix of curiosity and admiration, clearly appreciating what he had been staring at. His intense gaze made Roshawn smile, and for a brief minute, as the closing elevator doors blocked him from view, she was tempted to go back and ride the elevator back up for a second time.

It was normal for Roshawn to be fashionably late as she sauntered through the doors of The Lotus Room at half past eight o'clock. Nina sat at a center table with a pleasant-looking black man when Roshawn caught her eye from the other side of the room. The woman waved excitedly and when she pointed in Roshawn's direction, her companion spun around in his seat to see where it was she stared.

As Roshawn made her way to the table an attractive man with flaming red hair appeared at her side and gripped her elbow. She recognized him from his publicity photos and smiled warmly. His Southern accent was as big as he was as he greeted her. "From the way my wife is actin', you must be that new best friend she's been ravin' about all night. Hi, I'm Patrick Tracy."

Roshawn stepped out of the warm hug he'd wrapped around her. "It's very nice to meet you, Patrick. I'm Roshawn."

The man guided her to the table, stepping out of the way as his wife jumped from her seat to give Roshawn a quick hug. "I was afraid you'd forgotten about us," Nina said.

Roshawn shook her head. "Not at all. I'm still learning my way around town."

Patrick gestured toward his friend. "Roshawn, this is Cedric Guy. My agent."

"It's nice to meet you, Cedric," Roshawn said as she extended her hand toward the man who was sizing her up as if she were his next meal. His grin was cocky as he leaned in to grip her fingers and kiss the back of her hand. His voice was deep, tinged with a self-assurance that said he intended for her to be his next conquest. "Roshawn. A beautiful name for a beautiful woman."

Roshawn's chin rose ever so slightly as she appraised him. She smiled sweetly. She could see it was going to be necessary to shut him down early. Her instincts were shouting that this was a man she wanted absolutely nothing to do with. She pulled her hand from his and reached for a paper napkin sitting on the table, wiping at the spot where his lips had touched. When she finished, she pressed the napkin into the palm of his hand, closing his fingers tightly around it.

Nina burst out laughing. "I keep telling you that tired approach is never going to get you anywhere."

"Ouch, that hurt," Cedric said as he shrugged. He pulled his drink to his lips and took a large gulp, then used Roshawn's napkin to wipe his mouth.

Nina was still chuckling. "Roshawn, what do you drink?"

"A chocolate martini would do nicely right about now."

The woman nodded her head, shaking her new hairdo comfortably. "Cedric, you'll take care of that for us, won't you, darling? And I'll have another vodka-tonic." She reached for Roshawn's hand. "There are some wives here that you just have to meet, Roshawn. Gentlemen, we'll be right back. Have those drinks ready."

Roshawn gave the man a quick wink as she came to her feet. She smiled sweetly. "I appreciate that, Cedric. And I prefer top shelf. Thank you."

The man shook his head and grinned stupidly as Patrick tapped him in empathy on the back. As the two women walked away, the man could do nothing but chuckle under his breath.

The Lotus Room was a small, intimate nightclub that boasted a regular clientele of baseball players, baseball fans and groupies, and an occasional tourist. The setting was low-key, inspiring just a hint of seduction and intimacy, if one desired. Seating areas were comprised of circular booths upholstered in lush, chenille fabrics with large pillows for guests to relax against. The evening's musical selections were a nice mixture of jazz and blues; easy, sensual beats that made a woman want to dance if the right opportunity presented itself. The clientele was clearly upscale and mature, no hint of any teeny boppers lurking in the background. It was obvious from the bouncer at the door and the scrutiny she'd been made to endure to gain entrance, that the management didn't fool around. Roshawn wasn't partial to nightclubs, but she could see herself spending a good deal of her downtime in a place like this one.

Thirty minutes later, Nina had introduced her to half the room. Roshawn was ready for her drink, the names and faces no longer connecting in her head. The beat of the music was intoxicating and Roshawn found herself drunk with wanting, imagining the experience against a perfectly proportioned, exceptionally hard male body. She suddenly thought about the man in the elevator and a quiver of hope coursed through her bloodstream. She appraised the sports manager for a second time and the thoughts instantly flew from her mind. As the two women took their seats, Cedric excused himself, rising to go test his pickup lines on a voluptuous blonde at the bar.

Patrick gave his wife a quick kiss. He leaned in Roshawn's direction. "I apologize for my friend, Roshawn. He can't help himself sometimes."

Roshawn smiled as she took a sip of her drink. "Not a problem. He's nothing I can't handle."

"So, Nina tells me you're new to this area. What brings you to our neck of the woods?"

"My daughter. She's relocating here to live with her father while she attends the University of Phoenix. I'm just here for the summer to help her get settled."

"You lucked into a great temp job," Nina mused. "They say

John Chen is great to work for even when he's acting like a man!"

The two women chuckled.

"Well," Roshawn said, setting her glass against the wooden table. "John is my ex-husband. I kind of had an inside track."

Nina's eyes widened in surprise. "Your ex? You actually work for your ex-husband and you get along?"

"We're great friends."

Nina laughed. "Oh, this is too good! So, how do you get along with his wife?" Nina queried, leaning in closer to Roshawn. "She's not very friendly. Doesn't hang out with us wives much."

Her husband shook his head. "Don't start, Nina." He turned to Roshawn. "Don't answer that. She's spends more time in other people's business!"

Roshawn laughed. "Allison's very nice. She and I don't have any problems. Trust me, it's not as strange as it seems."

"You go, girl! I have to give it to you. I can't stand Patrick's ex-wife. It's a good thing they didn't have any kids."

The man shuddered. "Patrick can't stand his ex-wife."

The trio chatted comfortably for a few minutes and then the DJ shifted the mood with a classic Sam Cooke selection. When Sam started pleading for his woman to bring her love on home, Roshawn needed to get out of her seat. Her new friends were thinking the same thing as they followed behind her and headed hand in hand to the dance floor. The DJ had set a seductive mood and Roshawn found herself wishing for someone to hold her close as she shut her eyes and moved in time to the music.

Angel Rios caught sight of the ebony-toned woman the minute he walked into the room. It was the woman from the elevator and she was dancing alone. Alone on the dance floor and for a moment he and every other man in the room was transfixed by her movements. Smooth black skin glistened under the faint lights as she moved slowly and suggestively, her body bending in sync with the beat of the music whispering out of the speakers. The sheer, caramel-colored dress she wore was skintight, clinging like mist to her lean frame. Barely a size four thick, her bustline amounted to just a mouthful, her paper-thin waist magnifying just a hint of hips supported by lean, sculpted legs. Her regal presence was undeniable as she moved with a liquid fluidity that held him hostage where he stood.

Savoring the sight, Angel was grateful for the darkness that concealed his obvious interest. Taking a quick glance around the room, he noted the wealth of attention the woman was garnering, admirers sitting straighter in their seats as each contemplated making a move on the beautiful woman. He took a step closer himself before movement out of the corner of his eye pulled his attention. Everyone spied the man who was almost racing to the dance floor to catch up with her.

Angel recognized the sports agent who had moved quickly to the woman's side, his large hands falling possessively against the line of her hips as he pulled her close. Her eyes opened to acknowledge the man, but they were cold, no hint of desire emanating from them. Angel smiled ever so slightly. That woman would surely not be possessed by that man that night. In fact, Angel mused as he continued to study her body language, that man would not possess her ever.

A manicured hand fell against his own forearm, breaking his thoughts. The woman who smiled up at him was eager for his attention, her bright red fingernails lightly grazing the length of his arm. Angel smiled back as she pulled him toward the bar. Her intentions were clear. His would be also. He turned one last time to stare back at the dance floor, catching one final glimpse of the exquisite woman as she disappeared out the front door, leaving her admirer doubled over in pain in the center of the room.

It was close to midnight and her two friends were laughing over the telephone as Roshawn gave them an update on everything that had transpired since her arrival.

"The last straw was when the brother starting grinding on me. He has the audacity to whisper in my ear that we needed to take it back to his apartment because he was much better doing a horizontal mambo."

Bridget laughed. "Please, don't tell me you went home with him."

Roshawn sucked her teeth. "Of course not. That fool got all he was getting from me. I left him slumped over after giving him one well-placed knee to where it hurt him the most. He won't be trying that with me ever again."

Jeneva chuckled. "You haven't been there for two weeks and already you're assaulting people. Brings back memories," she laughed.

"Ha, ha, ha," Roshawn chimed sarcastically. "You are so funny."

"How is the job?" Bridget asked.

"Not bad actually. And I think I might be doing hair on the side every now and then."

"Now that brings back memories," Bridget said. "You use to hook up some hair in your mother's kitchen. Remember that, Jeneva?"

"I sure do. Roshawn learned how to do her first weave on

Connie Brimm's big head. She did Connie and Connie cleaned out Mrs. Bradsher's refrigerator."

The trio giggled.

"Well, you sound great Roshawn," Jeneva said.

"Yes, you do," Bridget agreed.

"I'm feeling good, although…" Roshawn hesitated.

"Although, what?" Bridget prodded.

Roshawn paused, searching for the words. She heaved a deep sigh before she spoke. "I was actually lonely tonight. It was strange. For a quick minute I was missing Chen, and then I realized it really wasn't Chen I was missing, it was…"

"Not having a man," Bridget finished for her.

Roshawn sighed again. "Yeah."

Jeneva nodded into the receiver. "You'll meet someone, Roshawn. You just have to give it time. It'll happen when it's supposed to."

"I don't know about all that now," Bridget interjected. "I'm still waiting, and it's been how long? You've had two husbands, Roshawn's had one, and I'm still trying to get a date who lasts longer than the appetizer and dinner."

"If you'd talk to the man, you wouldn't have that problem," Jeneva stated.

"What man?"

Roshawn laughed. "You know what man. Is he still in Louisiana?"

"Oh, please!" Bridget said, her eyes rolling.

"Darwin's back in a few weeks," Jeneva responded. "Then we'll see what's up."

Roshawn giggled. The moment went quiet for a quick second before she spoke. "I miss you guys," she said softly. "I miss you two a lot."

"We miss you, too," they both responded.

"Call us next week," Bridget commanded. "Okay?"

"I will. Jeneva, kiss my baby for me, and tell Mac I said hello."

"I will. Enjoy it, Roshawn. Everything will work out just fine."

After hanging up the receiver, Roshawn looked out onto the moonlit patio. The house was eerie, nothing but the quiet of darkness surrounding her. Closing the blinds, she headed toward the back of the house and the master bedroom, thinking that maybe tomorrow night wouldn't feel so empty.

Chapter 7

Chen met Roshawn at the office door, a long list of things for her to do in his hand.

"Where are you off to?" Roshawn asked, noting the airline tickets peeking from his breast pocket.

"Cancun. Allison has a few days off so we're taking Ming for a quick trip."

Roshawn slowly nodded her head. "Thanks for telling me."

The man studied her for a quick minute, noting her tightened jaw and the abrasive glare washing over him. "It was a spur-of-the-moment decision, and it's only for the weekend."

"I didn't say anything yet, Chen."

"You didn't have to. Your face is saying it for you."

Roshawn cut her eye at him as she moved to the seat behind the desk. "Chen, you don't have to get my permission to take your wife and our daughter on a trip. But having the courtesy to tell me before you're walking onto the plane would have been nice."

"I'm telling you now."

"You could have called me last night, Chen. I was hoping to spend time with Ming this weekend."

The man tossed his head back against his shoulders, exasperation shadowing his expression. "Is this going to be a fight?"

"Only if you make it one."

Chen closed his eyes for a quick moment, then refocused his gaze back on Roshawn's face, her eyes piercing straight through him. "I apologize. You're right. I should have called you last night."

Roshawn nodded. "Don't make that mistake again, please. I wouldn't do it to you, so don't do it to me."

Chen waved his head from side to side then took a seat against the corner of her desk. "I heard you had a problem with Cedric Guy last night."

Roshawn rolled her eyes. "It wouldn't have been a problem if he had just kept his crotch off my thigh. The man was humping my leg like a Chihuahua in heat."

Chen nodded, fighting not to laugh. "We're a tight-knit organization, Roshawn. News travels fast. Bad news travels even faster."

Roshawn shrugged. "My body, Chen. My rules. I don't play that unless I want to. Mr. Guy had to learn that the hard way. He should have just backed up like I politely asked him to do in the first place."

"Well, if you have any more problems you just let me know, okay?"

"I do know how to take care of myself."

Chen sighed. He muttered under his breath in Cantonese.

Roshawn smiled. "Stop fussing. I'll be fine. You can relax."

Chen stood back on his feet. "If you need me, just call my cell phone. It'll be on. I'll drop Ming by to see you when we get back on Sunday."

Roshawn nodded.

Chen continued. "Angel Rios will be calling to confirm I received his paperwork from Santo Domingo. Let him know everything has been taken care of and he can pick up his documents anytime."

Roshawn lifted the neatly typed paper from the desk, giving the rest of Chen's to-do list a quick review. "I guess I need to get busy. You have a good trip and keep my daughter safe, please."

Chen held her gaze for another quick minute and smiled. "Thanks, Roshawn."

She winked. "Tell that woman of yours I said hello."

Roshawn was well past ready to leave when Angel Rios finally called. The man greeted her warmly, his deep voice resonating with Latino bravado. The tone was low and seductive and it caught Roshawn completely off guard.

"Good afternoon. This is Angel Rios. Is Mr. Chen there, please?"

Roshawn paused without realizing it. The voice on the other end was the epitome of sexy and as she reflected on the sensuality of it everything else went right out of her head.

"Hello?"

She cleared her throat, a wave of embarrassment sweeping over her. "I'm sorry, Mr. Rios. No, Mr. Chen is gone for the weekend but he did leave a message for you." The man nodded into the receiver as Roshawn relayed the information. "Will you be coming this afternoon?" she asked.

This time Angel hesitated before answering. "No. I'm very sorry. I need to keep practicing," he said. "I don't think I can get away anytime soon."

"I can bring them to you," Roshawn volunteered, the words flying out of her mouth before she could catch them.

"Thank you," the man responded. "That would be very helpful."

"I'll be there as soon as I can."

Hanging up the telephone, Roshawn shook her head. The stadium in Tucson was almost a two-hour drive from the corporate office. What in the world had she been thinking?

After a half-dozen wrong turns and one missed exit, Roshawn finally found her way to Tucson Electric Park. By the time she pulled her car into a parking spot and shut down the engine, all she could think of was finding her way to a restroom. The guard at the entrance door was less than accommodating until she flashed him her employee identification card and dropped Angel Rios's and John Chen's names in the same sentence.

"Take the elevator to the upper level," he said, pointing his index finger. "Bathrooms will be on your right."

"Thank you," Roshawn said, rushing past him in the direction he pointed her in.

Ten minutes later, with relief found, Roshawn took in the expanse of the stadium, which was considered the centerpiece of the Pima County Sports Complex. The ballpark was renowned for its proximity to Chase Field, home of the Titans during the playing season, and its six-field practice facilities that the Titans and the Chicago White Sox made use of during spring training. Within Tucson Electric Park there was a major league clubhouse, where the Titans would dress daily, plus clubhouses for visiting teams and umpires. The home clubhouse also boasted an indoor batting cage located on the lower level on the way to the playing field.

From where she stood on the mezzanine, Roshawn could take in the full spectrum of the ball field. The playing surface was symmetrical, measuring some 340 feet down each foul line and 405 feet straightaway to center field. With the meticulously manicured lawns it was truly a sight to behold for any baseball aficionado.

There were a number of players on the field still practicing. A few were pitching balls to other players, one or two squatting in catcher's masks, and there was one player standing outside the batter's cage in deep discussion with a man Roshawn assumed was probably one of the coaches from the way he was gesturing with his hands.

Nina had been right about eye candy, Roshawn thought, as she removed her darkened sunshades for a better view. These boys were nicely packaged, she mused, an appreciative hum rising from her midsection as she slowly appraised each one. One man in particular had caught Roshawn's full attention, the player swinging a wooden bat inside the cage. Easing her way down the steps, she made her way to the gate and gestured for attention. The coach looked up curiously before easing his way to where she stood.

"I'm sorry, miss, but the park is closed to the public. You're not supposed to be on the field."

Roshawn raised her eyebrows ever so slightly. "I'm looking for Angel Rios. He's expecting me. I'm John Chen's assistant."

The man nodded. "Sorry about that. We can't be too careful. I'm sure you understand."

Roshawn looked him up and down, her gaze racing the

length of his slightly overweight frame. She didn't bother to respond.

The coach called Angel's name, gesturing for him to join her.

"Thank you," Roshawn said, dismissing him with a quick nod of her head.

The man left, heading in the direction of two players who appeared to be winding down for the day. Roshawn barely noticed what was going on with them as her stare was locked on the beautiful black man sauntering in her direction. The man from the elevator.

Angel Rios was smiling widely, full lips that complemented flawless white teeth lifting easily. As he drew closer he pulled the sweat-stained T-shirt from his body and Roshawn heard herself gasp out loud. His chest was like two slices of a dark oak tree, each pectoral muscle nearly round beneath tight, oiled skin. His upper body was a profusion of muscle, each sinew clearly defined and in perfect proportion. Roshawn marveled at his deep, honey-toned complexion, the color of his skin bronzed warm and golden from the intense sun. His waist narrowed dramatically down toward his hips, his body bulging out again in powerful thighs accentuated by the snug fit of his striped baseball pants. His behind was a tight, rounded mass of solid muscle that one could have easily bounced a quarter off of and there was an exceptionally large and definite bulge in the front of his pants that promised mysteries Roshawn could only wonder about.

Angel recognized her instantly, his gaze running from her head to her feet. She was even more beautiful than he remembered, he thought, admiring the gold silk top and deep purple skirt that hugged her diminutive body. Her dark complexion was flawless, her skin like polished black marble. Her features were delicate, a button nose, dimpled cheeks and full lips that appeared ready to be kissed. He was drawn to the energy that spun in her eyes, light shimmering against her retina. He extended his hand in greeting. "Hello. I'm Angel Rios. It's nice to meet you finally."

Roshawn pressed her palm tightly to his, noting the firmness of his fingers as they locked around hers. A current of electricity surged through her as they held the handshake longer than necessary. Energy spun a fine web of heat through her and it shone vibrantly from her eyes as she looked him up and down. "Hello, I'm Roshawn. Roshawn Bradsher. Here is your paperwork," she said, extending the folder toward him as they finally broke the handshake.

Angel grinned shyly, his heart suddenly beating with anticipation. "Thank you. I really appreciate you bringing this. I hope it wasn't too much trouble."

Roshawn gave him one of her brightest smiles, dropping her eyes ever so slightly. "No, it wasn't any trouble at all." Her gaze was lingering, drawing him in so deep the man felt as if he would suddenly lose himself beneath the depths of it.

Angel suddenly stood nervously, perspiration beading against his forehead. He swiped at the rise of moisture with the back of his hand, his eyes skating anxiously from side to side. His tongue seemed to thicken in his mouth, holding back his words and thoughts as he struggled with what to say. The anxiety of a schoolboy's crush seemed to rise from nowhere to consume his usual confidence and bravado. The emotion was foreign to him, and as she stared curiously, still studying him, Angel found himself wishing for someplace to turn and run. "Well, thanks again. I've got to get back to practice," he heard himself say, the words rushing past his lips as if on a mission of their own.

Roshawn watched as Angel Rios nodded his head in appreciation before turning back to the batting cage, rushing to get back to whatever it was he needed to do. She stood watching for only a brief moment as he picked up his bat and signaled for the pitching machine to be turned back on, briefly turning to stare in her direction one last time. Ten minutes later, she was back on the road headed for home.

Roshawn had barely made it past the signs announcing the town of Paradise Valley when her cell phone rang. As she paused at a stop sign she pushed the hands-free speaker to answer the call.

"Hello?"

"Roshawn, it's me, Nina. What are you doing?"

"Hi, Nina. I just got back from Tucson. I had to go to Electric Park to meet Angel Rios."

"Ohhh, the team's new crown prince! I hear that he is just absolutely divine. Is he cute?"

Roshawn grinned as an image of the man flashed through her mind. She pulled her car into the driveway and turned off the engine. "Yes, he's very nice."

"I hear he's quite the Lothario though. They say he's never seen with the same woman twice and he's usually seen with a lot of women. One hangs off each arm as a matter of fact. Those big-busted, implant-wearing, wannabe Barbie doll types."

Roshawn chuckled at the idea. "Really? He didn't come across as much of a ladies' man to me. In fact, he seemed to be a little shy."

Her friend giggled. "I don't know anything about shy. In fact, I was given the impression that he's a little too confident, downright cocky and very alpha-male macho. Maybe you scared him?"

Roshawn shook her head at the thought. "Maybe. So, what's up?"

"Do you feel like hanging out? A few of the wives are coming over to my house for dinner. Nothing fancy, just pizza and wine coolers. I'd love for you to come."

"It sounds like fun."

"That's great. You'll have a good time. I promise," the woman gushed, digressing into lengthy detail about each and every female who would be attending.

By the time Nina was ready to give her directions, Roshawn and her cell phone had made it into her home. "I'll see you in an hour," Roshawn said just before disconnecting the call.

She flipped quickly through the stack of letters that had been in her mailbox. The temporary mail transfer had finally kicked in and her correspondence had been redirected from her Seattle address. The latest issue of *Essence* magazine was all she had any real interest in, she thought as she tossed everything else onto the kitchen counter.

In want of a hot shower, Roshawn dropped her clothes to the floor as she headed into the master bath. The trail of her garments started with her silk shirt in the hallway and ended with her blue thong falling on the floor just outside the bathroom door. As she waited for the water to warm she studied her naked reflection in the floor-to-ceiling mirror. "I look hot for thirty-six," she mused out loud, grateful for the thin genes she'd inherited from her mother and her grandmother. Even when she'd been pregnant with Ming, Roshawn could have gotten lost in the folds of a size six garment.

Roshawn stepped beneath the flow of hot water, allowing the rising steam to rain around her. The rush of fluid felt great against her skin as she spun in a slow circle beneath the dual showerheads. Thoughts of Angel Rios suddenly washed over her. The man had been polite but had barely paid her an ounce of attention. The sight of him though had incited a rage of wanting between her thighs and Roshawn was dismayed that such a blatant rush of desire had so readily consumed her. John Chen had been the only other man to ever do that to her.

The tips of her fingers lightly grazed the rise of candy-hard nipple, then slid to her abdomen resting atop the flat of her stomach. How her best friend Jeneva had ever endured fourteen years without a man's touch was beyond her comprehension. It had been a long time since she had been intimate with a man, and Roshawn had no intentions of letting it drag on for too much longer. The last time she'd been touched had been right before Allison waltzed into John Chen's life and took control. Since then, there hadn't been a man she'd found worthy of what she had to offer and definitely not one who caused butterflies to flutter out of control in the pit of her stomach.

But Angel Rios had managed to light a low flame through her. Roshawn pondered the possibilities. The man was surely intriguing, but she was reluctant to see whether or not he was capable of a full, raging fire. Clearly, there could be nothing between them. His youth dispelled any maturity, the rumors of his playboy behavior indicative of a man still set on sowing whatever oats he thought were due him. She wasn't interested in playing that game with a man. Roshawn Bradsher had never been a notch on any man's belt, and shy, or not, Angel Rios surely would not be the first.

The drive from the ballpark to the hotel always calmed him. Angel was enamored with the magnificence of the land-

scape. The dry desert terrain and magnanimous rock formations were so unlike his tropical home in Santo Domingo
where the pristine beaches stretch for nearly a thousand miles
along the blue coastline. He enjoyed the stark contrasts
between the two. He glanced to the clock radio, noting the
time. It was still early. He could have practiced for another
hour or so but the coach had sent him away, telling him to
save his energy for Monday and opening day of the major
league season.

Angel was so ready to show everyone what he could do
on the ball field. It had been his father's dream for him since
he'd been knee-high to play major league baseball in the
United States. Angel was anxious for his father to witness
him not only do that, but to be a success at it, his reputation
in the game likened to the careers of Hank Aaron, Barry
Bonds, Roberto Clemente and all the other great players that
had preceded him. Angel had been all of twelve years old the
day he'd promised his father that one day his name would be
inked in the Baseball Hall of Fame roster.

His father's love of the game had been the catalyst for his
love of it. The old man could rattle statistics and trivia like
other men breathed. Before he could read or write, Angel had
known that Ozzie Virgil had been the first player from his
native Dominican Republic to play professional ball in the
United States, his nine season career starting with the New
York Giants in 1956. His father could tell you the man's
hitting and fielding statistics as easily as he rattled off his own
name and birth date.

The two had followed the careers of all the men of color,
from Jamaican native Chili Davis to Cuba's Rafael Almeida
and Armando Marsans. Both had idolized the likes of African-
Americans Jackie Robinson, Satchel Paige and Don New-

combe, men whose determination and persistence had set a
standard Angel was intent on maintaining and eventually ex-
ceeding. Angel was determined that nothing and no one would
ever keep him from achieving his goals. He would not be distracted.

That woman though had clearly been a distraction. As he
navigated his car down AZ-143-N toward North 44th Street
and the Doubletree Hotel, he couldn't stop himself from
thinking of her, remembering the look she'd given him, her
eyes searching his. The moment had thrown him and he'd had
to turn away from her, to hurl himself toward the batting
cages in order to regain control. No woman had ever had that
effect on him before, inciting an interest that had nothing to
do with the raging hardness that pressed taut in his pants.
Angel shook his head, determined to think of anything but
Roshawn Bradsher.

Making his way into the hotel he greeted the concierge and
the desk staff who had come to know both him and his father
well. Their stay had already exceeded twelve weeks, courtesy
of his new employer, having begun just after the New Year
when the Titans had negotiated a trade to secure him. He'd
had about enough of hotel living, he thought, as another
guest and his family rushed him for an autograph.

The desk clerk, a slim blond man named Bryan Harvey
gestured for his attention. "Good evening, Mr. Rios. We have
a few messages for you, sir."

"Thank you, Bryan," Angel responded, taking the pink
message slips from the man's hands.

"And your father wanted you to know that he'd be in the
lounge."

Angel nodded. "Thank you."

He made his way across the lobby toward the hotel's bar

and restaurant. Business was booming in The Belvedere Lounge and Grill, singles, couples and families savoring their evening meal and the cooling flow of a wet beverage. Israel Rios was in his usual spot, perched on a bar stool at the far end of the bar. Angel heaved a deep sigh. His father was missing home, longing for the companionship of his old fishing buddies and the easy camaraderie that existed between him and the street vendors who peddled everything from cashews to electronic appliances. Angel was more determined than ever to find them a real home where his father could garden and cook to his heart's content. He made himself a promise to see John Chen first thing Monday morning for advice.

"Hey, *Papí*. What are you doing?" Angel asked, taking the seat beside his father.

Israel wrapped his arms around his son's shoulders in a quick embrace. "I was just talking to the peoples here," he said, fighting his first desire to respond in Spanish. "Just talking while I wait here for you. How was your practice, *hijo?*"

Angel nodded. "It was good." He reached for the cocktail glass sitting in front of his father and lifted it to his nose. "What are you drinking?" he asked.

The man smiled. "My friend, Lisa, she make me a fruit punch. Not as good as home, but good," he said, gesturing toward the bartender at the other end of the bar.

Angel waved as the woman headed in their direction.

"Your regular, Mr. Rios?" she asked, a wide grin spreading over her face.

"Not tonight, Lisa. I need to go rest. We'll just have the check, please."

She gave him a bright smile, tossing her red hair over her

shoulders as she spun back to the register and her computerized order pad.

"Did you eat, *Papí?*"

The older man nodded. *"Sí."*

After drawing his signature across the check, Angel and his father rose from their seat and headed toward the elevators to their second floor room. Once inside, Angel dropped to a chair and pulled the folder from his gym bag. He sat quiet as he perused its contents.

"What is that?" his father asked, taking the seat across from him.

"Just some papers they need me to sign," his son answered. "Mr. Chen's assistant brought them to me at the ballpark today."

"Oh, she's a very nice girl," Israel exclaimed. "She is having her third baby. Her husband, he must be very proud. He has two sons and another on the way."

Angel shook his head. "Not her. She's not working for him for a while. Not until after she has her child. A new woman is working for him now. Her name is Roshawn."

With mention of her name, a strange expression crossed his face as Angel remembered his reaction to her, every fiber of his being turned sensitive to her presence. The look was not lost on his father who eyed him curiously.

"She is pretty, this new woman?" the man asked.

His son nodded. *"Sí, muy bonita, Papí."*

"Tiene un esposo?"

Angel shrugged, cutting an eye toward his father. "I don't know if she has a husband. I don't know anything about her."

"But you'd like to?"

He turned to face the older man. "She's a woman. There's not much else I need to know."

The old man shook his head, slipping into his native language to lecture his son. "You need to settle down, son. A wife will be good for you. Someone to keep you warm at night. To be with you during the day. You need a woman like your mother, God rest her soul. Someone to love you and give you sons of your own. "

Angel sighed. "One day, *Papí,* maybe."

The man tossed his hand up in exasperation. "One day, yes! These women you keep taking to your bed aren't good women. You need one who will challenge you, make you be a better man. A good woman will do that for you. But you will not find a woman like that if you don't take time to know her heart. You have to invest your time."

"All I have time for right now is the game, *Papí.* Nothing else. *Nada!*" Angel came to his feet, indicating the conversation had ended as he wished his father a good night.

His father watched as Angel disappeared into his bedroom and closed the door behind him. Sitting back against his seat, Israel clasped his hands in prayer, his elbows resting against his upper thigh. He thought about his son, and that look, a mixture of confusion and interest, that had spun across his face. Whoever this woman was, she had touched a nerve, he thought to himself, suddenly curious to know more about her. He would have to meet this woman for himself and maybe help his son find his way to love.

Chapter 8

Roshawn had only promised them two hours of her time and had already given up half a day when the youth director of the Phoenix Children's Center asked if she wouldn't mind staying for just a little while longer. Marshall Tucker, a blond and blue-eyed college student smiled at her brightly, the length of his sandy-blond hair swaying back and forth against his thin shoulders.

"We could really use you, Roshawn," Marshall implored, pointing at a group of young boys who were kicking a rubber ball back and forth in the playground of the center's grassy yard. "Two of our volunteers cancelled on us at the last minute and we're not expecting any of the ball players to fill in until this afternoon. I promise you can take off the minute they get here."

"Pretty, pretty, please?" a bespeckled twelve-year-old begged, an expensive pair of sunshades perched on the end of his nose. "We can eat lunch together," the boy grinned.

Roshawn smiled back. "I usually like my lunch dates to be a little older," she said jokingly as she tousled his thick curls.

"I got an older brother," the child said, his infectious grin filling his round face, "but he's not as cute as I am."

Roshawn shook her head as Marshall pointed the child in the opposite direction. "Joshua, go play. Miss Bradsher is not interested in dating you or your brother."

The boy winked at her as he eased off. "Don't know what you're missing, pretty lady," he chimed, laughter pulling at his thin lips.

"Oh, I know exactly what I'm missing," Roshawn said, laughing with him. She nodded her head at Marshall. "I'm out of here as soon as my relief shows up."

The young man smiled broadly. "You're a lifesaver. Thanks, Roshawn."

She watched as he scurried back to the main office to report that an extra pair of hands would be around for just a little while longer. This was the third time Roshawn had volunteered at the center. Ming had brought her the first time, excited for her mother to share in the experience.

It had taken the girl less than a week after her arrival to secure a part-time job as a youth counselor, mentoring a group of girls ages nine to thirteen. Both Roshawn and Chen had been duly impressed with their only child, and after spending that initial afternoon, Roshawn had understood Ming's attraction to the place. The kids were great, happy and good-natured as they bantered back and forth with one another, and the staff was just a wonderful mix of college students, parents and adult volunteers, many of them affiliated with the Titans organization, who genuinely liked being of service to the community. Roshawn had readily agreed to come back to volunteer during her spare time. With her daughter being gone for the weekend and nothing else to do with herself, Roshawn had figured this Saturday morning would be as good as any other.

Making her way to the center of the play area, she jumped into the fray of arms and legs battling for possession of the ball. An impromptu game of soccer ensued with Roshawn racing down the field shuffling the ball with her feet and the youngsters cheering and yelling excitedly as they raced after her in hot pursuit. Thirty minutes later, Roshawn fell to the ground, panting for air, as her playmates fell down beside her.

"No fair," one boy protested, his face skewed in a tight pout. "I didn't get to shoot a goal."

"Is too fair," another professed, his head bobbing up and down excitedly. "Isn't it fair, Miss Bradsher?"

She nodded. "Very fair. You'll get to shoot next time, Charlie."

"Can we play again?" another child asked, coming to wrap his arms around Roshawn's neck. "Please?"

She rolled her eyes. "Aren't you tired, little bit? I think we should rest for a minute."

"Then can we play again?"

Roshawn smiled. "We'll see. Right now, I need you to go check with Marshall to see if he's ready for you guys to eat lunch."

"I'll go," the boy named Charlie said as he and a companion both jumped up and raced toward the main building.

The child with the kung fu grip around her neck peered around to look in her face. "Why you cut all your hair off? You look like a boy."

Roshawn laughed as she peeled his fingers apart and guided him to sit in her lap. She rubbed a palm against his own closely cropped hairdo. "I cut it all off because I like the way it looks. Don't you think it looks good on me?"

"Girls is supposed to have long hair."

"Yeah," the group of them echoed.

She shook her head. "Girls and boys should have hair that looks good on them and makes them feel good about themselves."

The child persisted. "Girls is prettier with long hair."

"What? Are you saying I'm not pretty?"

The boy grinned, a goofy smile spreading across his chubby cheeks. He shrugged his shoulders. "You looks okay, I guess."

Roshawn began to tickle the youngster, inciting a rush of giggles. "Just okay?"

"Yes, you're pretty!" he exclaimed, fighting to catch his breath, still laughing hysterically.

"How come you don't act like no real girl?" another boy asked. "You play ball and stuff and you like to have fun."

"Girls play ball and they like to have fun. That's just not a boy thing."

"Well, my big brother says girls need to stay home and cook and clean and do girl things and they need to stop acting like us boys all the time," one young man said, the comment coming in a rush out of his mouth.

Roshawn laughed. "Well, your big brother is wrong and you can tell him I said so."

They were still laughing and chatting as Marshall and Charlie made their way back to the group.

"Lunch is served," Marshall said, gesturing toward the main building. "And Roshawn, your relief has arrived."

"Yeah, food!" the kids exclaimed, all of them jumping up to race back inside.

"Everyone needs to wash their hands first!" Roshawn shouted loudly. "And I'm going to check each and every finger!"

Marshall extended a hand to help pull her back onto her feet as the gathering disappeared from view, racing to beat each other into the dining hall. "You're really good with them. They all adore you."

She smiled. "They're sweet kids and I enjoy being with them."

The man grinned. "I think a few of them even have a little crush on you. Charlie was just inside telling Angel Rios and two of the other players how much he likes you."

Roshawn cut her eye in his direction. "Mr. Rios is here?"

Marshall nodded. "He's volunteering this afternoon. They're in the kitchen helping to serve. Do you know him?"

"We've met."

Marshall tapped her lightly against the shoulder. "Well, thank you again. There's plenty to eat if you want to hang out and have lunch with us, otherwise we'll see you next time."

"Thanks, Marshall."

As Roshawn made her way inside, she smoothed a hand down the front of her T-shirt, tucking the garment neatly into her denim shorts. Although she knew she didn't look bad, she also knew she didn't look good enough to want to run into Angel Rios. She'd had every intention of ensuring Angel Rios not only gave her a second look the next time they had run into each other but a third and fourth glance as well. Her casual attire was hardly worthy of being remembered, she thought as she eased her way into the ladies' room and stood before the mirror. She ran a quick palm across her head and then a finger beneath her eyes. A damp paper towel against her neck and over the length of her arms and legs cooled her body temperature and rid her of the grass stains and flecks of dirt she'd garnered from playing outside.

With any luck, she thought as she made her way out of the restroom and down the corridor toward the main office and her purse, she could bypass the lunchroom and Angel Rios altogether. As she passed the entrance to the cafeteria she hurried by, almost racing to reach the other end of the hallway. Thinking she was only a few feet from getting away without being seen, she didn't notice the man standing on the other side of the office door as she pushed her way inside. Angel Rios turned abruptly as Roshawn pushed her way through the entrance, and the duo smacked straight into each other.

"Excuse me," Angel said as the woman crashed into his chest, the whole of her small body brushing up against his. Instinctively, he cradled a protective arm around her torso to catch her.

"I'm so sorry," Roshawn apologized as she stood staring up at him, recognition flashing in her dark eyes. The sudden rush of warmth from his body was disconcerting and she wished for a hole in the floor to drop herself straight down into. "Mr. Rios. I …didn't see…you," Roshawn stammered. "Sorry about that."

"No. It was my fault. I should have been looking." He smiled seductively as he tightened the grip he had around her waist.

Roshawn could only imagine the possibilities as she became aware of her pelvis and legs pressed to his, the spread of his fingers burning hot against the cotton fabric of her T-shirt. Her flesh felt as if it had been caught on fire. Without thinking she stepped in even closer, her palms moving to his broad chest as she looked up into his face. Heat surged from the apex of her feminine quadrant into every nerve and muscle that ran through her body. Roshawn felt herself shudder as she struggled to catch her breath.

Angel grinned. "How are you, Ms. Bradsher?"

Roshawn flashed him a quick smile. "Well, thank you. How about yourself?"

He shrugged, nodding his head at the same time. "I am very well, thank you." His hand danced against her lower back, the urge to let his palm glide down and across the round of her buttocks tempting.

The air in the room was suddenly thick, waves of wanting seeming to billow though the atmosphere with an agenda of its own. Both were suddenly aware that it had taken very little for them to fall into the moment with each other, trading easy caresses as if it were the most natural thing for the two of them to do.

Someone laughing rang out from the other side of the door, suddenly bringing the moment back into focus. Roshawn pulled herself from his grasp as Angel reluctantly let her go. An awkward silence filled the space between them as they both struggled not to stare at each other. Roshawn wasn't accustomed to being so nervous in a man's presence and it was obvious as she stood there with him that his being so close was having an effect on her. She took another step back as she shot him a quick glance, her smile widening.

"Do you volunteer often?" Angel finally asked, breaking the silence.

"Once in awhile," she responded. "They needed an extra hand today so I came to play ball with the boys."

"The boys?" Surprise painted his expression.

Roshawn nodded. "Yes. The boys."

Angel eyed her curiously. "I would think you should be

playing dolls and dress up with the girls. Maybe teaching them how to cook and sew."

Roshawn laughed. "I do that when it's needed, but today the boys needed attention and they wanted to play ball."

"But…" Angel paused.

"But what?"

He shrugged again, his broad shoulders pushing up toward the ceiling. "I'm a little old-fashioned about things. I just think it would be better if the women volunteers devoted their time to the girls doing girl things."

Roshawn met his gaze, staring intently. The man had hit a raw nerve. "Really now?"

"If the girls see you playing ball and being rough with the boys they may get the wrong ideas."

"And what idea might that be? That they can do anything the boys can do and probably do it better?" Roshawn could see the man bristle as he studied her. "Are you a proponent of male and female roles, Mr. Rios?" she asked, eyeing him curiously.

He shrugged, baffled by the sudden exchange between them and having no idea how the conversation had turned so serious. He answered, sensing that his response would only dig him into a hole that she would want to bury him beneath. "I believe there's a place for women and there's a place for men and that is how it should be. I also think the younger we begin to teach children this the better."

Roshawn nodded her head slowly. "I think you're a sexist pig. That thinking is so antiquated," she said, her arms folding across her chest.

"It's traditional, but you feminist types always want to disturb the status quo."

"It's archaic, pure and simple, and if it weren't for us feminist types, men like you would have us barefoot and pregnant without any consideration for what we can actually accomplish."

"Women who think like you are why we have so many problems with our family units. I'm sure you think it's okay for mothers to work instead of being home to raise their children."

"I think a woman should do what's right for her and her family and if that means working a job she enjoys then yes, she should."

The man shook his head in dismay. "It would seem that you and I don't agree, Ms. Bradsher."

Roshawn shrugged, her thin shoulders easing slowly upward. "Where are you from, Mr. Rios?"

"The Dominican Republic. I was born and raised right outside Santo Domingo."

"A very traditional country, I take it."

"Very."

"You'll find that we're a little more open-minded here in the United States."

"Perhaps, but open-minded doesn't necessarily mean you are right." Angel smiled slightly, the faint bend to his lips teasing.

Roshawn struggled not to stare at his mouth. He had beautiful lips, full, plush pillows that she suddenly longed to press her own mouth against to see just how soft they were. She stared into his eyes, then quickly shifted her gaze. Heat rose for a second time burning through her, the temperature steadily rising.

Angel shifted his body, displacing his weight from one foot to the other, his own anxiety sweeping through him as he struggled to stall the rise of an erection that was pressing anxiously against the front of his slacks.

"I should be going," he finally said, his eyes locking with hers for a second time.

Roshawn nodded, moving out of his way. "Have a good afternoon, Mr. Rios," she said as she eased behind the counter to get her purse. "Maybe I'll see you here again sometime. In fact, perhaps you'll join me and we can entertain both the boys and the girls. I'm sure the young women could learn much from your influence, particularly what kind of male attitudes would not be in their best interest."

Angel chuckled ever so softly. "Perhaps and maybe you'll come to understand why I feel as strongly as I do. And, it was a pleasure to see you again as well, Ms. Bradsher," he concluded as she brushed past him.

Angel watched as she made her way out the door and down the hallway. He shook his head from side to side. That one could drive him completely crazy. Clearly, she wasn't his type, he mused as he headed back to the kitchen. The woman was too opinionated and exceptionally outspoken. Women like that usually had too much of nothing to say and much more than he was interested in hearing, he thought to himself. As he watched her exit the building, he couldn't help but appreciate the sway of her hips in her tight shorts and the toned muscles that comprised the length of her legs. No, she clearly wasn't his type, but why did she have to be so darn sexy?

As Roshawn pulled her car out of the parking lot, she reflected on her conversation with Rios. He had barely opened his mouth for a second and she knew cute or not, he was surely not the man for her. One man telling her what a woman should and should not do had been enough to last her a lifetime. She had no interest in trying to beat some sanity into any other. Angel Rios was clearly a lost cause, even if he did have one of the nicest bodies of any man she'd ever known.

Chapter 9

Ming sat on a kitchen chair in front of her mother as Roshawn combed the tangles from the girl's waist-length hair. She massaged a creamy concoction of mango and coconut oil through the lengths to moisturize the sun-streaked strands.

"You swam in salt water, didn't you?" Roshawn asked.

The girl nodded.

"The salt and now all this heat and sunshine has dried your hair out. We'll need to give it a few deep conditioning treatments for a while to strengthen it back or it's going to start breaking off."

"I like that conditioner," Ming chimed. "It smells so good."

Roshawn took a deep inhale of breath. "It does, doesn't it?"

"Nina says you need to bottle it. She loves what it does to her hair."

Roshawn shrugged. "I never really thought about it."

The girl laughed. "Did you see Daddy's face when we

came in and those two guys were sitting here getting their hair cut? He was so funny!"

Roshawn rolled her eyes. "Remind me to talk to your father about that. Just because I'm borrowing his house for a while doesn't give him any right to be walking in and out of here any time he feels like it. He doesn't even bother to knock. He's going to need to lose that key."

Ming giggled. "Allison said the same thing."

"She did?"

The girl nodded. "I think they had a fight about it. I asked Daddy but he said it was just a difference of opinion. But I don't think Allison likes having you so close by."

Roshawn raised an eyebrow, contemplating her daughter's comment. She wrapped a plastic cap around the girl's head, then gestured toward the hair dryer sitting on the kitchen table. "You need to sit under the hood for ten minutes, then we'll rinse your hair out, and blow it dry, okay?"

"Thanks, Mommy."

As Ming settled herself under the dryer, grabbing one of her teen magazines in her hands, Roshawn reached for the telephone and dialed a number Nina had left for her. The phone rang repeatedly and when there was no answer she hung up the receiver. She reviewed her appointment book for a second time, then jotted a quick notation into the margin.

Nina had been referring clients to her faster than she could handle them all. The evening before last, Patrick Tracy and two of the outfielders had come to get their hair cut, the only time they'd had available on their one day off. John Chen had not been amused when he'd arrived, unannounced, their teenage daughter in tow. And, Allison had seemed equally annoyed, but Roshawn's instincts told her that Allison's unhappiness was due to Chen's attitude and behavior more than anything else. Roshawn shook her head. She was sure Allison had some issues with her moving to Arizona, living in their old house and working for Chen. What woman wouldn't?

Glancing over to the clock on the wall, Roshawn thought about giving Chen a call but decided against it. If Allison was unhappy, that was his problem, but if there was any truth to what Ming suspected, she surely didn't want to be responsible for Chen and Allison fighting about it. She'd always gone out of her way to make the woman feel comfortable. Maybe the next time they were together, she would pull Allison aside for a heart-to-heart and let her knew she wasn't interested in Chen, Roshawn thought to herself. At the moment though, she had other issues to deal with. Juggling her home salon schedule being foremost in her mind.

Yesterday, one of the baseball wives and a secretary from the team's president's office had come for two haircuts, one perm and one roller set. Five heads, two days, and almost a thousand dollars later and Roshawn was quickly warming up to her side business. She had always been good at what she did and for the first time in a very long while she was enjoying it. She grinned.

Her temporary assistant's position was also going nicely; she and Chen working easily together despite an occasional difference of opinion, as Chen would prefer to call their somewhat heated battles. Ming was happier than she'd been in months and her relationship with her mother seemed to have regained its stride, the girl enjoying her mother's company without the teenage attitude and belligerent behavior. Roshawn was more than grateful for that blessing.

The telephone interrupted her thoughts and Roshawn pulled the receiver into her hand to answer it. "Hello?"

"Yes, hello," the male voice said, "may I speak to Mrs. Bradsher, please?"

"It's Ms. Bradsher. How may I help you?"

"Nina Tracy gave me your name and number. I'm interested in scheduling an appointment for a haircut, if that's possible."

Roshawn nodded into the receiver. "It is. What's your name?"

"My name's Bryan and I'm with the Doubletree Hotel. The appointment is actually for one of our guests and his son who are visiting with us for a brief period."

"And Nina gave you my number?"

"Yes, she and her husband, Patrick both spoke very highly of you."

"When would they like to come?"

"Would Thursday evening be a problem?"

Roshawn reached for her book and gave it a quick glance. "I can do them both at seven."

There was a brief pause. "That would be fine."

"Do you know where I'm located?" Roshawn asked. The answer was negative and she provided an address and quick directions when asked. The man named Bryan extended his thanks and disconnected the call. As she hung up the receiver Roshawn realized she'd not gotten the names of her two appointments. Oh well, she thought, crossing back to the other side of the room to check on her daughter's head. She'd worry about it later. Right now she wanted to finish Ming's hair so the two of them could get out of the house to enjoy what was left of a beautiful day.

Israel Rios grinned as Bryan Harvey passed him the scrap of paper with the woman's address and appointment time.

"Gracias, Bryan."

"Not a problem, Mr. Rios. Is there anything else I can

assist you with?" the young man asked, his dark eyes shining his eagerness to be of further assistance.

The elderly man shook his head. "That will be all for now," he said as he took a slow walk across the lobby and out the front door.

The day was exceptionally warm, the sun settled high in the deep blue sky. Had there been the roar of the ocean, deep blue waters to kiss a sandy shoreline, he would have thought he was back home in his native Santo Domingo. Israel took a deep breath, filling his lungs with dry heat. Taking a seat on an empty bench in front of the building he pulled the day's newspaper from his back pocket, opening it to the sports section. He reread the article for the umpteenth time, one paragraph in particular filling his chest with pride— Newcomer Angel Rios knocked two homers off pitcher Arnie Munoz to lead the Titans past the White Sox, 5-3, on Tuesday afternoon in front of a packed crowd at Bank One Ballpark.

He refolded the paper, laying it against the bench at his side. Thursday would be Angel's last day home. Then his son would have to be on the road for a week, the team playing five consecutive away games before returning to Phoenix. It would be the only opportunity Israel would have to bring his son face-to-face with the beautiful black woman. He smiled as he thought about her.

Israel had gone to John Chen's office to meet her for himself. As he remembered the moment he couldn't stop himself from grinning wider, fully understanding what it was about Roshawn Bradsher that had knocked his son right off sides.

He could hear the two of them outside the office door. John Chen hadn't been happy about something and it had been clear to anyone within earshot that Roshawn hadn't been bothered in the least by his disapproval. The woman had stood her ground, almost defiant as she made her point and stood fast behind it, never once wavering from her position. Chen had tossed his hands up in exasperation while she had stared him down, clearly amused, her arms folded firmly across her chest.

Israel had poked his head in cautiously, peering around the wooden door to ensure it was safe to enter. The old man had smiled in greeting, waving gingerly as Mr. Chen had invited him inside.

"Mr. Rios, please come in. How are you, sir?"

"*Gracias.* I am well, Mr. Chen. I hope I am not interrupting?"

"Not at all," the man said as he tossed a look in Roshawn's direction.

The exquisite woman had smiled warmly, her gaze scrutinizing him from head to toe. She'd extended her hand, introducing herself before Chen could even think about doing so. "Hello, sir. I'm Roshawn Bradsher."

Israel had pressed her manicured fingers between his lightly callused palms, gently caressing the appendage between his own. "It is a pleasure to meet you, Señorita Bradsher."

"Please, just call me Roshawn. Can I get you something to drink, Mr. Rios? A cup of coffee or maybe some tea?"

He shook his head. "No, thank you. I only stopped by to say hello. Mr. Chen has been a good friend to me and my son."

Her smile had warmed him, the sweetness of it like a soothing touch.

"Are you and your son settling in comfortably?" Roshawn asked.

The man nodded. "Yes, thank you. We will be better once we are in a home of our own. Do you know my son?"

"We've met briefly. You must be very proud."

The old man beamed. "That I am," he boasted, his chest expanding. "He is a good son, my Angel."

Chen had taken that moment to interject. "Mr. Rios, why don't you have a seat so you and I can catch up." He turned to Roshawn. "We can finish our conversation later."

The woman had chuckled lightly. "I think you know my position, *Mr.* Chen. It's not going to change," she stated firmly, spinning out of the room.

Israel had watched as John Chen's jaw had tightened ever so slightly. The Asian man had fought the urge to call after her. Israel had laughed out loud as he dropped into one of the leather chairs in front of the man's desk. "She's full of fire, that one, no?" he'd said, gesturing toward the door the woman had just closed.

Chen had nodded, a smile pulling at his lips. "Fire and then some," he'd responded. "That's why she and I are no longer married," he had added unconsciously. "She drives me crazy."

"She was your wife, this woman?"

Chen took a seat opposite the man. "Many years ago. We're divorced now, but we remained good friends. Most times at least."

Israel nodded. "Do you have children together?"

"One daughter. Ming will be eighteen this year."

"You had your child very young."

"Too young, but we were very much in love." A wistful look crossed Chen's face. "Probably too much in love."

Israel smiled slightly.

Chen noted the look on the old man's face, his expression a cross between curiosity and amusement. Suddenly embarrassed, he struggled to explain himself. "Marriage was a huge responsibility. Roshawn saw it one way and I saw it another. We just weren't able to make it work for us."

"You still have love for her," Israel stated matter-of-factly.

Chen smiled. "Roshawn is the type of woman you never really get out of your system. One day though she'll find a man who can handle all that fire in her. When that happens I will be as happy for her as she has been for me and my new wife."

A moment of silence wafted into the room.

Chen smiled sheepishly. "So, now that I've spilled my soul, what can I do for you today?"

The two men laughed.

Israel shook his head. "I really did just stop by to say hello."

"Angel spoke to me about finding a home for you two. I know with his schedule things haven't been easy. I'm trying to see what I can do to help you out."

"My son worries about too many things. He shouldn't but I cannot tell him so."

Chen smiled. "It is what we sons should do, Mr. Rios."

Israel returned the smile as he rose to his feet. "Thank you, Mr. Chen. It has been good to talk with you again."

Chen extended his hand, both men shaking firmly. Back in the reception area, Roshawn greeted him warmly, her down-to-earth personality overly engaging. "Was he any help to you, Mr. Rios, or do I need to take over?" she'd asked jokingly.

The man grinned. "A beautiful woman who takes charge. You could hurt a man's heart."

"Only the right man," she had answered coyly.

"And who might that be?" Israel asked.

Roshawn shrugged, a smile still filling her face. "I don't know yet. Have you been spoken for, Mr. Rios?"

He laughed. "I am much too old for you, little one," he responded.

Roshawn laughed with him. "What's that old saying? Just because there's snow on the roof, doesn't mean there isn't fire down below?"

He shook his head and chuckled. "I don't know this saying, but I like it. I must remember this one." His head waved from side to side. "But no, I am not available, but I do have a son who is," he said, humor dancing in his eyes.

Roshawn could feel herself blushing, the heat of it warming her cheeks as thoughts of Angel danced through her mind. "I have met that son of yours. I don't know that he and I would get along very well. Plus, they say that he's quite the ladies' man. It doesn't sound like he's interested in any one woman having his heart."

"Do you believe everything they say?"

She shook her own head. "Not at all. Finding out for myself is always so much more fun."

"Then perhaps you should. Find out for yourself, that is."

Roshawn giggled. "Are you playing matchmaker for your son, Mr. Rios?"

The man leaned in close, taking a quick glance over his shoulder as he did. He rested his hands against her shoulders as he whispered into her ear. "My son needs much help, but don't tell him I told you so."

The two laughed easily.

"I like you, Mr. Rios. I think you and I are going to be great friends."

"We most definitely will be, but only if you call me Israel. We share a secret now, so we can only be on first names."

"Then Israel it is," Roshawn said as she walked with him toward the elevator.

As they reached the elevator doors and he pushed the button for the lobby, he reached out to give her a quick hug. "It has been very nice to meet you, Roshawn."

"The pleasure has been all mine, Israel. I hope I'll see you again soon." As the elevator doors had closed, both were still waving at each other.

Israel picked up his newspaper, tucking it easily beneath his arm as he made his way back inside the hotel. He was looking forward to his haircut on Thursday. But he was looking forward to his son and the woman being in the same room together more.

Ming had decided to spend the night, making herself comfortable in the guest bedroom. The two had talked for hours, watching movies on cable and consuming a large bowl of Orville Redenbacher's movie butter popcorn mixed with plain M&M's. The salt-and-sugar rush had been the perfect touch to end the evening. Ming had enjoyed her mother's company and her mother had relished their time together as well.

By the stroke of midnight Ming was sound asleep. Roshawn tiptoed into the room to open a side window so a breeze of fresh air could billow through the young woman's dreams. Ming stirred ever so slightly, rolling from one side of the double bed to the other, settling deeper against the plush pillows. Her mother smiled as she pulled the cotton sheet up over the child's shoulders and tiptoed her way out, closing the door gently behind her.

In her own bed, Roshawn tossed and turned about, her body restless. She had taken Ming to the ball game, both cheering excitedly from the bleachers. Angel Rios had hit a home run and bunt sacrifice to help the Titans take another win. The man had been running through her thoughts ever since.

She grinned as she thought about his father. Roshawn's mother had often told her that if you wanted to know what kind of man you were getting for the long haul, then you only needed to take a long look at his father. If the father was aging well, chances were, there was a thread of hope for his offspring. If there was any truth to that, then Angel Rios would surely age like an expensive bottle of fine wine. Israel Rios was a nice-looking man. With his silvery head, bronze complexion, well-maintained body and classic features, it was clear from where his son had inherited his good looks. Too bad, she thought, he hadn't gotten an ounce of his father's charm.

The next day mother and daughter headed over to the Children's Center together to spend some time. Ming had organized an afternoon tea party for the little girls in her youth group and both women were excited. The young ladies had all been instructed to come attired in their best dresses to coordinate with the wide-brimmed hats they'd constructed and decorated during the week. Roshawn had been thrilled when Ming had asked her to join them. The day before the duo had scoured the thrift shops and dollar stores, coming up with enough pairs of white gloves to add the finishing touch to the event.

As Ming drove them to the center, she was regaling her mother with details about her recent date with one of the center's volunteers, a college sophomore named Dixon Perry, who her father had taken an instant disliking to.

"Daddy's being unreasonable," Ming said, tossing her mother a quick glance as her attention fluctuated between the road and the conversation.

"Your father is being protective of you. That's what fathers are supposed to do."

Ming rolled her eyes. "But he won't even make an effort to get to know Dix."

"Ming, your father has very traditional views about relationships and I don't care how progressive he may want to think he is. Chen isn't ready for you to be dating at all, let alone dating a boy who's older than you are. You're barely out of high school and he's been in college for two years. Your dad's just not ready to see you grow up yet."

"You don't have a problem with it."

Roshawn chuckled. "Actually, I'm not crazy about it either. But I know you well enough to know that if your father and I were both against you seeing this boy, you'd marry him out of sheer spite."

Ming laughed. "No, I wouldn't."

Her mother rolled her eyes. "I raised you, remember?"

"Well, I think I should be allowed to see Dix whenever I want."

"What you will be allowed to do is whatever your father decides. You're living in his house, under his rules, and you have to respect that, Ming."

"I could move out."

"Where would you go?"

"I could live with you."

"You could, but I have rules, too. And one of my rules would definitely be that you couldn't see this Dix boy or any other boy whenever you wanted. Besides, I'm moving back to Seattle in a few weeks. Do you want to go back to Seattle?"

Ming tightened her grip on the steering wheel. "You parents are a pain."

Roshawn smiled, nodding her head. "It comes with your birth certificate. Once they stamp that seal on it, you belong to us until you're eighteen. You have a few more weeks to go before the law considers you grown, baby girl, and until then we get to make your life absolutely miserable. It's our duty."

The girl cast another look toward her mother. Roshawn reached out a hand to stroke her child's shoulder. The space between them went quiet for a brief minute. Roshawn reached to adjust the automobile's radio, turning up the volume on the local rap station. Ludacris was rhyming a new tune with Chingy and both women were bopping their heads in time to the beat. Roshawn suddenly broke the reverie, turning the radio back down.

"Ming, I know you like this boy a lot and I hope you're remembering what we taught you about protecting yourself."

"I'm not having sex with him, Mom," Ming responded, annoyance tainting her words.

"I'm not just talking about sex, baby girl. I want to make sure you're thinking about your emotional health as well as your physical health. Yes, if you decide to have sex definitely make sure you're protected. AIDS is still a major concern for black females as well as herpes, chlamydia and all the other diseases out there. But I also want to make sure you're using your common sense and ensuring this boy is treating you well and respecting you as a woman. You don't need any man beating down your spirit."

Ming nodded. "I love you, Mommy. And I promise, I will use the good sense you taught me. And if I'm not sure about something, you'll be the first one I come to talk to. Now can we please change the subject?"

Roshawn sighed. "I don't like worrying about you, Ming."

"I know. I also know that no matter what I do you're still going to find something to worry about."

"Well, I guess you know me well then."

"When are you going to start dating?" Ming asked, turning the tables on her mother.

Roshawn turned to give the girl a quick look, her mouth sputtering open and then closed.

Ming asked again. "You do plan to date sometime soon, I hope."

"I'll date as soon as I meet someone I'm interested in."

"Why don't you ask Daddy to introduce you to someone?"

"I'm not interested in your father fixing me up with anyone but thank you for the suggestion."

Ming giggled. "How about Nina? I bet she knows a lot of men she could introduce you to. Maybe one of the ball players?"

"The ball players are too young for me. Most of them aren't much older than you are."

"So what's wrong with that?"

Roshawn shook her head. "Why all the questions about my love life all of a sudden?"

Ming paused, her gaze dancing around the intersection as they sat in wait at a red light. "Because I'm worried about you," the girl said, her eyes meeting her mother's intense stare.

"Me? Why are you worried about me?"

Ming paused for a second time. "If I ask you something, promise me you won't get mad?"

Roshawn tossed her a look of irritation. "What, Ming?"

"Are you hoping you and Daddy will get back together? Is that why you won't date anyone else?"

Roshawn was thrown by the question, her surprise registering on her face. "No," she said, shaking her head emphatically. "Where did you get that idea?"

"I know you and Daddy were still seeing each other before

he married Allison. I used to hope you two might get back together myself, but Daddy's happy with Allison. I want you to be happy, too, and I don't want you wishing for something that will probably never happen."

Roshawn sat back against her seat, her body suddenly feeling very heavy where she sat. Her daughter's astute candor had taken her aback. She could feel her child waiting anxiously for her to respond. Roshawn's head bobbed slowly against her shoulders.

"Your father and I had a very special relationship. I can't deny that. And maybe there was a part of me that wasn't ready to let him go, but I have. I know how much Allison means to him. I can see how happy he is with her and I love and respect your father enough to want him to be happy. What I had with Chen has nothing whatsoever to do with why I'm not dating now. I just haven't found the right man. But when I do, I'll let you know."

Ming smiled. "You're not being too picky, are you?"

Roshawn smiled back. "Being picky is why you have such a wonderful father. I will be as picky as I have to be."

"You're waiting for the butterflies, aren't you?"

Roshawn's smile widened. "You remembered that?" she said softly, her gaze searching her daughter's profile.

Ming nodded. "Yes. And I understand now because Dixon gives me butterflies," she said softly.

Roshawn could feel the tears rising against her eyes. Ming had only been twelve when they'd had one of their first mother-daughter conversations about boys, love and sex. Ming had asked her how she'd known she'd been in love with Chen and Roshawn had told her that when true love touches you, butterflies dance in your heart. She'd told her when the butterflies made her want to dance with them, then she'd know the man who had put them there was a man who was worthy of her love. But these aren't ordinary butterflies, Roshawn had intoned. In fact, they were special butterflies, winged angels that would make her want to be a better person, that would make her want to do what was right and good. These butterflies would make her want to build dreams and wishes with the man whose own butterflies danced alongside hers. Roshawn had hugged her twelve-year-old tightly. "You'll know," Roshawn had said, "because it won't be about how your body feels when he's close to you, but how your spirit feels when he isn't. The butterflies will keep you floating on top of the world because you will have found friendship that will last you a lifetime."

Ming pulled into an empty parking space in the center's partially filled lot. She leaned to kiss her mother's cheek, saying nothing else as she made her way out of the car. Roshawn sat alone for a quick minute before she followed her child through the front doors of the center, thinking that she and Chen would have to have a long talk about Ming and Mr. Dixon Perry.

Chapter 10

He should have been packing, getting his mind focused on the task ahead of him. Their next five games would not be easy, the San Diego Padres, Texas Rangers and Los Angeles Angels, giving them a real run for the pennant. Instead, he was navigating his way to some woman's home in Paradise Valley so that his father could get his hair cut. Angel took a deep breath to calm his annoyance, holding it briefly before letting it ease back out past his lips.

"What was wrong with the barber at the shopping center, *Papí?*" he asked.

Israel shrugged, his gaze focused on the views beyond the passenger side window of Angel's car. "I am told this woman is much better. She will have us looking like kings when she is done."

"And who told you this?"

"That very nice Señora Tracy."

"When did you see her?"

"After the game the other evening. We were admiring her husband's new haircut. He looks much better by the way," the man interjected, cutting an eye toward his son before continuing. "She and I, we were talking together and she told me about this new stylist. She said I would be very pleased."

Angel shook his head. "I don't know about this, *Papí*."

The old man laughed. "What is there to know, *hijo?* We will still be handsome men when she is done." He brushed his fingers against his chin, pulling at a nonexistent beard.

They were both laughing as they pulled into the driveway and exited the car. Both men took in the surroundings, admiring the house and its location.

"This is a very nice area, *hijo*. And a very nice house. We should look for a home near this one."

Angel nodded. "We just might do that, *Papí*. We'll have to wait and see."

They made their way to the front door and pushed the bell. The doorbell chimed softly, a low tinkle of bells rippling through the air. A very pretty young woman answered, smiling as she recognized Angel.

"Hi, may I help you?" she asked politely.

Angel nodded. "Hello. We have an appointment for a haircut. I think we are in the right place…"

The teenager nodded her head. "My mom is in the kitchen. Please, come on in."

As they entered the room, the girl's excitement bubbled. "I can't believe you're here! You're Angel Rios, aren't you? Great game the other night. Mom didn't say you were her appointment."

"That's because Mom had no idea," a soft voice said from the doorway.

Both men turned to see who had spoken and Israel beamed at the surprised look on both her and Angel's faces.

"Roshawn, my new friend! How are you?"

Roshawn smiled. "Very well. How are you, Israel?"

Israel nodded, looking from her to his son and back. "We did not know our appointment was with you," he said, his smile and the gleam in his eye saying otherwise.

Roshawn caught the look he gave her and she shook her head as she walked to his side. Wrapping her arms around him, she hugged him tightly as she whispered into his ear. "You are so bad!"

The man chuckled as he whispered back. "I can be so at times."

Roshawn turned her attention toward Angel. "Mr. Rios, it's a pleasure to see you again, as well."

The man nodded. "You and my father know each other?"

"We met earlier this week. We had a wonderful time together. Didn't we, Israel?"

"Yes, we did," he said, still beaming.

Roshawn gestured in Ming's direction, the girl brimming with excitement. "This is my daughter, Ming. Ming, this is Mr. Rios and his son, Angel Rios."

Israel pressed his palms to Ming's cheeks and kissed her forehead. "She is a beauty this one. Like her mother. John Chen must be very proud."

Ming's smile widened. "Thank you."

"It's very nice to meet you," Angel said, his tone still overly polite. Curiosity graced his face as he tried to make the connection between the girl, Roshawn and the Titans' scouting director.

Roshawn answered as if having read his mind. "Chen is my ex-husband and Ming's father," she said.

He nodded, suddenly connecting the girl's features to her parents.

"So," Roshawn said, gesturing for the two of them to follow her toward the back of the house. "What are you gentlemen having done this evening?"

"We desire two of your special haircuts," Israel answered. "We are told that you are the very best. And you also do the shaving?"

Roshawn nodded.

"I wasn't planning—" Angel started before being interrupted by his father.

"Two haircuts," the older man stated firmly, "and two shaves."

Roshawn reached to pull her fingers through Angel's thick, black curls. His gaze locked with hers and he held it for just a quick minute before having to drop his eyes to the floor, a current of electricity consuming him. Roshawn felt it as well and pulled her hand back as if burned. She clasped it tightly beneath the palm of her other hand and turned back toward Israel.

"Why don't we do you first, Israel," she said.

The old man took a seat on the high stool that Roshawn had placed in the center of the floor. A towel across his back and shoulders was followed by a plastic apron over his clothes that Roshawn tied easily at the nape of his neck. She motioned toward Angel with her eyes, gesturing for him to take a seat and relax.

"Make yourself comfortable, Mr. Rios," she said.

"Angel," he answered as he took a seat at the marble counter. "Please, call me Angel."

"Are you?" Roshawn asked.

"Am I what?"

"An angel?"

Israel chuckled. "Since he was a baby," the man responded. "That is why his mother gave him the name. It suited his personality."

Roshawn tossed Angel a wry smile. Reaching for a pair of scissors on the counter she began to cut hair, snipping quickly at the man's excess length.

"You have beautiful hair," she said, her fingers gliding through the locks. "It has a beautiful curl pattern."

"Gracias."

Behind her Angel grunted, a low snarl that caused her to turn to stare in his direction. His eyes skated around the room, focusing everywhere except on her as she stood watching him, her hands and the scissors frozen in midair.

"Is there something wrong, Angel?"

He shook his head, glancing down to his watch. "We are just on a tight schedule if you can please hurry this up," he said, his tone just a shade of gruff.

"Are you always this pleasant to be around or do you have to work at it?"

Angel eyed her, taken aback by her obvious sarcasm. "I don't know what you mean."

Israel interjected. "My son needs to learn how to relax. He doesn't know how to enjoy himself."

Angel rolled his eyes, biting his tongue not to respond.

Roshawn turned her attention back to Israel, continuing with his haircut. The two chatted easily as Angel sat stone-faced. He struggled not to stare. The oversize T-shirt she wore draped loosely over her body, stopping just at the bend of her knee. Her legs were bare, short shorts hidden beneath the cotton fabric. Every so often the T-shirt would pull tight against her body and he could see that she wore no bra, her small bustline having no need for one. At one point he detected the slight rise of her nipples and his body reacted without warning, energy surging below his waistline.

Angel closed his eyes and began to count, Roshawn's laughter further irritating his senses. When he felt in control enough to open them again, Roshawn was wrapping a plush white towel around his father's face, the aroma of aftershave filtering through the air. Israel had gone quiet, relaxing beneath the warm, moist fabric. As Angel sat watching her work, his gaze locked with hers and the two stared, neither saying one word. Just as quickly, Roshawn broke the connection, moving her attention back to his father.

Angel closed his eyes again, the image of Roshawn lost in his arms filling his thoughts. He was suddenly consumed with a desire to feel her against him. He wanted to touch her, to taste her, and as he fell into the fantasy, energy surged. Angel shook his head from side to side and began to count all over again.

Roshawn watched him out of the corner of her eye as he sat with his palms cupped tightly together in his lap and his eyes shut. He appeared completely lost in thought, oblivious to her and everything else around him. At one point he bit down against his bottom lip and then he gasped for air, opening his eyes wide to see if anyone had been watching him. Roshawn fought the urge to blatantly stare but the sight of him was causing her blood pressure to rise, warmth wafting through her body.

She passed a hand mirror to Israel as the man beamed his approval, coming to his feet. Gesturing, she pointed to the full-length mirror and watched as the old man eased his way to take a look at his reflection.

"Whenever you're ready, Angel," Roshawn said as she

stood beside the now empty chair, gesturing for him to come take a seat. Israel stood at the end of the hallway, admiring himself in the mirror.

Once again her stare was penetrating and he felt his legs quiver as he rose from his seat. Taking two quick strides he dropped heavily onto the seat beside her. Roshawn pulled both hands through his hair, her fingers lightly brushing against his hairline before easing through his thick mane. At the nape of his neck she gently caressed the rise of fuzz with the tips of her fingers. The motion caused him to jump ever so slightly.

Roshawn reached for a second towel and the plastic drape, wrapping both around him. "Your hair texture is curlier and heavier than your father's. I would prefer to use the clippers on your head. That way I can clean up your back hairline at the same time."

He nodded. "Whatever you think best."

"You're not much of a talker, are you?"

"Only when I have something that needs to be said."

"Well, do you prefer a certain cut over another?" Roshawn asked.

He shrugged. "It is usually cut the same, round all over. But not too short. I don't want too short."

Roshawn reached around him to pull at the cord to the electric clippers, easing it out of the way behind the chair. Angel caught a whiff of her perfume, the light floral scent wafting through his bloodstream. It made him dizzy with sudden wanting and he struggled against the sensations flooding through him.

"I'd like to change the style just a little, if you'll permit me to," Roshawn said, interrupting his thoughts. "I think it would look better on you and the curl pattern would lay better if I tapered it lower in the back and on the sides and removed just a bit more of the fullness out of the top. I think the style now is just a little too heavy for your face."

"I said not too short," the man responded curtly.

Roshawn heaved a light sigh. *This is like pulling teeth,* she thought to herself. *Why does he have to be so good-looking?*

From the other side of the room she could feel Israel staring at them. She turned to toss the man a look, shaking her head in his direction. He laughed, motioning toward the family room where Ming was watching television. "I think I will go watch this movie with your daughter, if that is all right with you, Roshawn?"

She nodded. "Of course. Please, make yourself right at home, Israel."

He gave her a quick wink as he headed into the other room leaving the two of them alone.

"Your father is something else," Roshawn said with a light laugh. "He must be great company for you."

"I do not appreciate you using my father to get next to me," Angel said, looking at her.

Roshawn laughed. "Boy, you must have fallen down and bumped this big head of yours," she said, the amusement shimmering in her voice.

Angel bristled. "I know how all you women are. You don't fool me."

"And pray tell, Mr. Rios. What do you think you know about all women?"

"I know that you will do anything to bleed a man dry. You will steal him blind and whisper in his ear at the same time to distract him. Women can't be trusted. You will get what you want by any means necessary. That makes you dangerous and a dangerous woman should never be trusted. None of you."

"And you have personally met and experienced every woman in the world to come to such a profound opinion of us?"

"It only takes one to shake her breasts and behind in a man's face to understand just how far you will go to deceive him. Like you are doing now. Making nice to an old man to see how far you can get with his son."

After a quick blade change, the clippers hummed in Roshawn's hand. "Well, Mr. Rios, let me enlighten you. I… am…not…like…all…women…" she said, slowly enunciating each word. "In fact, I'm not like any woman you have ever met, and I'm about to make an impression you won't soon forget."

With that said, Roshawn swiped the blades of the clippers across Angel's head, hacking at the significant length of every strand of hair. Angel gasped in shock, his hands flying to his head. The cut was a spectrum of high and low spots with a single bald patch of scalp that split down the middle of his skull, running from his hairline back. Roshawn cut the power to her tools, tossing him an angry glare as she stomped out of the room. Angel raged in Spanish, cursing profusely. Ming and Israel both jumped to their feet, racing past Roshawn to see what had happened. At the sight of him, Ming's hands flew to her mouth to stifle a sudden rush of giggles. Israel laughed outright, throwing back his head in glee.

Angel was not amused as he snatched the apron and towel from around his neck. He hurled himself into the room behind her, still raging in his native tongue. Roshawn had reclined her body against a chenille settee, clicking the television remote in her hand. She barely gave him a glance as he hovered angrily above her. Israel and Ming were still laughing in the doorway.

"I cannot believe this," Angel spewed harshly, switching from Spanish to English. "I am not paying you a dime for what you have done."

Roshawn cut her eye up at him. She leaned forward ever so slightly. "Your haircut was on the house. Consider it my personal gift to you. But you owe me one hundred dollars for your father's haircut and shave."

Angel snarled, his nostrils flaring and his eyes wide with fury. He turned toward his father, fuming in Spanish for a second time. "This woman is crazy. Look at what she has done to my head. I look like a buffoon. I am not paying her one cent. Not one. Look at her. She's sitting there like it's nothing. A gift she says. She's a lunatic," he screamed, the comments meant only for his father to understand.

Israel motioned with both hands, his palms waving his son to calm down. He responded in Spanish. "You need to relax, son. It is nothing that can't be fixed. We will shave it all when we get back to the hotel. No one will ever know. It will grow back, eventually."

Angel threw up his hands in frustration. Behind him, Roshawn came to her feet, her hands falling against the lean lines of her hips. As Angel turned back around to face her, she stepped directly in front of him, her gaze locking with his.

"Señor Rios," she started, her Spanish as close to perfect as his. "I am neither crazy, nor a lunatic. You got exactly what you deserved. And you look like the arrogant, pompous ass that you are. Just more trendy and definitely stylish. Now, pay me my money and get out of my house."

Behind her, Israel beamed, reaching into his pocket for five twenty-dollar bills. He passed her the cash as Angel stormed toward the front door. Laughter still danced in Israel's eyes.

Roshawn called after him, still speaking in Spanish. "Once you shave your head I suggest you use a quality sunscreen for the next few weeks. You'll burn badly if you get too much sun too fast. We wouldn't want that to happen. It might hurt."

Tossing her one last glare, Angel stomped from the house, calling for his father to hurry up. As the door slammed closed, Roshawn burst out laughing, falling into Israel's outstretched arms. The man hugged her warmly.

"You are much fun, *chica!*" he said.

"Your son is a spoiled brat. He needed to be put into his place. I don't know how you put up with him."

The man smiled. "My son, he likes you. And I think you like him. You two will be good for each other."

"I don't think so. I like you much more than I like your son," she said teasingly.

The man chuckled. "But my son is the only one who is available." He moved toward the front door, pulling her by the hand behind him.

Roshawn kissed his cheek. "You should come for dinner while Angel is gone. Ming and I will call you to make plans."

"I look forward to it," he said. He gave Ming a quick wink as she waved goodbye. *"Buenos noches, señoritas!"*

"Adios, Israel. Adios."

Angel was still fuming as he waited in the car for his father, a baseball cap sitting low on his head. He was angry, but what confused him was that the sentiment was not directed at that woman. He was more upset with himself and the conflict of emotions coursing through his bloodstream. As much as he had wanted to push her as far away as he could muster, there had still been a larger part of him that had wanted to pull her to him, to drop headfirst into that spellbinding gaze that rendered him totally useless. It was as if he'd been hungry for her, the eagerness nearing starvation as he purposely denied himself fulfillment. And then he had lashed out, unnecessarily ugly. Through it all she'd not been moved in the least, her emotions held in check. Even as she'd butchered his head, she had been in control, wielding dominion over him. His whole body shivered, continuing to shake with one rush of emotion after another.

As his father got into the vehicle, Angel's eyes were shut tight. Moisture pressed hot against the back of his eyelids. As if sensing his conflict, Israel patted him easily against his forearm. The two sat quietly for a quick minute. Then Angel began to laugh first, his father joining in until both of them were wiping the tears of it from their faces. Angel shifted the car into Drive and eased his way back onto the main road. Beside him, Israel eyed him smugly. He caught his father's gaze, holding it for a second before turning his attention back to the road.

"What?" he asked, a hint of tension still straining in his voice.

Israel chuckled. "You are lucky. It is a good thing you made her mad before she got to your shave. She might have cut your throat instead of just your hair." The man laughed again, the sound of it resonating in the space of the car.

"Did you know she could speak Spanish?" Angel asked, calm having returned to his voice.

Israel shook his head. "No. That was also a surprise to me."

Angel nodded his agreement as Israel chuckled under his breath. "She's full of fire, that woman is," his father muttered softly. "Full of fire!"

Chapter 11

The two women were laughing shamelessly in Nordstrom's dressing room as Nina gave Roshawn a gossip update. "That *girl* he was with looked like a man in drag. A very pretty man, but a man," she giggled, flouncing in front of the mirror in a red-checked gingham sundress.

Roshawn shook her head. "You look like a picnic table," she said, adjusting the top of a yellow capri set she was modeling.

"Look who's talking, Big Bird!" Nina chuckled.

Both women stood side by side studying each others' reflection in the mirror. Both burst out laughing at the same time.

"Oh, oh, oh!" Nina chimed as Roshawn stepped back into her own changing cubicle. "Have you seen Angel Rios? Boyfriend shaved his head!"

Roshawn grinned behind her curtain. "Oh, really?" she said, fighting to keep her voice as nonchalant as she could.

"He's as bald as a baby's butt. Talk about a hottie! That

man was gorgeous before, but this look has taken him to a whole new level of scrumptious!"

Roshawn rolled her eyes as Nina leaned in to her cubicle, passing her a striped Juicy Couture halter dress. "You should try this on. It will look much better on you than on me," Nina said.

Roshawn took the garment from her friend's hands and pulled it on over her head. She adjusted it against her lean frame, admiring it in the mirror. "I do like this."

"Told you. I think Angel would like it on you, too."

"You're obsessed with that man."

"No, I'm not. I just think you two would be cute together."

Roshawn rolled her eyes again.

"His father was asking about you, you know."

The woman laughed. "What did Israel want to know about me?"

"He was just interested in knowing if you were dating anyone, what you liked, what you didn't like."

"And you told him what?"

"I told him I thought his son would be perfect for you and he agreed."

Roshawn shook her head. "So, now both of you are playing matchmaker?"

Nina grinned. "Isn't it great!"

Roshawn smoothed the lines of the dress down against her body. "I don't think Angel Rios and I will be hooking up any time soon. I don't like anything about that man," she said firmly, spinning into a lengthy discourse about all she found wrong with him, starting with the obvious difference in their ages and ending with the man's arrogant attitude.

Nina eyed her curiously as she listened. A moment of

silence passed between them as Roshawn finished and stood staring at her friend for a response.

Nina chuckled. "Now, who were you trying to convince—you or me?"

Roshawn spun toward the wall, reaching for the clothes she'd arrived in. "Oh, please."

"You got it bad and you don't even know it."

Roshawn sucked her teeth. "Got what bad?"

"The hots for Angel Rios. You like the man. You like the man a lot."

"You're crazy. You and his father both are nuts if you think there will ever be anything between me and that man."

Nina was still grinning as they made their way out of the changing area toward the checkout counter. "Uh-huh!"

Israel had been invited to the Bradsher home for Sunday supper. He was excited and told his son so when the two had spoken by telephone earlier that day. Their conversation had taken place in the early hours of the morning as both were preparing for Sunday Mass, Israel headed to Iglesia del Nazareno, and Angel to one of the local Catholic churches in Dallas, Texas where the team was scheduled to play the Rangers later that afternoon.

His son had gone quiet at the mention of Roshawn's name, then made it clear he had no interest in discussing her with his father or anyone else, ever again. "Look, *Papí,*" he'd professed. "I'm not interested in that woman. If you like her, fine. That's your choice. I don't have to like anything about her."

Israel had chuckled under his breath, knowing what Angel wasn't yet willing to admit: Roshawn excited him. The woman had a choke hold on his attention and Angel really had no interest in her ever letting go. It was times like this Israel wanted to give his boy a good swift whack upside his hard, bald head. The old man laughed out loud as he stepped out of a taxi in Roshawn's driveway and paid the driver.

Ming answered the front door, greeting him warmly. "Hi, Mr. Rios. Please, come on in."

"*Hola!* How are you, precious?"

"Fine, thank you, sir."

"Please. You no call me sir, or Mr. Rios. You call me, *Abuelo,* okay?" he said wrapping an arm around her shoulder. "*Abuelo* is grandfather in Spanish."

Ming grinned. "Yes, sir," she said.

Israel held up his index finger shaking it and his head. "*Abuelo.*"

"Yes, *Abuelo,*" she said, reaching to kiss his cheek.

The man smiled, then took a deep inhale of breath. "Something smells very good," he said, following the girl into the kitchen.

Roshawn stood at the stove, waving hello with a wooden spoon. "Israel, welcome! How are you today?" she asked, moving to his side to give the man a quick hug.

"I am dining with two beautiful women. I am a happy man."

Roshawn laughed. "Well, I hope you're still happy after you've eaten."

"It smells very good," he said, peering over her shoulder toward the casserole pot that simmered on a low burner. He looked at her questioningly. "It reminds me of home. A dish my wife use to make for me."

Roshawn smiled. "I had to do a little research, but I'm told it's a very popular dish in the Dominican Republic."

Israel clasped his hands together excitedly, moving to the stove to peer beneath the pot's lid. "*Puerco Guisado!*" he said.

Roshawn nodded her head. "That's right. Pork stew, and if you're ready to eat, it's ready to be served."

Israel and Ming took a seat at the dining room table, the two chatting about Ming's plans for school, her summer holiday, and the new boyfriend she had taken an interest in. Israel tossed his hands up, skewing his face in disapproval. "You are too young for boys," he declared, tossing a look toward Roshawn. "She is too young for boys!"

The girl giggled. "That's what my dad says."

"You must listen to your father. John Chen is a very wise man. Your father, he will always tell you what is best," the man said, his head bobbing up and down against his shoulders.

Roshawn had transferred the stew to a soup tureen, garnishing the mixture of pork, tomatoes and spices with a sprinkling of parsley. A warm plate of flour tortillas and a garden salad completed the meal. As she served their plates, Israel hummed his approval. *"Muy bueno,"* he said as he dropped a cloth napkin into his lap. "Very good. Very good."

The woman gestured toward her daughter. "Ming, would you please bless the table," she commanded.

They all bowed their heads in prayer as Ming said the grace. From the first bite to the last, Israel felt more at home than he had felt in a long while. The hearty meal brought back fond memories of home and his late wife and as he settled back against his chair, his palms folded over a bulging belly, he said so.

"Roshawn, you have made me a very happy man tonight. Now, if you would only marry my son, I could die in peace knowing all would be well for Angel and for you."

Ming giggled and Roshawn laughed loudly. "You don't want much, do you Israel?"

The two chuckled as if they shared a secret. Ming asked to be excused from the table, heading back to her room to get on the new cell phone her father had given her.

"Why don't you and I have dessert and coffee on the patio," Roshawn said, pointing toward the outdoors. Israel nodded, then headed out the glass doors to settle himself comfortably against the cushioned seats.

The sun was just beginning to set and the early evening sky glistened in vibrant shades of red, orange and gold. The mountains in the distance appeared to be on fire from the intensity. Israel took a deep breath, the hot afternoon air starting to cool comfortably. Roshawn soon joined him with two cups of chicory coffee and two servings of caramel flan situated on a rattan tray. As she settled down beside him both allowed the quiet and the rich custard to rule the moment.

As Israel savored his last bite, Roshawn broke the silence. "Please, tell me about Angel's mother. It sounds like your wife was an incredible woman."

He took a slow sip of his coffee, a moment of deep reflection crossing his face. Roshawn turned in her seat to face him, pulling her legs beneath her body as she watched him. When he spoke, he did so in Spanish, the comfort of his native tongue obvious. Roshawn smiled ever so slightly.

"A man is blessed when he finds the one love who changes his whole world for the better. My beautiful wife, Graciella, she was my one great love. We were just babies when we fell in love. Our families both came from a long line of farmers and our two fathers owned land side by side. She and her sister use to run and play in the fields and I would watch them as I helped my father tend to the gardens. Oh, she was so beautiful, she was!

"She had beautiful skin like you. It had been kissed dark

by the sun, and her hair was long and thick, hanging to her waist. And she had the most beautiful eyes!" The man gasped at the memory, his own eyes glistening with moisture. He pulled a hand to his chest as if it hurt him to remember. Roshawn's eyes fell to the spot over his heart where he rubbed. The moment passed as he continued.

"I knew from the moment I first saw her that she would be my wife. She used to tell people that I only knew after she told me that it would be so." He chuckled lightly. "We were married very young and we were so happy. Few will ever know that kind of happiness.

"We had wanted many children but my wife had much female sickness. We lost three babies from female problems and that broke both of our hearts. But we had much love for each other and we knew that it would be God's will if we were to be blessed with babies and we would accept whatever he would want for us."

The man paused as Roshawn reached out to rest a palm against his arm. The gesture was comforting as he continued. "Many years passed and we accepted that it was just not to be. Then one day, my Graciella was pregnant with our Angel. She called him Angel from the moment she knew he was coming and that has been his name ever since."

Roshawn smiled. A moment of silence wafted over them for a second time. "Angel must have made you both very happy," she said softly.

He nodded. "We were very excited about his coming. My Graciella wanted so much to be a good mother. But God had other plans for her. She passed away in childbirth. She became very sick and it was too much for her delicate body."

Roshawn clasped her fingers to her lips, tears rising in her eyes. "I'm so sorry, Israel," she said softly.

The man shook his head, wiping at the moisture that had filled his eyes. "She was the love of my life and she gave me a beautiful son. And I will be with her again one day when God is finished with me here. But I would very much like to see you and my Angel married before I go, and I would like to hold my grandson at least once."

Roshawn shook her head as she raised her eyebrows at the man.

He laughed. "You two will make beautiful babies together."

She flipped her hand at him. "I am too old to even be thinking about a baby. Ming will be eighteen for goodness sake!"

The man waved his head up and down. "You will see," he said. "A father knows these things."

"So, tell me," Roshawn asked, quickly changing the subject. "Why does Angel think all women are evil and out to get him?"

The man shifted forward in his seat and sighed. "My son has not had good experiences with women. Many have tried to take advantage of his kindness. I have taught him that he has to be careful to wait for a woman who will love him because of what is in his heart and not because of what he does, or the money and land he has. He needs a woman who will challenge him and make him be a stronger man. A woman like you."

Israel could see her mulling over what he had said, the comment churning through her mind. They both drifted comfortably back into the silence, watching as the last ray of sunlight drifted out of view. As if on cue the timer for the outside patio lights initiated and the soft glow of light flicked on, casting an easy glow across the landscape.

"Now, you must tell me something," Israel said, resuming the conversation.

"What's that?"

"Where did you learn to speak Spanish?"

Roshawn grinned. "I studied it in school, then I spent a year in Portugal and Spain studying abroad. I had followed Chen there on a student internship the year before we were married. I also speak Chinese and some French."

The man nodded, clearly impressed. There was definitely more to the woman than what may have met the eye. And what met the eye was clearly imposing.

Roshawn shrugged. "It's really no big deal. I only learned Chinese so I'd know when Chen and his parents were talking about me and he taught me what little French I know."

The man gave her a wide grin as he came to his feet, Roshawn joining him. "My son will do well to marry such a beautiful, intelligent woman who can also cook. He will do very, very well."

The duo had talked for a long while. The evening ended when Chen had come to retrieve his daughter, offering Israel a ride back to his hotel at the same time. As Roshawn rinsed the last of the dirty dishes, stacking them neatly into the dishwasher, she couldn't help but think about the old man and the conversation they'd shared over the evening. Inevitably, thinking about Israel meant thinking about Angel. She heaved a deep sigh as she moved from the back door to the front, ensuring each was latched securely for the night.

Roshawn would never admit it out loud, but Angel Rios had constantly been on her mind. She woke up thinking about him, went to bed wondering about him, thoughts of him flooding her senses throughout the day. They had watched the game on television and she'd been excited to see him, observing him in action on the baseball field. And she had suppressed the emotion, denying it to Israel, and Ming, and mostly to herself.

Stripping out of her clothes, she ran a bath, filling the over-size tub with hot water and jasmine-scented bath beads. Strolling naked into the bedroom she switched on the CD player, flooding the room with music. Her LL Cool J CD was in the player and the heavy beat of "Move Somethin'" suddenly rocked the room. She stood listening for a brief moment, her head and body bouncing in time to the beat.

Roshawn adjusted the volume, raising it just a touch before heading back into the bathroom and lowering her body into the tub. The music felt good, almost tactile, as the vibration coursed through her body. In combination with the misty heat that filled the space and the gentle waves of moisture that flowed over her skin, Roshawn found herself breathing heavily, Angel Rios once again dominating her thoughts.

Curiosity was getting the better of her. She was curious to know what moved him, to discover what lay beneath his staunch exterior. Angel Rios was intriguing and Roshawn was challenged to know what it would take to break him down, to get into his head, and maybe even move his heart.

She swiped a damp palm across her brow, brushing at the rise of moisture that beaded over her skin. A faint smile lifted the lines of her mouth as LL teased her with "Apple Cobbler." The sexual innuendo was anything but subtle as the man likened an intimate oral act to his favorite dessert. Thoughts of Angel surged through her femaleness and made her stomach quiver with excitement. Goose bumps prickled the length of her arms.

The night of his haircut, as her fingers had danced through his hair, her body leaning against his, her nipples had blossomed rock hard against the cotton fabric of her T-shirt. Heat had billowed through her pores and had the opportunity presented itself she would have gladly explored every square inch of Angel Rios. Roshawn's smile widened at the thought.

A sudden realization consumed her. Sitting upright, she pulled her knees to her chest, wrapping her arms tightly around her legs. One tear trickled the length of her cheek, dancing with the steamy mist in the room. Her emotions were a sudden whirlwind as she reflected on what was happening with her.

John Chen was clearly out of her system. Roshawn had loved him so hard and for so long, that even when she knew it was better for them to not be married, she had been unwilling to completely let him go. John had been the one man she had welcomed into her bed without thought or reservation as he had full occupancy over her heart. And it suddenly dawned on her that she had finally let him go, opening herself to the possibility of letting someone else in. And whether she said it out loud or not, Angel Rios had moved her spirit and was clearly in playing position to tighten a firm grip around her heart.

Angel dropped to the bed, stretching the length of his body across the mattress. The hotel room was neither extravagant nor elaborate, simply comfortable and accommodating. A king-size bed, two chairs, a desk and the requisite television comprised the bulk of the furniture. As hotel rooms went, it was a very nice one but Angel barely noticed, having grown weary of them all.

The team had played well and his body was now feeling

the effects. A massage would have been nice but he had no interest in any of the team's physical therapists putting their hands on him. After the ride from the home team's stadium, he had left a few of the players in the hotel bar celebrating their win. And now he was alone, staring up at the ceiling, his thoughts lost on that woman. He pulled his palm across the smooth flesh on his head. He actually liked the look, surprised that a shaved head was flattering on him.

He reflected back on the dialogue he had just had with his father. The man had boasted about his evening, singing Roshawn's praises. It had become increasingly clear to Angel during the course of their conversation that his father's obsession with that woman was about him being concerned for his son's future. The old man whole-heartedly believed that Roshawn Bradsher was the perfect woman for his only child.

After the hair debacle Angel had ventured to call her, dialing both her office and home numbers. Voice mail and an answering machine had picked up the first three calls. He'd hung up on the last one, the only time she'd actually answered. The sound of her voice had left him flustered, his voice catching in his throat and he'd hung up, not having a clue what he wanted to say.

A rush of heat surged through his groin and he cupped his hand over his crotch to stall the sudden rise of wanting. It seemed almost a lifetime ago when he would just have found a willing, pretty face to relieve his tension, sending his playmate on her way when the moment was over. For this trip, he had not even bothered to pack his usual supply of condoms. He had known as he sat in her kitchen watching her that until the two of them tested the waters to see what might happen between them, he had no further interest whatsoever in any other woman. Maybe they could make something work. And maybe they couldn't, but he had to know and he was more than willing to wait until he could make that happen.

Chapter 12

His door was partially closed and Chen was calling for her attention as she made her way into the outer office. All the telephone lines were ringing at the same time and Roshawn gestured with her index finger for him to give her one quick minute to get a handle on things. After taking one message, transferring a second call, and then answering a question for an assistant coach, Roshawn made her way into Chen's office.

"Good morning," she said, greeting him cheerfully as she pushed the office door open wider.

"Good morning," the man responded. "Roshawn, I believe you know Angel Rios," he said, gesturing to the occupied seat across from his desk.

Angel came to his feet, his body stiffening as he extended his hand politely. "It's very nice to see you again, Roshawn," he said softly, his gaze piercing hers.

Roshawn held the stare, both holding the handshake two

seconds longer than necessary. Chen stared from one to the other, his gaze landing back on his ex-wife's face as he noted the sudden rise of tension between the two. He cleared his throat to regain their attention. As if caught with her fingers in the cookie jar, Roshawn dropped her eyes to the floor, pulling her hand back to her side before looking back up again. "It's very nice to see you again as well, Angel," she finally responded.

Angel nodded ever so slightly as he sat back down. Chen gestured for Roshawn to take the empty seat beside the man.

"I need to put you on a special assignment, Roshawn. Angel and his father need to find a permanent home here in the area, but with the season having started he doesn't have the time to spend with a real estate agent the way he would like. We need you to narrow down a few selections for them to look at." Chen passed her a folder of documents. "This is a complete listing of everything that's on the market currently that falls within Angel's price range. You need to view them, figure out which two or three you think might be best, and then catch up with Angel to arrange time for him and his father to see them."

Roshawn nodded. "Is there anything special that you'd like me to look for, Angel?" she asked.

"You two might want to sit down together to talk about that," Chen said, taking a quick glance down at his gold wristwatch. "Please feel free to use my office. Right now, I have a meeting I need to get to so I'm going to leave you two to figure out the details. Roshawn, the name and telephone number for the realty agency is in the folder. The agent's name is Chelsea and she's very good." He turned to Angel. "Angel, you're in very good hands. If you need anything else you know where to find me."

Roshawn was still nodding as Chen grabbed his briefcase,

his suit jacket and his car keys before he raced out the door. There was an awkward moment of quiet as the two watched him until he rounded the corner and disappeared from sight. Roshawn broke the silence as she turned back toward Angel and eyed him smugly. "I like your haircut," she said. "Looks like your stylist did you a favor."

A smirk crossed his face as he moved a hand over his head. He shrugged. "I think you owe me an apology," he answered, sitting straighter in his seat.

Roshawn scoffed. "Don't hold your breath."

"Why are you so difficult?"

"Why are you so annoying?"

Angel sat staring at her, one leg crossed over his knee, his hands clasped prayerlike in front of him. He drew his fingers to his lips, blowing breath into the air. She was stunning, he thought to himself, eyeing her from head to toe. She wore a black, sleeveless, spandex turtleneck that fell just above her navel. A jeweled belly button ring shimmered against her dark skin as the light hit it just so. A linen skirt with an asymmetric hemline stopped at her knees, the low-waisted garment tied neatly on the side. Ballet flats in a black-and-taupe leopard print completed her ensemble. He could not stop staring into her eyes, the dark orbs dancing with laughter. He couldn't begin to imagine how so much energy could be packed in such a tiny body.

Roshawn leaned back in her seat, eyeing him just as intensely. A wooden toothpick hung from his mouth and he swirled it easily across his lips, manipulating it slowly in and out of his mouth. As she watched him, the motion was so erotic that it took her breath away. It took every ounce of willpower she possessed not to rise from her seat to rub her palms across his bald dome, wanting to feel his flesh against hers.

Nina couldn't have been more on the mark when she'd said the new style had elevated him to a whole new level of good-looking. The man was intoxicating, and sitting there in his black, Hugo Boss denim jeans, white silk shirt and black leather boots, he was oozing raw, unadulterated sensuality.

The emotions wafting between the two of them were so intense, so profoundly seductive, so hypnotic, that neither of them could think straight. The telephone ringing on Chen's desk pulled them both back from the moment. Roshawn jumped to her feet to reach for the receiver. "Good morning! John Chen's office."

Angel stood up, moving to stand by the window, staring out over the landscape. The palms of his hands were damp with perspiration. Never before had any one woman caused him to feel so much inner conflict. As she hung up the telephone he turned back around to face her. When he spoke, his voice was a throaty whisper, the seductive lull of his Spanish sending a chill straight through her.

"I'd prefer a single-story home, ideally in a gated community. I'm not looking to move again so I need a nice-sized house with space for expansion, if that becomes necessary. Two master suites would be great, but if that's not available then I need to be able to expand a second bedroom and bath for my father. Three additional bedrooms would be good to have as well. I don't plan to be single forever. A home I could easily move a wife into and possibly raise a family in would be perfect." He paused, his gaze penetrating, and then he licked his lips, his tongue swinging that toothpick from one side of his mouth to the other.

Roshawn took a deep breath and held it, intent on maintaining every bit of her composure. She released it slowly before responding. "Since you're thinking about a family, I'm sure a sizeable backyard would also be important. I know your father would enjoy an area for a garden as well. And, let's not forget the kitchen," she responded. "Israel would want a nice kitchen."

Angel nodded. "I'm glad that you can be professional about this. I've had some concerns since the other night. You seem to lack control. Your behavior has been irrational and…" he started, pausing as he cut his eyes away from the glare she threw him. He didn't bother to finish his statement.

Roshawn bit her tongue, her next comment coming with more bitterness than she'd intended, but she was suddenly feeling defensive. "Look, you don't like me and I'm not crazy about you either, but when it comes to this ball club, my day job and Chen's business, not even you could push me to do anything that might jeopardize that. Now, I'll find you a home. I may even help you move, but after that I think the less we have to do with each other, the better."

He stood silent, appraising the sudden rush of anger that had washed over her. "As you wish." He took three long strides toward the door. "Thank you. I'll be in town this week and then I'm on the road for two weeks," he said curtly.

"I know the team's schedule," Roshawn answered, crossing her arms over her chest. "I'll call you when I find something I think you'd be interested in seeing, Mr. Rios."

Taking one last look at her, Angel spun around on his heels and out the door, closing it firmly behind him. Roshawn tossed the folder she was holding to the desktop. Where did he get off calling her irrational? The man didn't know a thing about her and there he'd been passing judgment. If only he knew, she thought, thinking back to the night she'd clipped his hair. Angel Rios needed to learn that she never did anything without good reason.

She stormed back to her desk, booting up her computer. She shook her head in annoyance as confusion washed over her spirit. Each time she was in his company all she wanted was to give the arrogant fool a good, swift kick in his very round, very high, exceptionally delectable behind. The man was infuriating. Why did Angel Rios have to be so alluring?

Angel stomped to his car. How could one woman continually make him want to pull his hair out? If he'd had hair, he thought as he ran a palm across his scalp. And where did she get off getting an attitude with him just because he didn't take too kindly to her flamboyant behavior. Spoiled, that's what was wrong with her. Probably used to always getting her own way whether she should have it or not. He shook his head as he eased himself into his vehicle. Why, he thought, as he shifted into gear and pulled onto the main road, did she have to be so extraordinarily beautiful?

Later that afternoon Roshawn was sifting through the stack of MLS home listings and coordinating times to preview them with the Realtor. A few were immediately eliminated, clearly not meeting the family's needs as far as Roshawn was concerned. A couple stood out as perfect, she thought, and she was excited to be able to sneak a peek inside the million-dollar listings.

As she scheduled her last appointment and hung up the telephone, Chen dropped down to his favorite seat against the corner of her desk. "So, what's going on with you and Angel Rios?" he asked.

Roshawn cut her eye at the man, then focused back on the papers in front of her, refusing to meet his stare. She shrugged. "I don't know what you're talking about."

Chen smiled. "You were never a good liar, Roshawn."

She looked up at him, taking a deep inhale of breath. "I don't believe there is anything going on with Mr. Rios and myself. We don't particularly get along with one another. Nothing else."

Chen chuckled softly. "His father believes otherwise. So does Ming."

"Is this some kind of conspiracy?"

"We all want to see you happy, Roshawn."

"Then stay out of my business and we will all be happy."

Chen nodded slowly, standing back on his feet. "Nina called while you were on the other line. She wants you to call her. Something about meeting her at The Lotus Room tonight."

Roshawn nodded her thanks, sorting once again through the pile of papers. Chen stood watching her from the doorway. Her gaze locked with his as he called her name.

"Yes, Chen?"

"I want you to be happy more than anyone else, Roshawn. He's a little young," Chen said teasingly, "but I think you might need a younger man to keep up with you. Plus, he's got a promising future. I wouldn't have to worry about him taking care of you. I like him. In fact, there's a lot about him that I like."

Roshawn said nothing as they continued to stare at one another. Chen smiled again as he headed back into his office. *"Wo ai ni,* Roshawn."

She continued to stare after him, emotion catching tightly in her chest. "I love you, too, Chen. I love you, too."

Roshawn desperately needed the mood of The Lotus Room. She had already been on edge after her brief encoun-

ter with Angel and when Chen had felt it necessary to offer
his approval of the man, she had almost lost it completely.
Nina was on the dance floor with a husky blonde when she
arrived. Roshawn recognized him as a player from one of the
minor league teams who was being evaluated by Chen and
the pitching staff. When her friend caught sight of her, she
pointed toward a rear booth where Patrick sat alone, tapping
his fingers in time to the music. Roshawn waved hello to the
woman and headed in the direction of the husband.

"Hi, Patrick. How are you?" she asked as she came to his
side.

The man rose slightly from his seat to kiss her cheek.
"I'm good. How you doin', Roshawn?"

She nodded. "I could complain but it wouldn't do any
good."

Patrick chuckled. "I hear ya'. Nobody ever listens anyway," he said, smiling widely.

Roshawn dropped down onto an empty seat, laying her
leather clutch against the table.

"Would you like a chocolate martini, Roshawn?"

She gave it a quick thought, then shook her head. "Not
tonight, thank you. I would like a bottle of Perrier with a twist
of lemon, though."

Patrick nodded as he excused himself and headed toward
the bar. As he stood ordering, Nina made her way to the
table. Her dance partner had headed in the opposite direction,
stopping to slap hands with Patrick before moving on to the
men's room. Nina lit a cigarette, turning to blow a ring of
smoke behind her.

"When did you start smoking?" Roshawn asked, eyeing
her friend curiously.

"I only do it when Patrick and I are fighting."

"Mmm! What happened?"

"I called his room this weekend when they were in Dallas and some woman answered the telephone. The witch hung up on me and when I called back, he picked up. He swears up and down that he was alone and they just connected me to the wrong room."

Roshawn looked toward the bar then turned back to her friend. "Do you believe him?"

Nina heaved a deep sigh. "Let's be for real, Roshawn. Patrick is a professional baseball player. Women throw themselves at him all the time. Sometimes right in front of my face. And, he's a man. Put the right temptation in front of him and anything is bound to happen. Ask his ex-wife. That's how he and I met in the first place."

Roshawn shook her head. "Patrick loves you and you love him, Nina."

Nina smiled, stubbing her cigarette out into an ashtray. She placed the half-empty pack back into her purse. "That's the only reason I haven't called my attorney yet and demanded half," the woman exclaimed. She changed the subject. "So, how are things going with you?"

Roshawn shrugged, not bothering to respond.

Nina smiled. "How are things going with you and Angel?"

She gave her friend an annoyed look. "They aren't. They won't be. Let's just move on."

Nina sighed. "You're probably better off anyway. It's not easy being the wife of a professional athlete."

Roshawn giggled. "As I remember, it was difficult just being a wife."

At that moment Patrick turned back to the table, two drinks in his hands. He grinned broadly as he approached, moving to place Roshawn's water down in front of her and a vodka-tonic before his wife. He gently squeezed the woman's shoulders before sitting back down.

No one spoke and all three turned to focus on the crowd gathering for happy hour. Everyone seemed genuinely enthused to be there and Roshawn couldn't help noting how distinguished a group they all were. In fact, she mused as her eyes skated slowly around the room, there might be some who would have ventured to call them a pretty crowd because everyone looked good.

Her eyes were focused on the entrance at the exact moment Angel came through the door. As if sensing her with radar his gaze fell directly on her and he stopped short, blatantly staring. Roshawn sat straighter in her seat as she returned the look and when he broke the connection, moving to a stool at the bar, she was only slightly disappointed. Nina didn't miss a trick.

"Would you like Patrick to go invite him over?" the woman asked, leaning over the table toward her.

Roshawn cut her gaze from Nina to Patrick and back again. She cast a quick glance toward Angel and shook her head. "No."

The couple gave each other a look, both noting the quick change in Roshawn's disposition. Carefree and relaxed had suddenly shifted to anxious and moody. Nina started to comment but Patrick interrupted her, pulling at her hand as he asked her to dance.

"Please?" he whined, his eyes pleading with her.

Roshawn waved them off. "Go dance with your husband. Have some fun. I'll be fine." She watched as Nina finally gave in, following eagerly behind the man. She tossed Angel another quick gaze, bristling when she saw him talking to a leggy redhead in a miniskirt that just covered her crotch line.

The woman had wrapped both arms around him as she whispered into his ear. Roshawn reached for her drink and took a heavy gulp, suddenly wishing for that martini. She closed her eyes and focused on the music.

The DJ had taken full control of the room. The man had been spinning bedroom ballads back to back, slow, sultry numbers that made a woman wish for a man if she didn't have one, and had a man begging for more attention than he probably deserved. It was suddenly so hot that Roshawn could hardly bear it. She glanced toward the bar for a third look, just in time to see Angel disengage himself from the woman's embrace. He reached into his pocket and pulled a billfold into his hands. He counted off a number of dollar bills that he tossed to the counter. The redheaded woman was eyeing him eagerly, her interest almost as intense as Roshawn's. The man met Roshawn's gaze for a second time and held it. He nodded boldly in her direction. He leaned to whisper something to his new friend and then he brushed rudely past her, leaving the woman standing with her mouth open, a look of pure surprise gracing her round face.

Roshawn watched as he slowly sauntered in her direction. He stopped as he reached the edge of the dance floor, his gaze still entwined tightly with hers. He gestured with his forefinger, beckoning her toward him. Theirs was a silent conversation as Roshawn rose from her seat and made a path through the crowded dance floor to meet him halfway, her movements enticingly slow. The moment was surreal as Roshawn focused on nothing but Angel, and the sultry, hedonistic rendition of "Drift Away" billowing through the room.

As she stepped before him, Angel placed his right hand against her hip and slowly eased her against his body. Roshawn closed her eyes and dropped into the sensation as her body pressed hot against the lines of his. His hips were rocking slowly back and forth, and she moved with him, intent on following him wherever it was he planned to lead her. She leaned into him, her arms still hanging loosely at her sides as they navigated an erotic bump and grind to the beat of the music. Roshawn could feel herself being consumed by the moment. She dropped her cheek to his broad chest and took a deep breath, inhaling the scent of him. The cologne was a light musk, filling her nostrils and sweeping through her bloodstream like a sensual narcotic. The moment had taken full control over them and when she felt his lips brush ever so lightly across her forehead, The Miracles were whispering what a wonderful world it could be.

Roshawn lifted her gaze to stare up at him, her arms reaching around to rest her hands against the shelf of his rear end. Angel smiled, never missing a step as his large palms wrapped around her back and pulled her tighter against him, his pelvis still rotating in sync with hers. Roshawn gasped as the sensations surging through her body threatened to drop her to the floor, her knees quivering in response. Her eyes fell shut once again as he tightened his grip around her torso, melding his body against hers. Angel pressed his cheek to her cheek and when the warmth of his breath blew lightly past her ear, Roshawn was no more good.

He could have lifted her off the floor with one hand, he thought as he held her tightly. She fit so neatly within his arms it was as if they'd been made just for her. As he held her, his body dancing easily against hers, he couldn't imagine the moment when he would have to let her go. Her body was warm, her skin like satin beneath his palms as he slowly caressed her bare arms, his fingers tiptoeing across her back and shoulders. He savored each sensation, energy surging from one end of his body to the other, converging en masse at the apex of his manhood.

Angel resisted the urge to kiss her mouth, wanting to taste her, knowing that if he did there would be no stopping. He was barely holding on as it was as he stared down at her. Her lips were parted ever so slightly, her breath coming in short gasps, her eyes closed tightly to shut out everything but the emotions surging like brush fire between them. He was so hungry for her that he felt as if the heat that had risen between them was swallowing his entire being whole.

The song changed, shifting the mood as couples began to bounce around the floor beside them. Angel was still holding on, reluctant to break the bond between them. He felt her sigh, her body quivering ever so gently against him and his gaze met hers one more time. Neither said a word and the moment was interrupted as Nina stepped up to greet them.

"Hi, guys," the woman said too cheerily, grinning from one to the other.

Roshawn was still staring up at Angel as he seemed to be waiting for her to say something. But she couldn't speak. Words were caught in the fog of wanting and blatant desire that had clouded her thoughts. She stood frozen, embarrassment starting to grow like a pesky weed throughout the garden of her spirit. Her gaze shifted toward her friend, her eyes begging the woman to say something that would help ease her out of the trance she seemed to be lost in. But Nina's gaze was still locked on Angel, oblivious to the waves of unease wafting between the couple.

The man suddenly leaned to kiss Roshawn's cheek, his full lips lingering against her skin. He took her hand and squeezed it, his fingers entwined between hers. "Thank you for the dance. I won't be a bother to you again," he said softly before pulling away from her. He gave Nina a quick smile, said goodbye, then turned, moving easily toward the door. As he made his exit, Roshawn was still standing in awe in the center of the room, someone singing something about a warm and tender love.

Bridget was rolling on the floor laughing hysterically at her. Roshawn was not amused as she switched the telephone receiver from one ear to the other. She curled over on her side, pulling a cotton sheet up over her legs.

"It wasn't funny, Bridget. I knew I should have called Jeneva."

"The brother sexes you up in public and then left you hanging, and you don't see what's funny about that?" her friend said, chuckling all over again.

"He didn't sex me up."

"What do you call it?"

Roshawn paused, reflecting back on the scene with Angel. She inhaled swiftly as the realization of what had happened overtook her. Her voice came in a low whisper. "Bridget, that man made love to me. It was the most sensual, most intimate thing I have ever experienced. We might not have been naked, but he made love to me on that dance floor."

"You were still in a public place."

"Girl, it was like the whole world disappeared and there was no one there but the two of us."

"But he left you hanging."

Roshawn groaned, rolling onto her back. "Like a load of wet laundry! If we had been naked and alone it would have been as if he'd rolled over, gotten out of bed and left me high and dry wanting more."

"At least he kissed you goodbye."

"Bridget, I have never been so disoriented in my entire life. I have never been so starstruck around a man. I couldn't even speak. He must have thought I was a complete fool."

"I doubt it. He probably thought you were a little ditzy though." Bridget laughed, the sound resonating through the receiver.

"I don't know what to do, Bridget. Tell me what to do!"

Bridget sighed and Roshawn could only imagine the eye roll her friend was giving her. "Stop playing hard to get," she said. "Obviously, you like this man and he likes you. Why not give it a try?"

"Because he irritates me."

"And I'm sure you're nothing but an annoying itch under his skin, too. Sounds like you two are going to be perfect for one another."

Roshawn heaved a deep sigh. "Hang up. I'm calling Jeneva."

"Jeneva's busy having real sex."

"Excuse me?"

"She and Mac are spending the week in a hotel room. Her mother-in-law is here taking care of the baby so the two of them decided to sneak off for some extracurricular activity."

"How is Mama Frances?"

"She's great. Having a blast with little Alexa. That child gets sweeter and sweeter every day."

Roshawn sighed again.

"You really like this man a lot, don't you Roshawn?" Bridget asked, a sudden awareness washing over her.

Her friend didn't respond and only the inhale and exhale of her breathing passed over the phone lines. "I don't know him that well, Bridget," she finally said softly.

"But you'd like to, wouldn't you?"

"I think I would just like to stop being celibate."

This time Bridget sighed. "You do need to call Jeneva. She is so much better at getting you to face your real feelings than I am."

They shared another moment of silence.

"You know how you say I always get everything I want and how I don't let anything get in my way? You're always joking about me being so strong?"

Bridget nodded into the receiver. "Yeah, because you are."

"Well, this time I'm scared, Bridget. I'm scared to death. For months now I have felt like my entire life has been at sea, drifting no place fast. And for the first time since Chen, I'm thinking about a man I may want around for longer than one meal and I'm scared. I don't know what to do, how to do it, or even if I should. I don't feel strong, Bridget."

Bridget would feel the tears that swelled in Roshawn's eyes, the ones her friend would never allow to fall. "That's what makes you a strong woman, Roshawn. You're always the first one to say what you're feeling, when you feel it. You don't hold back. I don't know any other woman who is as open, and as honest, and as fearless as you are. Even when you are scared, you own up to it. You face it and you get past it. That takes more strength than I could ever imagine."

Roshawn reflected on her friend's comments, the pregnant silence growing full as it swelled like new life between them.

"You really shouldn't shortchange yourself," Roshawn finally responded.

"What do you mean?"

"You're definitely as good at this as Jeneva is."

Bridget laughed. "I love you, too, heifer!"

Chapter 13

Angel was panting hard as he pushed open the doors to the men's lockers. The smell of male sweat hit him square in the face. Players were walking around in jockstraps and towels, or naked, whooping and whistling or snapping towels as they recovered from a hard practice. The coaches had put them all through their paces and there wasn't one of them who wasn't feeling it. Some more than others. A few sat in front of their lockers, heads hanging, muscles aching, in need of whatever or whoever might be able to bring them some relief. Others were skylarking, releasing the last remnants of energy that had managed to escape the ball field and the coaches' watchful eyes.

Personal equipment and gym bags lay ignored or forgotten across the benches and floor. In the other room, water was hissing from the showers, and the stink of old shoes, dirty gear and ripe perspiration filled the small space. Conversations were mixed and varied, some peppered with laughter, words of advice, or choice appraisals of the other jocks' girlfriends, wives and the female fans that worshipped them. Comments ranged from loud and bawdy to even-tempered and low-keyed. Angel grunted as the first baseman slapped him on the back and congratulated him on his game.

"You headed out tonight?" the man asked as he dried his freshly washed hair with a clean towel. "It's ladies' night at the club. I hear the honeys will be hungry for some beef tonight," the man exclaimed, palming his crotch as he laughed out loud.

It was late in the afternoon and with practice finished, all Angel wanted was a hot shower, a hot meal and his bed. "No, I need to get some rest."

"Your boy was out last night," the center fielder chimed in, intruding on the conversation. "Saw him dancing with a real cutie. Baby girl won't nothing but a mouthful, but she was hot as hell! It looked like someone had poured her into that dress she had on. You take that home with you last night, Rios? 'Cause if you didn't I sure plan to take her home with me the next time I see her." He high-fived another player, both of them cheering like they'd accomplished something.

Angel bristled as he cut an eye in the man's direction. His eyes narrowed to thin slits as venom filled his mouth to respond. Before he could answer, Patrick Tracy joined in the conversation. "Watch your mouth. That's family you're talking about. I can't having you talkin' like that 'bout my baby sister."

The center fielder laughed. "I see you got a little color in your family, Tracy. What happened to you?"

"Your mama is what happened to me, boy," Patrick responded, flicking his towel in the other man's direction.

KIMANI
ROMANCE

An Important Message from the Publisher

Dear Reader,

Because you've chosen to read one of our fine novels, I'd like to say "thank you"! And, as a special way to say thank you, I'm offering to send you two more Kimani Romance novels and two surprise gifts – absolutely FREE! These books will keep it real with true-to-life African American characters that turn up the heat and sizzle with passion.

Please enjoy the free books and gifts with our compliments...

Linda Gill

Publisher, Kimani Press

Peel off Seal and Place Inside...

We'd like to send you two free books to introduce you to our brand-new line – Kimani Romance™! These novels feature strong, sexy women, and African-American heroes that are charming, loving and true. Our authors fill each page with exceptional dialogue, exciting plot twists, and enough sizzling romance to keep you riveted until the very end!

KIMANI ROMANCE ... LOVE'S ULTIMATE DESTINATION

Your two books have a combined cover price of $11.98 in the U.S. and $13.98 in Canada, but are yours **FREE!** We'll even send you two wonderful surprise gifts. You can't lose

2 Free Bonus Gifts!

We'll send you two wonderful surprise gifts, absolutely FREE, just for giving KIMANI ROMANCE books a try! Don't miss out — **MAIL THE REPLY CARD TODAY!**

www.KimaniPress.com

The guys laughed as Mr. Center Field shook his head and rolled his eyes as he resumed dressing.

Patrick turned toward Angel as the others drifted off in other directions. "Hey, how you doin'?"

Angel shrugged, the noticeable wave of tension that had dropped down over his shoulders slowly dissipating.

"Don't pay these fools no attention. Most of 'em talk big, but there ain't no harm behind it."

"Are you close to Roshawn?" Angel asked as he pulled his baseball shirt over his head, tossing it into his gym bag.

"She and Nina, my wife, are really good friends. She's a sweet girl and I think she likes you."

Angel tossed the man a quick look, then turned back to untie the lacings of his baseball cleats.

"Maybe the four of us can get together some time. I think she'd like that. What do you say?"

Angel eyed him one last time. He shrugged again. "I don't think she would like that at all," he said as he headed into the showers, leaving Patrick staring curiously after him.

Israel stood off to the side, watching as Angel swung bat after bat inside the batting cage. Frustration colored the perspiration that dripped from his brow, the salt of it stinging his eyes and impeding his view. With the last ball and subsequent miss, Israel had seen enough and said so.

"*Hijo!* No more," the man said firmly, opening the cage door and gesturing in his son's direction. "You are going to damage your shoulder doing this."

Angel rested the end of the bat against the top of his athletic shoe. He swiped his sleeve across his brow, the dampness leaving a dark, wet stain against the cotton fabric. The two men stood staring at one another until Israel reached his hand and took the bat from his son's grip. He turned out the door as Angel followed obediently behind him.

Both remained silent as Israel helped his son pack his belongings in the rear storage area of the car. Even as they settled themselves in the vehicle neither one had anything to say. It was clear to Israel that something, or someone, was on his son's mind, all the man's focus centered around such. He also knew Angel would talk to him when he was ready and not one minute before. His son could be stubborn like that, a trait he'd inherited from his mother.

As Angel maneuvered the vehicle onto the expressway, Israel tapped his fingers against the center console, much to Angel's irritation. Angel shook his head. "*Papí!* Stop. You are driving me crazy."

Israel shrugged. "You will not talk to me and it is much too quiet in this car."

Angel cracked half a smile. "I have much on my mind, *Papí.*"

"What is bothering you, Angel?"

His son shrugged. "I can't focus, *Papí.* My swing is off. My head is not in the game. This is not good for me."

"But why, *hijo?* What is in your way?"

Angel sighed, his gaze shifting between the rearview mirror, the side mirror and the road. He struggled with what to say. Where were the words to tell the man that it was a woman who was disrupting his calm, just the thought of her sending him into a tailspin? It had always been easy before her. The women who had walked in and out of his life before had only been there for as long as his carnal needs dictated. He'd had no want of anything else from any of them. Baseball had always been his first priority. His father had been his second priority. All else was moot. Now, here was this woman upsetting the balance of all his life plans. Where were the words to explain all the emotions embodied in this turn of events with Roshawn? Emotions he himself had no understanding of. Angel shook his head and said all he could even think to begin to say.

"It is nothing for you to worry about, *Papí*. Things will be better soon."

Nina was putting the last touches on her dining room table when her husband Patrick came through the back door of their home.

"I'm in the dining room," she answered as he called out her name, searching out her whereabouts.

"Hi," Patrick said, coming to her side to see what it was she was doing. "Everything looks great."

Nina smiled her appreciation as she adjusted the last napkin against the table that was set for six. "Did you remember to pick up the wine?"

He nodded. "There are five bottles of Merlot on the kitchen counter."

She leaned to kiss his cheek. "Thank you."

"Are you sure you want to do this?" Patrick asked, dropping down to sit on one of the cushioned chairs.

"Do what?"

"Blindside Roshawn with this dinner date."

"I'm not blindsiding her. She knows we're just having a few friends over for a quiet dinner. And I told her there would be a single man here for her to meet."

"But they've already met and Angel's going to be the only single man here."

"And one is more than enough."

Patrick shook his head. "I sure hope you know what you're doing, baby doll."

Nina laughed. "I hope I'm making a love connection."

"The two of them might not be interested in being connected to each other. I told you how he reacted in the locker room the other day."

The woman shrugged. "Well, I think they'd be cute together, so what can it hurt to try?" She glanced over to the clock on the wall. "You need to go get ready. Our guests will be here soon."

"Just remember—" Patrick grinned as he came to his feet "—this was all your idea. Don't put me in it."

Nina rolled her eyes. "Chicken!"

Thirty minutes later the couple had greeted three of their four invited guests and were waiting for the last. As usual, Roshawn was late, her arrival timed to ensure that she would make an entrance that would not be soon forgotten. Angel was standing in conversation with Patrick and Evan Hoyle, the team's resident pitching ace. The men were talking shop, baseball lingo being bantered easily between them. Nina and John's wife, Candy, were sipping on their drinks, both lauding Roshawn's skills with a pair of scissors.

"I absolutely love what she did for Cindi Davis. I asked her about perming my hair and she told me not to do it. She thought it would make me look like a poodle."

Nina laughed. "That's what I love about her. She doesn't hold back." The woman glanced toward the men and then to her clock. As if on cue, the doorbell rang, signaling Roshawn's arrival. Nina jumped to her feet to answer the door, her excitement greeting her friend in the entrance. Grinning widely, Nina pulled her into the house. "It's about time!" she exclaimed.

Roshawn chuckled as she leaned to give her friend a quick hug. "Be glad I'm here."

Nina pointed her toward the formal living room. "Everyone's this way. Come meet my surprise."

Roshawn cut her eye at the woman. "If you did what I think you did I'm going to kill you."

Nina laughed, whispering as she linked her arm through Roshawn's. "I told you I couldn't have an odd number at the table. I just invited one of Patrick's friends to even us out."

Roshawn caught sight of Angel before she could form the words to respond to the woman beside her. She stopped short, nervous tension suddenly consuming her. She had not seen him since that night on the dance floor. As she stood there eyeing him, the memory of that night surged like brushfire through her. He was dressed in a pair of black dress slacks and a black knit shirt that nicely outlined the muscles of his chest. A wide smile filled his face as he laughed easily with his friends. There was no denying the expression that consumed Roshawn's face, intrigue and wanting swirling past her eyes in his direction.

Nina gave her arm a quick tug, her broad smile growing wider. "You and Angel Rios have met before, haven't you?" she said sarcastically as she gestured in the man's direction.

Roshawn glared at her friend, struggling to regain some composure. At that moment, Angel turned, noticing her arrival for the first time. The man's smile faded ever so slightly as he stood staring, a rise of perspiration suddenly beading against his palms. He spun the glass he was tightly holding between his hands and took a deep breath as he tossed a look in Patrick's direction. His friend noticed his sudden discomfort and smiled.

"It was Nina's idea. Since you and Roshawn are both new to the area and you know each other already, she figured it wouldn't be too awkward for you."

The other man standing with him eyed Roshawn curiously. He took a quick sip of his drink before speaking. "Now that's one beautiful woman. If I wasn't married myself I wouldn't mind being fixed up with her. I wouldn't mind at all," Evan stated, his voice low so that only his companions heard him.

All three men turned in greeting as Nina pushed Roshawn through the door to the patio, Candy following close behind them. "Gentlemen, do you all know Roshawn Bradsher?" Nina said brightly.

Evan extended his hand. "No. I don't think we've met."

Roshawn smiled coyly as she shook his hand. "Your reputation precedes you, Mr. Hoyle. That was a great game you pitched last week."

The man smiled back, his chest pushing forward ever so slightly. "Well, thank you. It's very nice to meet you, Roshawn. And, please, call me Evan."

Roshawn moved to kiss Patrick's cheek. She gave him a quick wink. "Hi, Patrick. How's it hanging?"

The man returned her greeting with a warm hug. "Hey there, darlin'. Glad you could make it."

She turned to Angel who was still staring at her. "Angel, it's very nice to see you again."

He nodded slowly. "It's a pleasure seeing you as well," he said, a sudden eagerness filling his eyes. He grinned shyly and Roshawn returned the smile with one of her own.

"Well, now that we're all here, I'm going to go check on our meal. If you'll all excuse me for a moment," Nina said, turning back toward the kitchen. "I shouldn't be too long."

Roshawn turned to her friend. "Do you need any help?"

The woman shook her head. "No. You stay and chat. Candy can give me a hand. Won't you, Candy?"

"Of course."

The group watched as the two women disappeared back inside. Roshawn turned her attention back to the three men. She shifted her body ever so slightly, trying to distance herself from the heat rising between her and Angel, who was standing just a touch too close for comfort.

Evan spoke first. "So, Roshawn, Candy tells me you're only visiting with us for the summer."

She nodded. "That's correct. Just until my daughter gets settled in the area. She'll be attending the University of Phoenix this fall."

"Nina is hoping you'll change your mind and stay here permanently," Patrick said.

"Maybe you'll change your mind?" Angel interjected, his tone soft, his eyes meeting hers with an intense gaze.

Roshawn shrugged. "I don't think so," she answered, avoiding the deep look he was giving her.

Evan took another sip of his drink. "Maybe we can change your mind."

"We're definitely going to try," Patrick added.

"So, Roshawn, have you been to the Children's Center lately?" Angel asked.

"Do you volunteer also?" Evan asked.

"Yes," she answered, nodding her head. "I was just there for a few hours this afternoon with my daughter."

"Volunteering with the boys?" Angel asked, amusement coating his words.

"As a matter of fact," Roshawn said, turning to stare directly at him.

Both Evan and Patrick looked from one to other, sensing that something about Roshawn's volunteering was an issue between them.

Patrick raised his eyebrows questioningly. "Did we miss something?" he asked.

Roshawn shook her head from side to side. "Angel has issues with women volunteering with the boys, doing boy things. He's a bit chauvinistic."

Patrick chuckled.

Evan nodded his head. "I don't know if that's being chauvinistic. I think I agree that there are some places women just don't need to be."

"Does your wife agree with you?" Roshawn asked.

"Candy knows her place."

Roshawn rolled her eyes. "Another one."

"Another what?" Nina asked as she and Candy returned to the conversation, both moving to stand by their men.

"Another man who thinks he knows what's best for the female population."

Nina laughed. "Evan's a little uptight about things like that. My Patrick hasn't rubbed off on him yet."

"Nor will he," Evan responded. He wrapped an arm around his wife's shoulder and leaned to kiss her cheek. "Rules and regulations are a good thing for you females," he said, humor in his tone. He winked an eye at Angel and Patrick as if they shared some inside joke.

Roshawn cast an eye toward Candy. "And you put up with this?"

Color suddenly flushed the woman's pale complexion as she fanned a hand in Roshawn's direction. "Don't pay him no attention. You know how boys can be!" she exclaimed, leaning into the man's side, her arms wrapping around his waist. "He bluffs a good game but he's really just a big, old teddy bear."

Evan grinned. "See, my baby's not complaining and I'm

happy. So I guess I know a little something about what's good for you women."

Angel tossed Roshawn a sly smile. "Shouldn't all women want that for their men? For them to be happy?"

"And what about men wanting their women to be happy?" Roshawn tossed back. "Or don't we count?"

"Oh, you count," Angel said, his accent thickening as his voice dropped low and deep. "You count where you're needed the most."

The duo stared at each other for a brief moment, energy spinning a thick line between them.

Nina laughed. "Well, let's take this conversation to the table. Dinner is served."

As she led the way, the others followed behind her. Angel moved to follow Roshawn, the palm of his hand pressing lightly against the small of her back as he held the door open for her. The touch sent a shiver up her spine and she felt her knees quivering ever so slightly. In the dining room, Nina had set the table so that the two would be sitting side by side. Angel held the chair out for her, pushing it in slightly as she took her seat.

"Thank you," she responded politely.

The man smiled again, the warmth of it flooding through her. "I am only doing what a good man should do for a woman," he said smugly.

Roshawn shook her head. "As long as that good man understands that a woman is capable of opening her own door and pulling out her own seat, then there's nothing wrong with it."

Angel shook his head, turning toward Nina as he spoke. "Is your friend always so stubborn?"

Nina laughed. "She might be asking the same thing about you."

Roshawn scowled, turning toward Patrick who was grate-
fully changing the subject.

"Angel, how's the house-hunting going?"

Angel turned to Roshawn. "Yes, Roshawn. How is my
house-hunting going?"

Roshawn dropped a napkin into her lap. "It's going," she
responded. "I'm sure you'll be very satisfied very soon."

Angel shrugged, looking back toward Patrick. "You know
as much as I do, my friend. It's difficult finding good help."

Roshawn tossed him an angry glare. "Excuse me?"

Angel shrugged, his thick shoulders moving skyward
toward his ears. "I wasn't talking about you, Roshawn," he
said smugly as a thin grin pulled at his mouth. "I don't mean
you any hurt at all. It is just that you are not the first woman
who has been helping me find a home. But like many of the
women, it is difficult for you to focus on what I need, and
your own issues as well. That is why I think women should
devote themselves to their children and their homes. Leave
the other things to us men. It is what we are here for."

"Here, here," Evan chimed, lifting his glass in salute.

Patrick laughed. "He's teasing you, Roshawn."

Angel dropped a heavy hand against her upper thigh. His
palm burned hot against her flesh. "I know that you are
working very hard for me, Roshawn. I have also learned that
you take some things far too serious. You need to…how is it
they say…lighten up?"

"That's funny," Roshawn answered. "I distinctly remember hearing the same things about you. But all jokes aside,
Angel," she continued as she turned ever so slightly in her
seat to face him, "do you really believe men should dominate
women? And that women are incapable of functioning as well
as men?"

Angel sat back in his seat, his hands folded comfortably in his lap. "All jokes aside, I have great respect for women who are tops in their field, or whatever it is they choose to do. I do however think that men are much better at handling explosive situations and issues than women are, which inevitably gives them an advantage. We men do a better job of taking the heat, so women should just stick to what they do better—cooking, cleaning, taking care of the children and satisfying their man." The coy smile on Angel's face widened as he gave her a quick nod of his head.

As he concluded, both Patrick and Evan came to their feet, clapping their hands loudly. "I'm converted," Patrick joked. "Sign me up."

"Here's to being a man!" Evan cheered, his glass clinking in salute with Angel's.

Candy giggled, her eyes rolling skyward.

Roshawn shook her head. "You're all a bunch of fools," she said.

"I'm so glad you two are hitting it off." Nina chuckled as both of them tossed her a look. "Roshawn, why don't you give me a hand with the soup," she suggested.

Roshawn nodded. "Yes, why don't I."

Out of sight and earshot, Roshawn gripped her friend by the shoulders and shook her where she stood. "I am going to kill you."

Nina laughed. "You need to stop giving the poor guy a hard time. It's obvious he likes you and you like him."

Roshawn rolled her eyes. "You don't know what you're talking about. And how am I giving him a hard time?"

"This tit-for-tat thing you two do. He only does it because you do and you do it because you'd rather be doing other things with him."

"I know you've lost your mind now," Roshawn said shaking her head as she watched her friend dip a thick, tomato-based soup into oversize bowls. "You know, that man doesn't have a clue just how hot things could get for him," Roshawn mused, putting a stalk of celery from Nina's serving tray into her mouth.

"Maybe you need to show him," Nina responded.

Roshawn met her friend's gaze, mischief floating across both their expressions. "Maybe I should." Roshawn looked around her friend's kitchen. "What all are you serving tonight?" she asked, leaning to peer into one of the pots.

"We're starting off with a cold tomato soup. Then we're having a chicken and vegetable risotto, and New York style cheesecake with fresh berries for dessert."

There was a devilish glimmer shining in Roshawn's eye. She reached for one of the soup bowls, then shuffled through Nina's spice cabinet.

"What are you going to do?" Nina asked, eyeing her curiously.

"I'm just going to see how well Mr. Rios can take some heat."

Minutes later, Roshawn helped her friend serve the dish, setting a bowl in front of Angel first, and then all the others. Sitting back down she dropped her cloth napkin back into her lap and pulled her wineglass to her lips.

"This looks very good, Nina," Angel said sweetly as he reached for his spoon.

"It's an old family recipe," Nina responded, an impish grin crossing her face. "It has just the right touch of tangy and spice to it."

Roshawn chuckled. "Nina says only real men who can handle fire can handle this dish. Isn't that right, Nina?" She brought her own spoon to her mouth as she took a taste.

Evan hummed. "This is very good. It has just enough heat to give it some flavor."

Both Nina and Roshawn watched as Angel took his first taste of the appetizer, swallowing a spoonful of the rich soup. Roshawn followed, taking another mouthful of her own as she gave him a slight smile. "It is good, Nina," she said cheerily. "You must give me the recipe."

Angel swallowed his first bite and then his second. As he reached to take his third, his eyes suddenly watered, the flavor hitting him with full force. He grabbed for his water glass, gulping the cold fluid quickly. "It's very spicy," he said, tossing his hostess a quick glance.

Roshawn pulled another spoonful into her own mouth. Still smiling, she nodded her head. "I would actually prefer it a bit hotter. What do you think, Patrick?"

The man nodded. "It's one of my favorites, but you're right. I like it a little hotter."

Roshawn looked back toward Angel who appeared to be turning green. She struggled not to bust out laughing. The man was still fighting to get the concoction down, not wanting to insult his host. The flavoring was intense, heat burning his lips and tongue and down into his stomach. He looked around at all the others who seemed to be enjoying theirs with gusto.

"I'm not partial to spicy foods myself," Candy was saying. "Evan likes a lot of pepper and Tabasco on his food. But this is very good, Nina."

"A dish like this takes a discerning palate," Roshawn said. She took another spoonful, swirling the liquid around in her mouth. "This just invigorates your tongue. Don't you agree, Angel?"

The man nodded, his discomfort becoming even more obvious.

"Don't you like spicy foods, Angel?" Roshawn asked sweetly.

"Yes, but this is very intense," he managed to say, taking a sip of his water, then his wine and another of water. "Very intense."

Roshawn chuckled. "Not this. This is just a little heat. I'm sure a big, strong man like you can handle twice this heat."

Angel laid his spoon against the table. He turned to stare at Roshawn first and then Nina. Both women burst out into laughter.

"What's so funny," Patrick asked, his gaze racing between them. "What did you two do?"

Angel shook his head. "I think I've been tricked," he said, reaching his spoon into Roshawn's bowl. His gaze locked on hers as he pulled a spoonful of her soup into his mouth. The flavoring was mellow, a tasty blend of tomato and just a hint of spice. The level of heat was nowhere near that of the mess remaining in his own bowl. He nodded his head slowly. "Yes," he said, dropping his spoon back to the table. "They have gotten me good."

Roshawn grinned, her palm dropping against his forearm. "You deserved that," she laughed.

He shook his head, her touch firing every nerve ending the spicy soup had missed. "What did you do to this soup?"

"I just gave it a little zing. I added some habanero seeds, Tabasco, red pepper, horseradish and a few other hot spices to flavor it up special. Just for you." Her gaze danced with his, the two staring boldly at each other. "I wanted to see what you were made of, Mr. Rios."

"And did I pass the test?" he asked, his voice dropping low, the seductive tone washing over Roshawn.

She shifted slightly in her seat, moisture puddling in every crevice of her body. "You were quite the sport," she said, her gaze dropping in admiration.

Patrick shook his head, giving his wife a stern look. Nina shrugged her shoulders. "I had nothing to do with it," she said, lifting her hands up in surrender.

Roshawn reached for the ladle in the ceramic tureen that sat in the center of the table. She filled her own bowl with more soup then passed it to Angel, exchanging his dish with hers. "Why don't you see if you can handle this?" she said.

Chapter 14

It was an extraordinary evening for a baseball game. The air was warm, the sky crystal-clear in a deep shade of ocean blue. There was a hint of a breeze blowing in the air and the stadium was afire with laughing, excited spectators. Roshawn and Ming had come in through the players' entrance, trailing behind Chen and Allison. Israel and Nina brought up the rear.

"This is so cool!" Ming exclaimed. "I can't believe we get to watch the game from the pool!"

Chen glanced over his shoulder, smiling at his daughter's enthusiasm. "Please remember to thank the club's president when you see him, Ming. Remember your manners, please."

Ming rolled her eyes, wrapping her arm through Roshawn's. "Yes, Daddy," she said mockingly, causing him to throw her a stern look.

Mother and daughter both burst out laughing. Roshawn

shook her head. "Relax, Chen. You are wound much too tight."

Up ahead of them, as if on cue, the doors to the locker room opened and the players began to head out in single file to the dugout. The group paused to let them all exit. Chen extended his wishes for a good game, directing individual comments to each of them as they waved a quick hello and goodbye. Nina jumped up excitedly when Patrick made his exit, blowing the man a kiss that he pretended to catch in midair. Angel was close on his heels and he stopped short at the sight of them all, acknowledging them with a quick nod before hurrying to catch up with the rest of his team.

When his gaze had landed on Roshawn, looking her up and down, she felt herself hold her breath. Biting down against her top lip, Roshawn spun from his sight, leaning down to brush at the back of her leg as if something had crawled against her skin. Israel's booming voice, encouraging his son's game, brought her back to the moment as she exhaled, air rushing past the line of her lips. As she stood upright she'd been glad that he was gone.

He had been a good sport at Nina's dinner party. The rest of the evening had been pleasant, despite the not-so-nice trick Roshawn had played on him. Their conversations had been engaging, only experiencing one other verbal battle during the course of the evening. Angel had departed just minutes before Roshawn and though she had hesitated, hopeful for a hint of his interest and attention, he had only wished her a warm good-night, disappearing before either had had an opportunity to even think about making plans to see each other again. Feigning disinterest in his presence was becoming harder and harder, and Roshawn feared her enthusiasm would not be received as eagerly. Had Angel Rios disregarded her in front of her family and friends, she would have been devastated.

As Chen stopped to have a quick conversation with one of the batting coaches, the rest of the group made their way to the Pool Pavilion. Located next to the outfield wall in right center, the pool area had been designed to recreate an upscale Arizona backyard. Besides the immaculate swimming pool, the area boasted a hot tub, fountains, and included catered dining with an assortment of personal amenities for about thirty-five select patrons and guests of the organization. What had fascinated Roshawn most the first time she saw it was its proximity to home plate. Sitting only some four hundred and fifteen feet away, the occasional home run had been known to make quite a splash, which in turn initiated a rush of water cannons that fired streams some thirty-five feet into the air.

In the home team's dugout, Angel was pacing the floor, anxiety sweeping through him. His father hadn't said anything about coming to the game with Roshawn and her family. Why such had been bothering him was a mystery, Angel thought. He took a deep breath, fighting to focus on the game. As he stepped on deck, ready for his next at bat, he watched as the opposing team's coach called for a time-out and slowly strolled toward the pitcher's mound. The man's expression was blank, the lines of his profile carved from the control that came with last-inning jitters where his team was ahead three runs to two and he had no intentions of losing.

The Titans had two players on base, one holding up the bag at third and their winning run at first. The batter up had a full count against him—three balls and two strikes, and with one out already secure, the coach had no interest in seeing the second potential out lost to them. With Angel on deck, most had reasoned the possibility that he could be the last Titans player to put the bat on the ball for this game. The Titans were hopeful he'd catch a good fastball that he could hammer home. Paramount on everybody's mind though was that Angel Rios's previous two at bats hadn't gone anywhere. For the first time in any game, Angel had been struck out, not once, but twice.

Angel scanned the crowd of spectators, eager faces cheering and catcalling out to the players. For some reason he found himself searching out the family seating area where the players' wives and children usually gathered. Even from where he stood it wasn't difficult to find her. Roshawn stood side by side with Patrick's wife, the two females laughing with the other women as everyone waited for the game to resume. He watched as the team's mascot, Baxter the Bobcat, jumped into the stands and motioned for her attention. The music blared as the duo did an impromptu dance, Roshawn shimmying every inch of her body around the stuffed creature. The crowd roared with laughter as the cameras caught the action on the Jumbotron screen, the outdoor LED video being panned around the stadium.

Angel bristled with jealousy. Everyone affiliated with the baseball organization knew the young man who donned the mascot's costume was a notorious flirt. The team teased him endlessly about the women he wrangled into dates by playing innocent in his bobcat costume. Angel could just imagine the tall, lanky, good-looking man slipping Roshawn his name and number after copping himself a squeeze and a tickle on the pretext of entertaining the audience. Angel bristled for a second time as Baxter leaned to kiss her cheek after bowing his gratitude for the dance. The audience might have been fooled, but Angel wasn't.

He heaved a deep sigh. She hadn't seemed happy at all to see him, he thought, as he found himself reflecting on their chance meeting before the game. She had barely given him a smile before turning her back to him as his father wished him a good game. Clearly, there was no interest there and he was wasting his time to think that there might be.

The crack of the bat hitting the ball drew his attention as he watched a high fly ball drop easily into the catcher's mitt. The catcher checked the base runners back to their bases and threw the ball easily back to the pitcher. With two outs, the crowd was cheering loudly for Angel as he stepped into the batter's box, shifting his athletic cup with his left hand as he dug his toe into the dirt. Angel lifted his bat over his right shoulder and adjusted his stance. Before he realized it, he'd taken one last glance in Roshawn's direction to see if she was watching. Three pitches later, Angel Rios was caught looking as the umpire called him out on strikes, the Titans losing their first game of the season.

The requisite "good game, good game" chants from the dugout to the locker room had grated on Angel's last nerve. It hadn't been a good game. In fact, it had been his personal worst game of all time and the hurt of it was all over his face. His teammates avoided him like the plague as he stormed into the locker room, throwing his gear to the floor. Even the coach hadn't bothered to comment during his wrap up speech, and Angel had refused all the media interviews.

Roshawn had felt his disappointment as if it were her own. She had hurt for him, sensing his dejection as he'd slammed his bat into home plate, his head and shoulders drooping low. His body was hunched as he'd exited the ball field. Standing outside the locker room door with Israel,

Roshawn wasn't sure if she should be there but the old man had pulled her along behind him after they'd wished Ming, Chen and Allison a good night. Nina had been waiting with them until Patrick had made his exit thirty minutes earlier. Roshawn had watched with just a hint of envy as the woman had embraced her husband, assuring him that the team would have better luck the next time. Before they'd headed in the direction of the exit, Patrick had asked if they needed a ride home, tossing her a curious stare. Israel had answered for her, declining the offer as he noted they would wait for Angel.

Roshawn had smiled, shaking her head. "I'll be fine, but thank you. I have my car and as soon as Mr. Rios catches up with his son I'll take off."

Patrick had smiled back warmly. "It may be a while. Angel's not in a good mood. This game was rough on him," he'd said as Nina had hugged them both goodbye.

Now, standing beside Israel, still waiting, Roshawn was questioning whether or not she should still be there or if she should have said goodbye some time ago. Israel seemed to read her mind as he dropped a hand against her arm.

"Thank you for waiting with me, Roshawn. I am sure Angel will not be too much longer."

Roshawn reached out to give the man a quick hug. "I'm glad I could stay with you. I wouldn't have wanted you to still be here all by your lonesome. Does he always take this long?"

Israel sighed, shrugging his shoulders. "Not usually, but I'm sure he's not doing well. He will take this game hard. Angel puts much pressure on himself. He will be unhappy with his performance for a very long time."

At that exact moment Angel stepped through the door. Startled, Roshawn jumped, the motion of it catching his immediate attention. She imagined that Angel's ears must have been burning because his appearance was as if he'd heard them call his name.

"Speak of the devil," she said cheerily, trying to make light of the moment.

Angel looked from her to his father and back. "Why are you here?"

Roshawn stiffened, pulling her five-feet-two-inch body upward. "Your father asked me to wait with him."

Angel shook his head, then brushed past the two of them, not bothering to utter another word. With the fresh memory of Nina and Patrick in her mind, Roshawn was put off by Angel's behavior. Tossing her hands up in frustration she rushed to catch up with him. Grabbing his arm, she threw the full weight of her body into the momentum and spun him around to face her. Angel stared down at her, his eyes ablaze.

"What is your problem? I was only trying to keep your father company," Roshawn said, her voice raised one octave, her hands clutching her hips.

"My father doesn't need your company."

"Maybe not, but that's what friends do for each other."

"You are not his friend."

"How would you know? I doubt you've ever had a friend."

"I don't need them."

"It wouldn't be ladylike for me to tell you what you do need," Roshawn said, taking a step closer to him as she threw up her hands. "But what the heck. You need to pull that stick out of your tight—"

Israel cut her off in midsentence. "Enough. Both of you," he said, his tone scolding.

Angel looked toward his father, then returned his gaze to Roshawn. He didn't say anything, his jaw locked tight with rage.

Roshawn bristled with her own anger.

"This is all your fault," Angel suddenly hissed at her. "You have done this. You have made me crazy!" Spinning on his heels, Angel stormed out of the building, leaving Roshawn and Israel both standing with their mouths wide open.

Angel had tossed and turned most of the night, sleep eluding him. He had watched shadows dance against the ceiling and the walls, infrequent flickers of light and dark skating around the room. As a little boy he had been afraid of the dark, crying out for his father when he thought the scary shadows were close to catching him in his bed. Comfort had always been as close as he either wanted or needed it to be. Last night what he had wanted he couldn't have. Frustration was walking a tightrope across his shoulders, his brow, and his chest, pulling tension through every nerve and tendon in his body.

He had listened to his father lecture him for hours, the words running one into the other as he had tuned the discourse on his bad behavior out of his mind. The monologue had run in one ear and out the other, lost behind the hurt and anger that had consumed him wholeheartedly. And it was her fault. He had no one else to blame but Roshawn. Before she had come insinuating herself into their lives, all had been well. She'd been there barely a minute and suddenly he was completely out of control. Who else did he have to blame? What else could explain his predicament?

Leaning up on his elbow he reached for his wristwatch on the nightstand. It was almost six-thirty and he needed to get ready for practice. He was grateful that there was no game. He couldn't have endured another devastation like the one he'd experienced yesterday. No one could understand what losing that game had done to him. Angel Rios had never let his team down. Angel Rios had never before allowed anyone or anything to breach his concentration. He was the man they could always count on. Always delivering when he was needed the most. And yesterday, he had failed them. Failed them because he'd been thinking about her.

He slammed a fist against the mattress, biting at his bottom lip. This had to end, he thought. He needed to get this settled once and for all. She needed to leave him and his father alone. That coy act of hers, like she didn't know what she was doing or how her presence was affecting him, was starting to wear thin. And his father wasn't helping the situation, the old man having fallen for her charms. But he knew better. He knew that if she stopped intruding, then he could go back to things being the way they had been. That would be the best thing for them all and he had every intentions of telling her so.

Roshawn was still lounging in her bed when the telephone rang. She reached for the receiver, her eyes still shut tight, avoiding the flood of light that was beginning to stream through her open windows. Heaving a deep sigh she pulled the instrument to her ear.

"Hello?"

Silence greeted her on the other end.

"Hello?" she repeated, annoyance growing in her tone.

When no one responded, Roshawn slammed the phone back down and rolled over on her side. It was way too early for people to be playing games, she thought to herself. At that hour of the morning someone could get cussed out. She reached for the sheet that she had kicked to the floor, pulling it back up over her body. She knew she needed to get up to get ready before Chen arrived with Ming, wanting her to go with them to pick out a new car for their daughter. But staying in her warm bed was too tempting and she intended to linger there for as long as she could.

An image of Angel Rios flashed across her memory and her body quivered ever so slightly. The man had been furious at her and she hadn't done anything to provoke him. Usually when a man was holding a grudge against her, Roshawn had some idea what for. Angel's anger however was totally irrational. Not only was the man rude, Roshawn thought, but clearly the elevator in that head of his didn't go all the way up to the top floor, stopping somewhere between crazy and crazier. She had attributed his behavior to plan old-fashioned immaturity, but was now thinking that the mere act of growing older might not do him any good at all. Medication or a sledgehammer to that thick skull of his might be his only recourse, she fathomed, an amused smile rising to her face. Taking a deep breath Roshawn stretched her body upward, lifting herself from the mattress and headed into the bathroom to wash her face and brush her teeth.

Minutes later the pounding against her front door pulled her out of the shower. After turning off the hot spray of water, she reached for the plush, terry bathrobe hanging on the bathroom door, wrapping it around her wet body. The banging continued, someone calling her name at the top of his lungs. As Roshawn headed down the hallway, the banging became more intense.

He would not leave until she opened the door, Angel reasoned. Not until he told her exactly what he thought about her. The woman had infuriated him, her antics clouding his judgment and impacting his game. He was not having any more of it. She would not move him from the path he'd set for himself. He stepped back, calling her name loudly for the third or fourth time. "Open the door, Roshawn."

Pulling the structure open, she eyed him curiously. "What in the world are you doing here?"

Angel brushed past her, pushing his way inside. Once inside the foyer, he spun back around to face her. The words caught in his throat and he felt himself gasp for air. He was taken aback by the sight of her seminakedness, her blush of black hair delightfully wet as rivulets of water ran from the the top of her head down the length of her body and fell in small puddles onto the hardwood floor. A light trickle of moisture ran down her cheek and along her neck. She was exquisite, her skin heated from the warm shower she'd just stepped out of.

The bathrobe was barely tied, gaping open and exposing just enough skin to send a shiver through his groin. Her eyes were bright, curiosity flickering simultaneously with rising ire. Her hands flew to her hips, causing the robe to open just a touch wider and Angel appraised her brashly, his gaze racing up and down the length of her torso.

"How dare you—" Roshawn started, but Angel cut off her words.

Before Roshawn realized what was happening, Angel had pulled her to him, hard, dropping his mouth abruptly against hers. The kiss was demanding, his lips anxious for a response as he plied her mouth open with his tongue. He danced inside the warm cavity, his tongue tasting hers and pleasure swelled out of control throughout his body. Roshawn was suddenly just as insistent, her own hunger doing battle with his. Clasping her hands behind his head, she licked the line of his full lips, grazing against the sharp edges of each tooth as she fell headfirst into the heat of his touch.

Angel's hands snaked beneath her robe, falling hot against her back as he nestled himself against her, and her against the bright white wall. Lifting her from the floor he pressed her pelvis against the rise of flesh in his crotch as he wrapped the length of her legs around his backside. With the wall to help support what little weight she carried, he allowed one of his hands to sneak between them, his fingers pulling at a nipple that had risen hard and full beneath his touch. The other gripped the round of her buttocks, his palm teasing her flesh.

Roshawn's own hands had fallen to his belt buckle, pulling hurriedly at the leather accessory. Angel kissed her eyelids, her cheek and the tip of her nose as his lips painted a trail down to her neck. He pulled back ever so slightly to stare into her eyes and Roshawn smiled, pulling his mouth back to her as she whispered his name, the lilt of it pleasing to his ear.

As Roshawn struggled with the zipper of his pants to release him, the moment was suddenly interrupted when Chen and Ming pushed open the front door, stepping inside. Chen's deep laugh stopped abruptly as the man stood staring. Ming's eyes widened in shock, her mouth falling open as she peered past her father's shoulder. Roshawn shook her head in disbelief, her forehead falling against Angel's chest as the man eased her back to the floor and moved to shield her nudity from view. He pulled anxiously at her opened bathrobe, closing it around her body. Roshawn tied the garment tight against her waist as Angel zipped and buckled his pants.

Ming eased herself past her father who still stood frozen in place. She giggled as she greeted them. "Hi, Mommy. Good morning, Angel. Daddy, would you please come help me with the coffeepot?" the young woman said, winking at her mother as she eased out of the room.

As if his daughter's voice had willed his legs to move, Chen turned to close the door, then marched past them, his displeasure evident on his face. "Roshawn. Angel," he said, curtly, a quick nod his only other greeting.

"Good morning, Chen," she said, staring after him as he disappeared through the door. She turned back toward Angel who was blushing profusely, color flooding his rich complexion a deep shade of burgundy. She smiled and moved to kiss his mouth one more time, stretching up on the tips of her toes to reach his lips. He gave her a quick peck in return, easing two steps back from the rise of heat between them.

"I'm so sorry," he whispered, throwing a cautious glance in the direction of the kitchen door.

She shook her head. "It's okay."

Angel waved his head back and forth. "No. I would never disrespect your family like that. I should have known better. It won't happen again."

Roshawn's gaze danced with his as she studied him, his disciplined demeanor resurfacing. "What? You won't kiss me again, or you won't kiss me in the doorway ever again?"

Angel had no answer, knowing that if given the opportunity he would definitely kiss her again, no matter where she might be. He closed his eyes and took a deep breath. This wasn't what he had come here for, he thought to himself. In fact, this wasn't at all what he'd intended to happen between them. Aloud, he said, "I must go."

Just as Roshawn opened her mouth to speak, Ming called to her from the other room. "Mom? Would you and Angel like a cup of coffee?"

"Just a minute, Ming," she answered as she turned toward the direction of her daughter's voice and then back to Angel.

"Why don't you come—" she started to say, stopping as Angel turned abruptly and raced out her front door as she called after him. "Angel! Wait!" Throwing up her hands in frustration she turned and headed into the other room.

Ming greeted her with a broad grin. "Cream in your coffee?" she asked smugly, laughter dancing in her eyes.

"You're not too grown to be smacked," Roshawn responded, reaching for the cup of hot fluid the girl passed to her.

"I wasn't the one getting my freak on in the hallway." Ming laughed as Roshawn swatted at her head.

Chen's booming voice interrupted them as he ordered Ming to her room so that he could speak with her mother in private. The smile faded from Ming's face as she looked from one to the other. "Now," Chen commanded in Cantonese, ordering her for a second time.

Roshawn gestured for the girl to obey, nodding her head as she gave Ming a slight smile. When she heard the bedroom door closing behind her child she spun to stare at her ex-husband, shaking her index finger from side to side. "Don't you dare, Chen," she chastised. "Don't you dare say one word."

The man sputtered, caught off guard by her outburst.

Roshawn ranted. "How dare you come into this house without knocking first? I don't care if you are the landlord, you have no right."

"I am Ming's father!" Chen shouted back.

"Yes, *Ming's* father, not mine. And you are not my husband or my lover anymore. You have no right to interfere in or comment on my private life unless I ask you to. No right at all."

"You need me…"

Roshawn interrupted him, her voice dropping back to a

normal tone. "All I need, Chen, is for you to be here for our daughter. And I need you to be happy for me when I move on with my life. You have Allison now and I don't want to waste any more of my time being alone. I just need you to understand that and be happy for me, no matter who I choose to be with. And I need you to respect my privacy."

Chen took a deep breath, a swift inhale of oxygen surging through his lungs. Moisture glistened in the narrowed lines of his gaze. Reaching into his pants pocket, he pulled out a key ring of assorted keys. Sifting through them, he pulled at one in particular, twisting it off the loop. Roshawn's gaze never left his as he extended his hand in her direction, holding the key out to her. As her hand met his, the key dropping into her palm, Chen clasped her fingers beneath his, holding tightly to her.

"I am happy for you, Roshawn. But I don't want you to be hurt." He smiled, pausing briefly before continuing. "And, our daughter has a lot of you in her. She will do things she sees you doing. I don't want you putting any crazy ideas into her head. I don't think my heart could handle it."

Roshawn smiled back. "I'll try to behave myself," she said softly.

Chen laughed. "That's like asking you not to breathe," he responded.

Roshawn shook her head. "Fix me another cup of coffee, please, while I go get dressed," she said, heading back toward the bedroom. "Your daughter said something about you buying her a Mustang convertible."

Israel met his son at the door. "*Hijo,* what is going on? The woman from the travel agency called to say you could pick up your plane tickets at the counter. Where are you going?"

"Home, *Papí*. I need to go home."

"But you have work."

Angel shook his head. "We have a few days off. I will be back on Wednesday. The coach has given his blessing."

Israel nodded. "What has happened, Angel?"

The man turned to stare at his father. "I need to think, *Papí*. I can't think here. I just need some space."

Israel nodded as Angel moved toward his bedroom. He stood in the doorway as his son tossed clothes into a small suitcase. The old man was moved to tears as he sensed the weight on his child's shoulders, stress creasing the lines in the young man's forehead. He eased through the doorway and took a seat on the edge of the bed. Angel stopped his packing and took a seat beside the old man, waiting patiently as Israel searched his thoughts for what he wanted to say. The comments came quickly.

"It is okay to love her, *hijo*. It is okay to open your heart and let her in. You know you want to. You know she is already there."

Angel shook his head. "Perhaps, *Papí*. But if I cannot have love like you and my mother, I don't want it at all."

Israel smiled. "Stop fighting this. She will make you a very happy man if you let her." Rising from his seat, Israel eased his way back out the door. Before he made his exit, he spun back around one last time. "Love her. Let her love you and you will have as much as your mother and I had, and more."

As Angel stood staring after the man it suddenly dawned on him. His father had never once called Roshawn by name. But Roshawn's had been the only name he heard.

Chapter 15

The morning couldn't have gone by any slower. Roshawn had stood back as Chen had settled on a 2006 Toyota RAV4 for Ming's eighteenth birthday present. Much to their daughter's liking, the salsa red vehicle came fully equipped with all the amenities and her very own Texaco gas card. The morning had ended after the trio had picked up Allison for a late lunch at Pizzeria Blanco.

Roshawn was barely inside her front door before she reached for the telephone and dialed the number for the Doubletree. The call was answered quickly and immediately connected to room 167. Israel answered on the second ring. *"Hola!"*

"Israel, hello. It's Roshawn. How are you?"

"I am well. But how are you doing?"

Roshawn smiled into the receiver. "I'm not sure. Is Angel there, please?"

The man shook his head as if she could see him. "He left for Santo Domingo an hour ago."

"Santo Domingo?"

"Yes. He said he needed time away to go think. So he went home."

A brief silence wafted between them before Roshawn spoke again. "When will he be back?" she asked.

"Wednesday."

They both fell silent for a second time.

"You know, Roshawn," Israel said matter-of-factly, "we have a beautiful home in Santo Domingo. And it is very nice there this time of year."

Roshawn chuckled. "No, Israel. I will speak with Angel when he gets back."

The man laughed heartily. "As you wish. But if you should change your mind, just let me know."

Frustration flooded over her as she said her goodbye and hung up the telephone. Pulling the receiver back into her hand, she dialed again, this time dialing her best friends in Seattle.

The afternoon sun was well on its way to settling down for the night. The outside air had shifted from excessively hot to unbearably warm. The central air-conditioning had been running nonstop for most of the day and didn't seem anywhere near stopping. Roshawn sat on the hardwood floor in the entrance of her home, staring at that spot on the wall where Angel had held her hostage in a moment of outright lust. Her skin still burned hot where he had touched her, teasing and tempting her out of every ounce of her sensibility. Whether she said it aloud or not, her wanting had been as intense as his had, maybe more so. Strangely though, it had been about something more than just reveling in the intoxication of his touch. At one point he had looked at her, his gaze so penetrating it had seared straight through every fiber of her being. She had gotten lost in it, the beauty of its magnitude washing like the spray of a waterfall over her.

Jeneva and Bridget had teased her and she had giggled along with them, although there had been a part of her that hadn't found any of it funny. Even the expression on Chen's face hadn't yet moved her to laugh, although she didn't doubt there would come a moment when just the memory of it would send her into hysterics. Like best friends do, they had given her a fountain of advice to mull over and she had been sitting there ever since, exploring and questioning every ounce of it.

She and Angel were both acting like this was some grade-school infatuation, she thought. Roshawn had played this game before, she mused, remembering back to sixth grade at Ordway Elementary School. Frankie Salley had been her first crush and on a daily basis the two had fought like cats and dogs. Every morning Frankie would greet her with a swift punch to the shoulder that she gladly reciprocated. How else was Frankie supposed to know she wanted to be his girlfriend? And now she and Angel were exchanging punches, unable to express what was really going on between them.

But after that morning's kiss, Roshawn was ready to change the rules. Angel had crossed the boundary lines and then retreated. But Roshawn knew there would be no going back for either one of them. She was more than ready to play until both of them could claim a win. She wanted him and had no doubts whatsoever that he wanted her just as much.

She looked around the space, suddenly aware of the quiet spinning a growing web through the room. When the telephone in her lap rang it startled her, pulling her back from her thoughts with such intensity that she jumped, dropping the receiver to the floor. Picking it up, she answered the call, catching it just seconds before the answering machine picked up.

"Hello?"

"Roshawn, it's me."

"Hi, Bridget. What's up?"

The woman on the other end took a deep breath before speaking. "Have you made a decision yet about what you're going to do?"

Her friend nodded into the receiver. "Yeah. I think I'm going to the Dominican Republic for a few days."

Bridget smiled. "We knew you would, so Jeneva and I thought we'd help you out."

"What did you two do?"

"Your flight leaves at ten. You need to be at the airport by eight o'clock. Unfortunately you have to change planes in Dallas, and then in Miami, so you won't get there until tomorrow afternoon. But you'll get there."

Roshawn's eyes widened in surprise. "You're kidding, right?"

"No, I'm not. You need to pack right now and get going. Jeneva's already talked to Chen, so you don't have to. He gave you Monday and Tuesday off. All you need to do is figure out where the man is once you get there."

Tears filled Roshawn's eyes. "Thanks, Bridget. I love you guys."

"We know. Go get your man, girl!"

Her call to Israel had taken only a few minutes. The man had told her to relax and enjoy her flight. Someone would be there on the other end to pick her up and take her to Angel. Excitement had colored his tone and just before disconnecting the call he had sent his love to Angel. "Tell my son I will be praying for the two of you," Israel had said with a wide smile in his voice.

"Thank you, *Papí*," Roshawn had answered.

The old man's grin had widened. "*Papí* sounds very good coming from your mouth, *niña*."

Roshawn's smile was as big. "I will see you soon," she'd said as she had hung up the telephone.

The elderly woman who woke him from his sleep did so with much noise, fussing nonstop as she pulled the covers from around his body. Angel rolled to his side, playing a game of tug of war with her as she reprimanded him, her thick Spanish echoing around the large room.

"Get up," his aunt said for the umpteenth time. "You are being lazy. I do not like lazy."

"Aunt Maria, let me be," Angel implored, pulling a plush pillow over his head.

"No. You must get up. There is much you need to do."

"What is there for me to do?"

"I promised that you would head to the farms to check on things today. You must go do this."

Angel sighed. "Yes, ma'am." He sat up slowly, his eyes barely open as he struggled to focus on her.

The large woman smiled warmly. "You are a good nephew. Now, hurry up. I have many things to prepare for today and then I must go into town. You need to eat your breakfast and be on your way before I leave."

He nodded slowly. "Where are you going?"

The woman hesitated, her eyes skipping around the room. "To the market. I have something I must pick up. Something special for your dinner tonight."

"You know I don't want you going to any trouble for me, Auntie."

The woman smiled, her wide grin filling her warm brown complexion. "This will be worth the effort to see you pleased."

Angel shook his head, shaking it at her and the sleep still trying to claim him.

"Up, nephew. Up now," she commanded once again. "I must leave soon," she said as she headed out the door. "My package will be arriving shortly and I must be there to meet it."

She had slept well on her trip, each flight and plane change easier than the last. Stepping from the plane, out into the late afternoon sun, Roshawn was stung with the delicate, yet smoldering heat of the Caribbean weather. As she maneuvered her way through the ultramodern airport she was taken by the vibrant energy and colors of the people making their way from one point to another. After retrieving her one bag from the claims area she looked around for the ride that had been promised to her, a sudden wave of nervous energy spinning through her midsection.

Roshawn would have known the buxom woman even if she hadn't been holding up the makeshift sign with her name misspelled. The spitting image of Israel, one could have mistaken this female image of him for an identical twin. The woman had his face, but with features that were clearly more feminine, more elegant, with thick, silvery hair that fell the length of her back.

Roshawn smiled warmly as she moved to greet her, making her way to the older woman's side. "*Holá*. I am Roshawn."

Maria Rios smiled, pulling the young woman into her arms and hugging her tightly. "Welcome," she said. "We are so excited to have you here with us."

"Thank you."

"My brother said you were a beauty. He spoke the truth," she said as she pulled Roshawn along beside her, leading them to a red minivan that she quickly maneuvered onto the road. Roshawn was duly impressed with the woman's driving as she aggressively moved them through the overwhelming amount of traffic. At one point the woman turned the wrong way, down a one-way street. Roshawn gripped the door handle with one hand and her chest with the other. Maria laughed. "Don't fret, child," she implored casually as if such were a common occurrence. "There are no police nearby!"

The woman talked incessantly, continuous chatter about Israel, Angel, their family, Angel, their home and Angel. Every so often she would ask Roshawn a question about herself and Arizona, but the moments were few and far between. Roshawn smiled sweetly, enjoying the company and the beauty of the tropical paradise they bypassed, occasionally asking about a site that caught her interest.

"Angel has been good to his family," the old woman was saying as they entered the outskirts of Santo Domingo. The ride from the airport to the northern coast of Santo Domingo and the Rios homestead had taken just under a half hour to complete and Roshawn looked up anxiously as her escort drove them through the entrance of Villa Rios. Her mouth fell open in awe, the sight before her totally unexpected. The woman beside her grinned broadly, her gray head bobbing up and down against her shoulders. "He has blessed us all with good fortune," she said softly. "His heart is pure gold."

The front gates opened on a winding driveway that circled

a massive marble fountain. From the roadside to the front door of the Spanish-style villa, the driveway, walkways and parking areas had been constructed of natural flagstone. The driveway was lined with towering manila palms that blew lazily beneath the warm breeze blowing in from the ocean. The home was surrounded by a series of exquisite gardens, the vibrant green vegetation beckoning one to walk between the brilliance of floral coloration and relax within the sheer beauty of it.

Maria parked the car and gestured for Roshawn to follow her inside. Roshawn was speechless as they stepped inside the front door, the expansive living space boasting a sweeping, circular staircase to the second floor, and three Spanish renaissance chandeliers that hung from the immense ceiling to light the room.

Roshawn followed her through the formal dining area, pausing to run her hand across the massive, kidney-shaped table with its twenty-four hand-carved chairs. A second flight of steps led them to the master bedroom suite that could have been a second home all on its own. It had its own bar, small kitchen, cedar-lined closets, separate office and television areas, plus a master bathroom with an oversize shower and Jacuzzi, and quadruple sinks.

Roshawn stood staring with her mouth open as Maria pointed out the amenities, opening the eight French doors to reveal the wraparound balcony that looked out to the swimming pool and gardens below, and the lush green mountains in the distance.

"This is where you will stay with Angel," the woman pronounced, dropping Roshawn's bag against the king-size bed.

Finding her voice, Roshawn shook her head. "I'm sure I should stay elsewhere."

Maria laughed, fanning her hand in Roshawn's direction. "We will see," she said, not bothering to move Roshawn's luggage from its resting spot. "But if you choose, we have two other bedrooms in this wing, and five in the other. We will find you someplace comfortable to rest."

"When will he be back?"

"Very soon. And I must go prepare supper for the two of you. Make yourself comfortable," she commanded as she stopped to give Roshawn a quick kiss on the cheek before exiting the room.

Minutes later Roshawn was still exploring the massive structure, ending her tour beneath a covered terrace that over-looked the swimming area. Roshawn was astonished by the size of the property, staring in wonder at not one, but three swimming pools of varying depths that flowed from top to bottom with three large waterfalls that spilled one pool into the other.

A large stone structure at the edge of the water caught her attention and Roshawn lifted herself to sit on top of it. Her legs dangled easily off the side and the vantage point gave her an incredible view of the landscape. Closing her eyes, she was suddenly consumed with the magnitude of where she was and why she had come. As the reality of her situation heightened her emotions she wasn't sure whether to laugh or cry at her predicament. What was forefront in her mind though was whether or not Angel would be happy to see her. She couldn't help but wonder if he would have any interest at all in her being there. Just as that very question crossed her thoughts she could sense his presence. She could feel him staring, his eyes piercing straight through her and when she opened her own to look, Angel stood on the other side of the swimming pool watching her.

Her gaze met his, locking for a brief minute. A minute that felt like a lifetime. His expression was a mixture of curiosity and surprise with twinges of apprehension and joy shadowing the lines of his profile. He tossed a quick glance over his shoulder to his aunt who stood in the doorway and the old woman was smiling. Roshawn could see her mouth something, appearing to urge him on, and then she closed the door, disappearing back into her kitchen.

Angel hesitated for just a second longer, then sauntered slowly toward her. Roshawn could feel herself holding her breath, almost afraid to release the influx of oxygen she'd taken until she had sense of his mood. She wanted to be prepared in case he pushed her away again, leaving her spirit and hopes bruised.

She was suddenly taken aback by the beauty of him, his skin darkened even more by the Caribbean sun. And there was something in his eyes that she had seen only once before, when he had kissed her so unabashedly in her doorway. It was sheer joy that tinted his dark brown eyes, shimmering light over everything his gaze fell on. The intensity of it was so overwhelming that her whole body seemed to ignite in flames. She squeezed her thighs tightly together, as if the heat forming between them would escape. Waves of fire scorched her from the inside out and suddenly there wasn't enough air, water, or cooling breezes to bring her any type of relief.

Angel stopped in front of her, one hand falling lightly against her knee as if he needed to assure himself that she was real and not a mirage he had created in his own mind. A smile pulled at his lips as he stepped in closer, easing himself between her parted legs. Roshawn wrapped her arms around his shoulders and pulled him close, dropping her mouth to his. Relief blew past her lips as she kissed him, just a light brushing of her flesh against his, the gesture easy, almost tentative, as she reacquainted her mouth to his.

Pulling away, Angel took a half step back and stared at her. He had known something was up the minute he'd come through the front door and his aunt Maria had come racing from the back of the house to greet him. The woman's excitement had painted her face, her enthusiasm spilling out in her laughter as she pulled him poolside, teasing him about a surprise. Never in his wildest dreams could he have imagined that Roshawn would be here, now, like this, waiting for him.

"What are you doing here?" he asked suddenly, bewilderment crossing his face.

"I came to see you." Roshawn smiled sweetly. "I wanted to be with you."

"But why…" the man paused, searching for words.

"Do you not want me here, Angel?"

He stared again, stepping back between her thighs. She tightened her embrace around his waist. He shook his head. "No, I want you with me," he answered, affirming the statement by kissing her again, this time with more ardor, a deep, long, luscious embrace that rose to a full swing of intensity. Roshawn relished the moment, finally breathing a sigh of relief that he had not turned her away.

"Walk with me," Angel said as he broke the kiss, lifting her from her perch. He pulled her hand into his and held it tightly as he led her down the stone path, and through the gardens. Flora bloomed in brilliant coloration, vibrant reds, yellows, oranges, and blues lavishing against the deep green backdrop. The aroma was overwhelming, the intense floral scents deluging her senses. As they walked he held her close, the gesture of his arm entwined with hers, their fingers clasped tightly one to the other, protective and endearing.

Roshawn appraised him. "Why did you leave? Obviously, you came to my home to see me, to talk to me and then you ran out. Why do you keep running away from me?"

Angel tossed her a quick glance, then focused his gaze on the landscape surrounding them. "I haven't been myself lately. And I didn't know how to tell you that you were the reason I was so out of sorts. I didn't think I could tell you or that you'd be interested."

She stopped, turning to stare up at him, her palms resting against his chest. "I was beginning to think you didn't like me. Every time we ran into each other we kept butting heads. But then that night we danced and when you came to my home and kissed me I felt like we were supposed to be together. It felt right. We felt right."

Angel smiled. "I like you very much. That's been the problem. I've been thinking you didn't like me and you've been such a nuisance. When I came to your home I was actually there to tell you what I thought about you. I wanted you to leave my father and me alone. You were too much of a distraction and I couldn't handle it."

Eyebrows raised, Roshawn eyed him curiously. "Oh? What else had you planned to say to me?"

He grinned, a wave of embarrassment sweeping over him as he shook his head. "I don't think you want to know. I think if I told you that you might leave and I don't want you to leave."

Roshawn smiled. "I'm not going anywhere. I'm here because I want to know you. My coming here was as good a place for us to get started as any other."

"Do you often chase after men you want to get to know?"

"I will do whatever it takes for the right man," she said matter-of-factly.

"Am I?" Angel asked, stopping to stare down at her. "The right man?"

Roshawn grinned. "I don't know yet. But I plan to have a great time while I find out."

Angel pulled her hand to his mouth and kissed the back of it, his lips lingering against the warmth of her skin. The gesture made her shiver and she drew her other palm along the side of his face. He smiled, the warmth of it filling his face.

"Since we're setting the record straight, I do owe you an apology," Roshawn said. "And I need to come clean about something."

"What?"

She reached to stroke the top of his head, her hands gently caressing his bald flesh. "I butchered your head on purpose but not because I was angry with you. You had beautiful hair, but the style was old. This suits you so much better and I didn't think you'd go for such a drastic change without a little push in the right direction."

The man's mouth dropped open and then he laughed, loudly, the sound rising from somewhere deep in his midsection. He wrapped his arms around her and hugged her tightly, his own palm caressing the back of her closely shaved head. "We look like two bowling balls," he chuckled, leaning his cheek against hers.

Roshawn nodded. "I like bowling balls," she said, laughing with him.

They continued walking as Angel gave her a tour of the property, guiding her down to the beach. Pulling off her sandals, Roshawn had walked barefoot in the sand, skipping along the shoreline where the water would occasionally rush up to kiss the land. Angel was enthralled by the comfort between them, an easy sharing of space that felt more than natural. He suddenly imagined himself very lost without her and he said so as they strolled hand in hand watching the sun beginning to dip low in the blue sky.

"You're the first woman who's ever been here like this. I like it. I like it a lot."

Roshawn pressed her fingers between his. "Now, you know it wouldn't be the same if it were just any woman here."

Angel leaned to kiss her forehead. "I know and I hope you're laying claim to your space."

She reached to wrap her arms around him. "I'm laying claim to whatever is meant to be mine."

Angel moved his lips against hers, drawing her breath into his body as he kissed her. A little shudder ran up the length of Roshawn's spine as she kissed him back. As the sun finally set, dipping low into the ocean until it disappeared from view, they stood holding tightly to each other, oblivious to everything except the roar of the sea and the lull of each other's heartbeat.

Back at the house, it was quiet, Maria having disappeared from sight. The kitchen table had been set for two, the meal sitting on the stovetop for them to enjoy. The abundance of food was tasty but by the third bite, it was clear that the baked salmon, steamed veggies and potatoes almandine were not on either of their minds. Roshawn rose from the table first, her gaze locking with his as she laid her napkin against the tabletop and turned toward the stairway. Slowly spinning back toward him, she tossed Angel a come-hither look that caused him to stop chewing in midbite. Angel swallowed the mouthful in one large gulp, almost choking to get it down.

Flinging his own napkin to the chair, he was right on her heels as she eased her way up the stairs.

Both stopped short in the entrance of the master bedroom. The room was aglow with candles that adorned every level surface and a fire burned in the fireplace, the vibrant glow of reds and yellows spinning light throughout the room. The bed had been turned down, a bouquet of roses laying against the pillows, and a bottle of wine and two glasses sat chilled and ready on the nightstand.

As they stood in the doorway, taking in the beauty of it all, Angel wrapped his arms around her waist, drawing her to him as he wrapped her in a deep embrace. He held on tightly, his face dropping against the back of her neck as he kissed her flesh, allowing his lips to run an easy path up to the lobe of her ear. Outside, it had begun to rain, the onslaught of precipitation tapping gently against the glass doors. The wind had picked up, blowing gusts over the horizon, and Roshawn could hear the faint tinkle of wind chimes announcing the onset of thunder crackling in the distance. She leaned back into the embrace, allowing the weight of her torso to fall against Angel's broad chest. Roshawn moaned ever so softly as Angel continued to tattoo kisses against her neck and across the width of her shoulders.

Spinning her around to face him, Angel kissed her tenderly, his mouth softly caressing hers. Together their tongues danced and he could feel the rush of heat as it extended down his torso and into his loins. Angel wrapped his body around hers, as she pulled him tighter against her. Her kiss had him on fire. Moaning deeply into her mouth, he couldn't get enough of her. Just hours earlier he'd been convinced that there would be nothing between them. He had resigned himself to not letting anything ever again happen that could leave him vulnerable and here he was now, so lost in the dynamics of her presence that he couldn't think about ever being away from her. The moment he had come through the door to see her waiting for him, he had been delighted to have her take him where he knew only she could.

Roshawn marveled at the gentleness of his touch as he dripped kisses down her chin to her open throat where he softly nibbled and tickled her flesh. His hands felt incredible as he slowly stroked her flesh through her clothes, his fingers gliding across her back and down her spine. He kneaded the tissue gently, his hands skating down to her buttocks as he palmed the lean tissue and pulled her tightly against him. Roshawn heard herself gasp his name, whispering it over her lips into the warm, evening air.

Taking a step back, Angel smiled down on her, the desire in his expression painting affection over every inch of her body. He could not imagine her face being any sweeter than at that very minute, and then it was, as she smiled wider, the rapture of it filling the beauty of her expression. He dropped down to his knees, pushing her T-shirt up to expose the bare flesh of her abdomen. He planted a soft kiss against her belly button as he pulled her to him, lapping his tongue over the taut tissue of her tummy. Roshawn gasped loudly as she cradled her arms around his head, her fingers gently kneading the bald flesh. Current surged through her body as Angel lightly nipped at her skin, sending a wave of electricity straight down to her feminine spirit.

Rising back up, Angel pushed her T-shirt up and over her head as she extended her arms upward, allowing him to undress her. Unclasping her bra, he grinned wickedly as he dropped it and her shirt to the floor. Roshawn grinned back as she undid the buttons of his shirt, pushing it from his chest and over his shoulders to join her clothing on the floor. Angel pulled her back to him, kissing her mouth with pure, unadulterated desire. Roshawn wrapped her arms tightly around him as he lifted her up and eased her down against the bed, pressing his bare chest against hers.

Easing slowly down her body, Angel left a trail of wet kisses against her neck, his tongue dancing against the indentation of her clavicle, down to the tissue of her breasts. He parted his lips ever so slightly to allow just the tip of her nipple inside. He suckled slowly, easing more and more of her into the warm basin of his mouth as he locked his lips around the whole of her. His desire was consuming and when he suckled harder, pulling her anxiously between his teeth, his tongue flicking over the hard rise of rock candy with quick, lashing repetitions, Roshawn's back arched in ecstasy. His hand reached to cradle her other breast against his fingertips and at the heat of his touch she could feel warm tears filling the corners of her eyes. Roshawn couldn't imagine the sensations shooting through her body being any more intense and then he shifted, moving his attention from one breast to the other and her body exploded in a wave of convulsions.

When Angel finally lifted himself from her, Roshawn had lost all sense of time and space. Her breathing was heavy, coming in ragged gasps as she sucked in air. Rising up on her elbows, she watched as Angel ambled over to the other side of the room and turned on the sound system. The music was a series of honey-toned ballads, sultry, haunting numbers that had a decisively Afro-Caribbean flair seasoned with strings, woodwinds and a virtuoso guitar. Tossing her a slow smile, he moved toward the bathroom, disappearing behind the closed door.

Roshawn lay back against the bed, curling both arms

above her head as she closed her eyes. In the distance she could hear water running, melding with the patter of rain that was still falling outside. Her chest was glowing from all the loving attention Angel had just paid her and the rest of her body was still burning hot from release. If the last few minutes were all the time she could have with him, Roshawn thought, then her trip would have been well worth her efforts. Angel's touch, his arms wrapped protectively around her, the tenderness of his gaze, and the sweetness of his smile had been as soothing as she could imagine any balm ever being.

The bathroom door opened and she turned toward him as he reentered the room. He stood naked in the doorway, his gaze locking tightly with hers. Roshawn lifted herself upward, staring as he stood in full glory, every dark muscle in his body hard and wanting. As he slowly moved toward her, Roshawn sprawled back against the bed, reaching both of her arms out to him. As he eased himself above her, lowering his body against hers, she pulled him close and Angel kissed her like she had never been kissed before. His lips covered her lips, his tongue seemingly everywhere at one time, filling her mouth, pushing for more space, lips pulling and releasing lips, teeth bumping, moans melting into one, deep, guttural cry. They kissed until dizziness claimed them both, the room spinning in a slow revolution around them.

Angel broke the connection, easing off to the side as he leaned to stare down at her. Roshawn gazed up at him anxiously, excitement spinning energy deep into the pit of her stomach. The anticipation was overwhelming as he teased her, his hands creeping beneath the short length of her skirt as hers danced the length of his arms and over his chest. His fingers skated in slow circles against her inner thigh and when he boldly pressed his hand against her secret treasure, sneaking his fingers beneath the line of her silk panties, Roshawn responded with a muffled gasp that she quickly silenced with a swallow. Angel smiled his appreciation, removing the last of her clothing from her body as he tossed her skirt and her panties to the floor at the end of the bed.

Perspiration beaded against both their nude bodies, moisture dripping into every crease and crevice of his and her body. Roshawn licked at the moisture against his chest, her tongue trailing slowly across the broad expansion of muscle. Tipping his head back slightly against his shoulders, Angel closed his eyes, relishing the sensation of her mouth upon him, her hands pressing against his back, the moderate length of her fingernails tightly gripping his flesh.

Roshawn pushed her palms against his chest, until he rolled onto his back, staring at her hungrily. She smiled coyly as she lifted her body above his, straddling him unabashedly. His palms moved to play with her breasts and she gripped him by the wrists, pushing his hands back behind his head. Shifting her body against his, Roshawn pushed and pulled her hips against him, teasing and taunting his manhood between her thighs. Angel could feel the rush of excitement building within him and he arched his hips up off the bed to stall her movements. Seduction wafted over her expression as she eyed him playfully, having gained full control over the moment. She leaned to whisper into his ear, biting lightly at his earlobe, her tongue tracing the outline of the appendage.

"Promise me your heart, Angel Rios," she said softly. "Promise it to me now."

Angel nodded, the splendor of her consuming his spirit. He muttered his response in Spanish, the lilt of the language sending shivers through her body. "I give you my heart," he whispered back, "now and always."

Roshawn smiled as he rolled her back against the bed, his mouth meeting hers for another kiss, blowing life into his promise as his breath blew past her lips and into her heart. No longer able to resist, Angel shifted his weight, reaching into the nightstand for a condom. Pulling it from his hand, Roshawn eased the prophylactic from the wrapper and sheathed him slowly, her fingers toying with the fullness of his manhood as he closed his eyes and reveled in the sensation of her hands upon him.

Plying her legs open easily, Angel covered her body with his, easing himself deep into her channel. He stared into her eyes as he fused his body into hers, her inner muscles spasming in sheer delight. Roshawn met him eagerly, craving every inch of him as he danced against her, every stroke drawing him deeper into the center of her being. He gripped her hands in his, his fingers entwined between hers as she called his name, calling it over and over again, the lilt of it like music to his ears. The moment was overwhelming as he felt as if his blood had turned into fire in his veins, every muscle in his body contracting at once.

Both cried out as the rush of their orgasm ripped through them. As they gave in to the moment, the sensation of relief was totally eclipsed by the mind-shattering waves of pleasure that poured through them. Neither could measure the time that elapsed as they lay holding each other tightly. Roshawn imagined it could have lasted just seconds or an eternity, the moment condensed down to just his body entwined with hers and the radiant pleasure of their two hearts beating in sync. As Angel held her, his body still locked tightly with hers, everything was disjointed, incoherent, as if he were outside himself, lost in a world of sheer bliss. He had opened his heart and let her in and he could never again see himself wanting to run from what Roshawn was willing to give.

Chapter 16

Roshawn was still sleeping soundly when the first rays of sunlight pierced through the room. The candles and fire had all burned out hours earlier, and the sudden shift from dark to light had pulled Angel from the comfort of his own slumber. He smiled down at her as she lay sprawled on her stomach, her naked body pressed into the mattress, one leg entwined tightly between his.

He'd lost count of the number of times they'd made love, each experience more intense than the previous. His last recollection of time had been when they'd raced down to the kitchen to gorge themselves on the vanilla custard and sugared strawberries his aunt Maria had left in the cooler for their dessert. It had been half past two o'clock in the morning. Roshawn had casually scooped the chilled confection onto his groin, and before he could react, had proceeded to eat and lick every drop from his body. The shock of the moment had quickly turned to sheer exhilaration as she had bathed him with her tongue, inciting a climactic rush through every nerve ending in his body. By the time they'd made it back upstairs and into the bed he'd been delightfully satiated and the experience had been far from finished.

Across the room, the local radio station had replaced the CD, the resident radio personality promising them a warm, sunny day with no further precipitation on the horizon. An advertisement for one of the local nightclubs caught Angel's attention and as he listened to the details he made tentative plans in his mind for him and Roshawn later on that evening. He leaned to press a kiss against her shoulder, gently easing his leg from beneath hers. She barely stirred as he eased his body off the mattress and headed into the bathroom to empty his bladder.

Minutes later as he stood beneath a flow of hot water, a much needed shower spraying down over him, his thoughts were still on the ethereal creature lying in rest in his bed. Never before had he known any woman with the vibrancy and energy Roshawn exuded. She was the perfect complement to his staid demeanor, challenging him in ways he'd thought unfathomable. He had shared more of himself in the short hours since her arrival than he had shared in his lifetime with anyone else. Even his father, who knew him better than anyone else was not privy to some of the secrets he'd found himself sharing with Roshawn as she had lain against him, her body curled tightly alongside his.

Her passion for life was undeniable. Angel sensed that Roshawn's spirited personality would be a constant source of energy for him to pull from. She had made it perfectly clear that she was not a woman who would be tamed by any man and if quiet and demure was what he wanted in his woman, then she was clearly the wrong choice to be in his life. He had kissed her, dropping himself deep inside her body, claiming every inch of her as his own and she had known without any doubts or reservations that he wanted her in his life more than he would ever be able to express in words.

The bathroom door opening interrupted his thoughts, Roshawn calling his name from the entrance.

"May I come in?" she said softly, sleep still clouding her voice. "I really need to use the bathroom."

"Of course," Angel exclaimed, peering out the frosted glass shower doors. "Good morning. I didn't think you'd ever wake up."

Roshawn laughed as she dropped her naked body to the commode. "I missed you. The bed got cold."

Angel chuckled with her. "That bed needed to cool down some."

Joining him in the oversize shower, Roshawn welcomed the spray of hot fluid. She stood like stone as Angel passed a soap-filled loofah sponge gently over her skin, suds spilling down her body and into the drain.

"Mmm," she purred as he followed each pass with a tender kiss. "If you keep this up that bed isn't going to stay cold for long."

Angel laughed. "Oh, yes, it is. I want to show you my home. You need to see Santo Domingo before we have to go back to the States. You can't do that from the bed."

Roshawn pressed the length of her body against his, savoring the sensation of his naked flesh as it kissed her own. Water showered over them much like the rain that had blessed the land just hours earlier. The gentle flow was nourishing them both with its sweet essence. Angel held her, wrapping his arms around her like the thick boughs of an ancient tree and the emotions that washed over Roshawn were like none she'd ever known before.

She leaned her cheek onto his chest and Angel pulled her closer as if the gesture could fuse them eternally together. There was something safe and protective in the curve of his embrace and Roshawn relished the enormity of it. When he pressed his lips to her forehead, and then her eyelids and cheeks, she imagined that she could stay lost in his space forever, the warmth of his body enveloping all of her senses with a radiance that felt comfortably familiar. She peered up to stare into his eyes and Angel kissed her with an easy smile as his palms stroked the length of her back. Roshawn caressed him with her gaze, a slow easy massage that connected every pore and danced along the length of his eyelashes as she committed his loving expression to memory.

She watched as his mouth curved up in appreciation, his full lips like plush pillows beckoning her to lay her own mouth atop his. And then he spoke, leaning close to her ear. "Thank you for coming after me," he whispered softly. "Last night was very special to me and I don't want it to ever end."

Santo Domingo was one of the most enchanting cities she had ever visited, Roshawn thought as they walked hand in hand through the streets. It was a profusion of modern sophistication, old-world charisma and Latin charm. As they had roamed the city, Angel had regaled her with story after story as he had taken her past the fortresses, the colonial palaces and the chapels that dated back to the early sixteenth century. His tales had been gallant, rich with innuendos of intense political intrigue and romance.

As they had walked along Las Damas Street, he recalled a time when the space had been populated by court ladies and soldiers, monks and noblemen, pirates and slaves. She had marveled at his knowledge of men like Hernán Cortés, Ponce de León and Rodrigo de Bastidas who had lived and plotted conquests, and found love in the very heart of the streets where they were now venturing. Roshawn had watched him, awe spilling out of her eyes as he'd enamoured her with tales of adventure and romance, taking her to another time and another place with the magic of his storytelling.

Side by side they'd wandered through a few of the museums and galleries that inhabited the old city, stopping for lunch in one of the local restaurants as the midday sun had peaked high in the clear sky. At one point Angel had pulled her into a secluded courtyard, the quaint space perfumed by the fragrance of blooming flora, and he had kissed her until her mind had been a puddle of mush, her body limp with desire.

Their last stop had been Los Tres Ojos, an exceptional fifty-foot deep cave with three lagoons surrounded by stalagmites and lush vegetation. The two had donned their swim gear, traipsing through the caverns as if it were something they did every day while they stole kisses and caresses behind the crags and rock formations. The day could have gone on forever, Angel had thought, as he pulled her hand to his lips and kissed the back of her fingers. Roshawn had found herself overwhelmed, not only by the warmth of the people who had greeted her with heartfelt wishes, and their native son with sincere reverence, but also by the sheer passion and seductive ambience that radiated throughout the city.

As the evening hours approached, Roshawn's body was fatigued, but her spirit had been abundantly exhilarated. The duo had finally fallen out from exhaustion, drifting happily to sleep as they'd dropped across Angel's bed, hands still entwined tightly together. Maria had looked in on them once, refreshing a bottle of wine and tray of cheese, crackers and fruit from the night before. She had smiled approvingly, withdrawing to her own room to call her brother and report that all was well with her beloved nephew and the woman who'd come from the States to claim his heart.

As the night unfolded, the sun falling off in the horizon, Roshawn opened her eyes and stretched the length of her body. For only a brief moment she was unsure of her whereabouts and just as she was thinking about panicking, Angel rolled his body closer to hers, his arms tightening around her torso in a protective embrace. Roshawn rolled to press her nose into the bend of his neck, inhaling deeply as she imbibed his scent deep into her lungs. An exhale of breath blew hot against the man's flesh.

Angel chuckled softly. "That tickles," he said, his own eyes still closed tightly.

Roshawn reached to kiss that space just beneath his chin. "So, you planning to sleep the night away?"

He shook his head. "Not at all. I have plans for you."

"I hope those plans involve food because I'm hungry."

He opened one eye and looked at her, shaking his head against the pillow. Roshawn lifted her body ever so slightly to lie across his chest. Angel tightened his hold around her. "We can get a shower, and then I'm sure there's food in the kitchen. My *tía* Maria cooks constantly."

Roshawn smiled. "She's so sweet. I imagine she and your father are quite a pair."

"They are. She raised me. She's the only mother I have ever known. I love her dearly. I don't think I would be here if it wasn't for her and my father."

"Family's very important."

"Tell me about your family. You don't ever talk much about them."

"Well, I was an only child also. My best friends, Bridget and Jeneva, became my sisters. None of us had any siblings and I think that's what drew us to each other. My parents were great. Both of them were teachers and now that they're retired they spend most of their time traveling around the world. In fact they're in Hong Kong right now with Chen's parents."

Angel nodded. "You and your ex-husband are very close."

"We're very good friends. I have a lot of respect for him. He's been an incredible father."

"He is very proud of Ming. He talks about her often."

"Ming is her daddy's heart. He adores that child. She couldn't have asked for a better father."

"I want someday to be a good father to my children."

Roshawn leaned up to stare into his face. "Children?"

Angel nodded. "I hope to have many children someday."

"How many is many?"

He grinned, shrugging his shoulders. "As many as you will allow me."

Roshawn grinned back. "Your father came at me with that mess. What would I look like having more babies now? Ming is eighteen years old. I'm thirty-six years old. For all I know, all my eggs are dried up by now."

The look Angel gave her was so consuming Roshawn felt her heart skip a beat and then two, picking up the pace as it restarted itself.

"You would look like the beautiful creature you are with my babies passing through your womb. Your age is of no consequence if your heart is open to the idea," he said softly, the convictions of his statement wafting through her. Roshawn said nothing, still staring into his eyes.

"Will you think about having my babies, Roshawn?" He pressed his palm to her abdomen, his fingers gliding over her flesh. "Will you honor my love for you with a son born of your heart?"

Silence whispered softly to them, his words a gentle echo sweeping over her spirit. "Do you love me? Do you, Angel?"

His smile brightened. "Did I not promise you my heart for now and always?"

"But do you love me?"

Angel pushed her back against the mattress, rolling his body above hers. He stared down at her, intoxicated by the sight of her. Her eyes glistened as they stared into his. "I love you with everything I have in me. It is why you and only you could have the effect that you do on me. You thrill me. You make me vulnerable. Only love could leave me feeling so empty when I'm not with you and so complete when you are so near to me. Of course, I love you."

Roshawn pressed a palm to his chest, reaching her other to stroke the side of his face. "Then with everything I have in me, I will honor that love. I will gladly think about having your daughters."

Angel laughed, tossing his head back against his shoulders. "I said my sons."

"And I said your daughters."

"Sons."

"Daughters."

"Stubborn."

"Irritating."

Angel lightly pressed his mouth to hers, his kiss barely a touch against her lips. He scanned her face, joy glistening in his eyes. "Say it," he said, his tone just shy of commanding. "Tell me now."

Roshawn grinned, her wide smile wrapped in sheer bliss, understanding seeping into her heart as she whispered her response into his soul. "I'm falling in love with you, Angel Rios. I am falling head over heels in love with you."

"So, where are you two off to this evening?" Maria asked as she lifted Angel's dinner plate from the table. She stood beside her nephew, balancing the plate in one hand, the other resting lightly against the man's shoulder.

"Guácara Taina," Angel responded, his eyebrows raising ever so slightly as he turned to look at Roshawn.

The older woman nodded. "They say that it is a very nice place."

"What is it?" Roshawn asked, eyeing him curiously as she pulled the last bite of her meal into her mouth.

Maria did a quick shuffle from the table to the kitchen sink. "It's the club for dancing the salsa and Merengue," the woman said as she dropped the plate against the counter and shimmed her way back to the table.

Roshawn grinned. "Merengue, huh?"

Angel leaned back against his seat, the front legs of his chair rising an inch or so off the floor. A broad smile filled the warmth of his brown face. "Roshawn is quite the dancer, *Tía*," he said teasingly. He smiled in jest as he chuckled softly and the look he gave Roshawn caused her to blush, the heat of it warming her dimpled cheeks.

She laughed. "It helps to have a great partner, Auntie."

Warmth from the old woman's smile beamed over the two of them. "I am sure you two will dance nicely together," she said softly, giving Roshawn a sly wink. "Do you know how to Merengue, Roshawn?" Maria asked. "It is our national dance, you know?"

"Really?" Roshawn said. "I've been salsa dancing before but I don't think I've ever done the Merengue."

Maria nodded her gray head. "If you can do the salsa then you can do the Merengue." She tapped Angel against the back. "Tell Roshawn about the Merengue, nephew. I have things to do in the other room." She leaned to kiss his cheek, then circled round the table to embrace Roshawn. The duo watched as she went out of the room toward the other end of the house.

"She does too much, my *tía*. Every time I try to get her some help she makes a fuss."

"She and your father are both very strong-willed," Roshawn said with a slight smile.

Angel smiled back. "They are more stubborn than you are," he said, lowering his chair back to the floor as he rested his forearms against the table, his hands clasped in prayer.

The two sat quietly, staring intently at each other, eyes dancing back and forth easily. The moment was endearing and as they both fell into the moment, Roshawn imagined that she could see her butterflies dancing sweetly with his.

Chapter 17

There was a line of cologned and perfumed, exotically dressed bodies extending from the entrance of Guácara Taina, the upscale dance club situated in the center of town. Angel pulled his car up to the door and got out. A cheer erupted from the crowd gathered as they recognized him, calling loudly for his attention. He smiled and waved his appreciation as he maneuvered his way around the vehicle to the passenger door. A club valet rushed to his side and greeted him by name, the two men shaking hands.

As Angel passed over the keys, he reached to open the car door. His smug expression was a mix of pride and joy as he extended his hand to help Roshawn to her feet. The man standing beside him eyed her from top to toe, his eyes widening brightly at the sight of her. Angel wrapped a possessive arm around her waist and guided her through the crown and toward the entrance. It was like the waters parting for Moses as people stepped aside to let them through. Two burly employees moved to open the door, greeting them both politely.

Once inside the multilevel cultural and dance center, they were guided deep into the caverns of an underground cave. From there they were led to a private table in the VIP section, a prime spot in the grand space illuminated by hints of light positioned strategically throughout the room. As Roshawn's eyes adjusted to the dim light, she held Angel's hand, moving to take a seat in the cushioned booth first.

Without Angel speaking one word, a bottle of champagne and two glasses were delivered to the table by an exotic young woman with skin the color of warm mahogany and licorice-colored hair that fell like silk strands down to the middle of her back. She smiled slyly, her gaze locked on Angel, never once bothering to toss a look in Roshawn's direction. Roshawn bristled, sitting straighter in her seat, her annoyance at the flagrant disrespect painting her face. The moment passed when Angel leaned and kissed her mouth, not once bothering to acknowledge the other woman's presence. Roshawn couldn't help but smile smugly as the female stormed off in a huff. After a brief conversation with the owners, the couple finally found themselves alone.

The dance floor just below them was packed with couples shimmying to the deep tempos of the music. Roshawn watched with awe at the proficiency of the young dancers spinning and gliding, hips and torsos shaking provocatively. She reached for Angel's hand and moved in closer as she talked into his ear, the volume of the music giving any attempts at conversation a good battle.

"So, tell me about the Merengue," she said, her mouth pressed close to his ear. She took a second to pass her tongue against the line of his face, smiling seductively before she pulled back.

Angel smiled, nodding his head as he leaned in even closer. Roshawn could not help but note the ease in which he slipped into his native tongue. "There are two stories that the old people tell about the Merengue. It is a very old dance and some say it came from the slaves who used to see the Europeans dance in the big houses. When these slaves were chained together they were forced to drag one leg as they cut sugar in the large cane fields. They would do this to the beat of the drums and from there, when they had their own festivities they would mimic the master's dances and improvise on the movements that they did in the fields. Their dance was more fun and brought them much joy.

"Others tell the story of a great war hero who was wounded in the leg during one of the many revolutions here in the Dominican Republic. A party of villagers welcomed him home with a victory celebration, and out of sympathy for his affliction, the guests felt obliged to limp and drag one foot as he did. The original Merengue was not danced by couples, but was a circle dance and the men and women would face each other and hold hands, but they did not hold each other too closely."

Roshawn nodded, still watching the action below. The music tempo had varied but the dances were similar. They seemed to enjoy the slower turns that would transition to a sharp quickening pace towards the latter part of the dance. There was much hip action and the energy was beyond definition.

She took a quick sip of her drink and reached for his hand. "Let's Merengue!" she chimed as she pulled him to his feet, leading the way toward the dance floor.

Angel grinned as he followed eagerly behind her, her exuberance matching the energy in the room. The surrounding
ambience was wild, enthusiasm as thick as the heat rising
through the packed crowd. In a matter of minutes, Roshawn
had mastered the step, her body shifting left, right, left, right,
in time with the tempo. Angel loved to watch her move, her
lithe frame moving easily with the heavy beat of the music,
seduction shining in her eyes as she stared at him, and that
incredible smile filling his spirit with warmth and energy.

At one point, the crowd parted, giving them a wealth of
space as all eyes stood watching. Since there was nothing shy
about either of them, they played to the audience, their performance on the dance floor one that would not only be the
talk of the nightclub, but would make the local gossip section
of the newspaper the next morning.

Before they knew it, the lights were flashing overhead, signaling the early hours of the morning. Angel leaned to give
her a quick kiss, then pulled her along toward the door,
stopping only briefly to wave goodbye to the management.
Thirty minutes later they were pulling into the driveway of
the Rios home and though she should have been exhausted,
Roshawn felt as if she were just getting her second wind.

"That was a lot of fun," she said, smiling brightly. "We
must do that again."

Angel smiled back. "We can do it as often as you like."

She reached for him, resting her hand against his upper
thigh as he guided the vehicle into its empty space, shifted
it into park, and cut off the engine. A glimmer of mischief
flickered over Roshawn's face as she suddenly jumped from
the car, racing up the walkway toward the back of the house.
Confused, Angel raced behind her, calling out her name.

"Roshawn? What are you doing?"

Her enigmatic laughter was the only response as she quickly disappeared from sight. Seconds later, there was a loud splash, the woman still giggling excitedly as he finally made it to her side. She floated naked against the cushion of water in the lower pool, the red silk dress and Ferragamo shoes she'd worn discarded poolside in one disheveled pile. Her arms paddled easily at her sides as her wide grin beckoned him to join her.

"What are you doing?" he asked, his arms folded across his chest.

"What's it look like? I felt like a swim," she said coyly, her tone oozing with eroticism.

He shook his head, staring intently at her, his body begging his mind to toss reason to the wind and jump right in beside her. Angel pulled at his necktie and unfastened the top buttons of his dress shirt. Roshawn's smile widened as she flipped her body in the water, her bare buttocks mooning him in the open air before twisting back around to face him. He couldn't help but grin back as he pulled the shirt and jacket off simultaneously, tossing both into the pile on top of Roshawn's garments. He rubbed a wide palm slowly across his chest and down to his abdomen, his hands finally falling against the waistband of his slacks.

"We have to fly this afternoon, Roshawn. You should be getting your rest."

"Rest isn't what I'm interested in getting," she said smugly, her own hands reaching to cup both her breasts as she stood upright, the water leveling off just beneath her nipples. She slowly cupped a palm in the warm water and guided the moisture over one shoulder and then the other. Her gaze locked with Angel's. "How long do you plan to keep me waiting?" she asked, her tongue gliding slowly over her bottom lip and back inside her mouth.

Angel pulled at his zipper, then pushed the rest of his clothes to the ground in one sweep. The length of his manhood protruded eagerly, a rock-hard erection quivering with an urgent need to feel her inner intimacy. Reaching back down for his suit jacket, Angel pulled his wallet from the inner pocket and searched its folds for the one and only condom he knew was hidden inside. Grasping his fury in his right hand for a brief second to stall his sudden yearning, he sheathed himself quickly. Moving to the far end of the pool he dove in headfirst, the water splashing its greeting. Swimming beneath the blue fluid, illuminated only by a full moon and the pool lights, he swam to her side. He resurfaced in front of her, every inch of his body glistening as it emerged from the water. He clasped her tightly around the waist and pulled her to him.

"I think the champagne has made you tipsy," he whispered, his eyes darting back and forth across her face.

"Oh, I'm very clearheaded," she said as she locked her legs around his waist and teased her femininity against his pelvis. "I know exactly what I'm doing," Roshawn said as she pressed her hands to his chest, her palms brushing lightly across his hardened nipples. The shiver that coursed through him caused his body to shake ever so slightly and Roshawn smiled with amusement as his expression intensified, his breathing starting to race as he sucked in deep breaths of air.

Roshawn giggled again and pulled away from him as she glided her lean body into an upward arch and propelled herself to the opposite end. The water seemed to part and make room for her presence, swirling around her face and breasts and thighs with delicious, rippling flourishes.

As she reached the end of the pool and looked back around, Angel was nowhere to be seen. Her gaze skipped across the surface of the water, trying to sense just where he lay beneath the liquid puddle. She was suddenly surprised, her body stiffening with pleasure as Angel swam between her legs, his mouth latching hungrily to her flesh as his hands clasped her buttocks, pulling her legs over his broad shoulders and back. For a moment, her head was pulled under the water and she held her breath tightly, intensifying the sensations that surged up through her torso and into her limbs from the intimate kiss. As she rose back to the surface, clutching at the side of the pool, she sucked in air, gasping loudly from the unexpected gratification. Control suddenly shifted between them. As she cried out his name it echoed loudly throughout the darkened air.

As quickly as he'd appeared, Angel was suddenly gone, disappearing stealthlike beneath the pool's deep warm flow. Roshawn shivered at the loss of his touch, spinning herself in a circle to see where he might appear next. She continued to kick her legs slowly, her arms fluttering in sync to keep her afloat. Just as a wave of nervous anxiety swept through her, Angel resurfaced behind her, clasping her tightly around the waist as he pushed her toward the side of the pool. Grasping the pool's edge, Roshawn panted her excitement as Angel pressed his body against hers, his chest brushing powerfully against her back and buttocks.

Angel reached round to kiss her mouth, pulling her head back against his chest as his lips moved feverishly against hers. Roshawn lost all sense of presence, feeling as if every inch of her flesh, every fiber of muscle, every drop of her blood was swimming in pure ecstasy. He leaned her forward, his mouth moving against the back of her neck, his tongue licking the moisture from her shoulders as she moaned with pure pleasure. As he pressed his hand against her, his fingers dancing intimately between her thighs, he took her from behind, his rigid body moving urgently against hers. The sensations raging through them both were intense, waves of lust and pleasure coming in a maddening rush before both dropped beneath the blanket of water, allowing it to swirl around them.

As the sun lifted slowly in the morning sky, Maria looked out the rear door, her head waving from side to side, her eyes rolling in disbelief. Searching a closet in the laundry room she found two lightweight blankets and pulled them from an upper shelf. Easing quietly outside she smiled down on the sleeping couple, their naked bodies curled closely together against a cushioned patio chair, Roshawn's head against his chest, Angel's arms embracing her tightly. Dropping both blankets around them, she reached for the clothes discarded on the other side of the pool, and headed back inside. Breakfast would soon need to be ready and there was much she had to do to prepare the lovers for their return trip back to the United States.

He could hear the two women laughing easily together. He and Roshawn had only been a touch embarrassed when they'd been awakened from their sleep to find that Maria had found them exposed, covering their nakedness as they'd slept. Together they'd gone inside the home, trying to tiptoe toward the back stairs and Maria had called out to them, announcing that breakfast was on the table and they would be late for the airport if they didn't soon get a move on it. She had chided them playfully, then had gone about her daily chores humming happily. And now she and Roshawn were laughing and giggling like they'd known each other their whole lifetimes.

He had called his father only to discover that the old man had been given frequent updates since Roshawn's arrival. Maria had called him daily to share the going-on in the house and Israel was tickled to death that his son and Roshawn had finally given in to what he had believed was inevitable. Angel shook his head, a slight smile pulling his full lips upward.

They only had another two and a half hours before it would be time to leave for the airport. Some quick maneuverings, with just a touch of begging and pleading had netted them tickets on the same flight. Both he and Roshawn had been thrilled that the return would be easier than their arrival had been, only one connection and plane change before landing back in Phoenix.

For the moment though, Angel needed to revive his muscles, to reinvigorate life back into them. Although he had thoroughly enjoyed his time with Roshawn, soon he would have to return to his game and redeem himself for the horrendous loss from the week before. He heaved a deep sigh as he thought back to the defeat, his swing sending the bat sailing above the ball as it had landed snugly in the opposing catcher's mitt. Angel could still hear the whir of it as it had buzzed past him and out of his reach.

He looked around the immaculate exercise room, his personal sanctuary whenever he was home. The room was large, a variety of expensive gym equipment decorating the space. At one end a large rack of free weights, barbells and a weight bench filled the corner. A treadmill, stationary bike and stair climber were situated room center. One wall was completely mirrored and a flat-screen plasma television was positioned on another. A sophisticated sound system was the last adornment in a far corner.

Stripping his T-shirt from his body, Angel turned to the mirror beside the bench. He raised his arms and flexed his biceps. They bulged obscenely and he smirked, admiring his reflection. He had done this often as a little boy, when his muscles had only been a fleeting wish. His father had laughed, then had cautioned him not to ever let his looks swell his already large head. Angel chuckled at the memories as he struck a bodybuilder's pose. A few more smirks in the mirror, a few more poses, and he was laughing out loud at the absurdity. Quiet from the other room made him look quickly over his shoulder to ensure neither Roshawn or Maria had sneaked up on him without his knowing. He would have been truly embarrassed if either had been watching his performance. He relaxed and posed one last time when Maria's voice rippled through the air.

He reclined on the bench to prepare for some chest presses knowing that there was nothing like pumping a little iron to stretch out his muscles after an extended period of just lounging around. After three sets of lifts, he was perspiring nicely, sweat beginning to bead against his brow and torso. Thirty minutes later he had moved from one station to the next with ease and he felt good, extraordinarily energized. In the distance he could still hear the two women chattering about everything and about nothing and it renewed the smile upon his face.

He was thrilled that Roshawn was so at ease with his family. His family was important to him. Everything he did, he did for the benefit of his father and his *tía* Maria and the many aunts, uncles and cousins that fruited his family tree. He paused for a brief second, midstride on the stair-stepper, a wide smile blossoming across his face.

The day before he had driven her to the country, the lands

that bordered the outskirts of Santo Domingo where almost half the country's population resided. Generations had farmed the lands there, living off the crops and livestock to support themselves. The original lands owned by his grandfathers and their grandfathers had been farmed so long that most of the soil lacked the necessary nutrients to sustain a crop for long-term farming. Angel's financial success had enabled his relatives to afford fields of grazing cattle that had become a viable source of income for them to build on. They supplemented that with growing bananas and tobacco and the family as a whole was thriving.

His cousin Tito had welcomed them both warmly, ushering them from the car to the stables and two waiting mules loaded with supplies that needed to be transported from one side of the vast acreage to the other. Tito had led the way, chattering his excitement as he and Roshawn had followed willingly behind. Roshawn had been a great sport, coaxing and coddling the stubborn beast when it had grown weary itself of the journey, digging in its hoofs to be left alone.

Before leaving, Roshawn had improvised a game of catch with a gathering of children who'd come to see them, laughing and cheering excitedly. She had emptied her handbag of chewing gum, mints, and even a chocolate bar, which she'd divvied into equal portions for them all to share, promising to send more as soon as she was able. On the return trip back to the city he'd driven along the southern coast toward Lago Enriquillo, which lay near the borders of neighboring Haiti. Roshawn had asked questions and had celebrated his homeland with her genuine interest in knowing about it and him.

Angel transitioned back to the bench to do one more rotation of arm curls with a heavy set of free weights. Roshawn's beautiful face smiling down at him pulled him from his reflections.

"Did you work out all them muscles?" she asked leaning to press her lips to his.

He grinned. "Even some I didn't know I had," he answered, dropping the fifty-pound weight to the floor. His hands fell to her hips as Roshawn straddled his body and sat down on his lap. One muscle in particular quivered ever so slightly.

"We should probably go get ready to leave," Roshawn said, wrapping her arms around his neck, her fingers dancing against the back of his head. "Or we'll be late for our flight."

He nodded, his gaze brushing the canvas of her face with light, even strokes. "Thank you," he said softly.

Her head tilted as she looked at him curiously. "For what?"

"For coming after me."

Roshawn smiled. "I'd do anything for the right man."

Angel grinned back. "Am I?"

She kissed him, their mouths lingering in the moment before she answered, her words singing sweetly in his ears. "Without a doubt."

Chapter 18

As they pulled into the driveway of her home, Roshawn had a feeling of contentment that she'd never before had. The flights home had been picture-perfect and even one stomach-churning moment of turbulence had been easily dismissed with Angel holding tightly to her hand. But as she stepped from the vehicle and took note of Ming's new car and a second familiar Chevy pickup truck, the dials on her parental radar suddenly spun into action. She tossed Angel a quick glance as he pulled her luggage from the trunk and followed behind her toward the front door.

"What's the matter?" he asked, noting the concerned expression that had crossed her face.

"I'm just wondering why my daughter is entertaining company when she's not even supposed to be here."

Angel nodded his head slowly, a heavy palm dropping against her shoulder to calm the rise of anxiety that had swept through her. As they made their way through the front door, they could hear Ming giggling, the sound of her laughter coming from the family room. The CD player was on full blast, the heavy beat of 50 Cent singing "Candy Shop" spinning over the airwaves. Stepping into the room, Roshawn could only shake her head as her daughter lay on the chenille settee in a string bikini that was more string than fabric. She lay parallel dancing with a tall young man who seemed even taller when you took into account the full foot of afro that sat atop his head. Neither noticed as Angel and Roshawn stood staring at them, the young man grinding his hips against her child as if he were trying to drill for oil.

Roshawn snapped off the music. "Ming, I know you have completely lost your mind."

"Mommy!" Ming cried out as the two of them jumped to their feet, shock registered across their faces.

"Does your father know you're here by yourself with this boy? And Dixon, *what,* pray tell, are you doing in my house groping my daughter?"

The young man sputtered, no sound coming past his lips as he looked from Roshawn to Angel and back again. "I…I…"

"She asked you a question. I think you need to answer it," Angel said, moving to take a seat against one of the high bar stools. "And I think you should answer it very quickly."

"I'm sorry, Ms. Bradsher. We didn't mean…" The young man paused, sweat beginning to bead against his brow.

Roshawn shook her head, her gaze still locked with Ming's.

"We weren't doing anything wrong, Mommy. I swear."

"That's not what it looked like. Did you have your father's permission to be here alone with Dix, Ming?"

"No, but…"

"Does he even know where you are?"

"He...I...we..." Tears filled Ming's eyes.

"I didn't think so. That was your first mistake. And where the hell are your clothes? I know damn well your father didn't buy you that swimsuit and I sure wouldn't have." Roshawn slammed her purse to the counter. "Don't answer that. Just go change. Now. Then we all need to have a serious talk."

Ming turned to Dix, the young man's gaze trying to offer her a hint of support.

"I think I should be going," he said softly, moving as if to take his leave.

"I don't think so, son," Angel said, pointing to the chenille settee. "Take a seat. She means you, too."

"Yes, I do," Roshawn stated, glaring at the boy, his mahogany complexion having paled substantially. She shook a finger in his direction, wanting to say something, but then stalling, the words seeming to catch in her throat. "I'll deal with you in a minute, Dixon," she said finally. She turned toward Angel. "You two need to excuse me for a minute. I need to speak with my daughter."

Turning an about-face, Roshawn headed down the hall behind Ming. The boy on the sofa closed his eyes, his hands cupped in prayer in front of him. As Angel stood staring at him, the man couldn't help but smile, a very slight bending of his lips pulling at his expression, remembering well what it felt like to be a teenaged boy caught with his hand in the cookie jar.

In the other room, Ming was muttering under her breath as she tossed a T-shirt and a pair of jeans over her bra and panties. The string bikini lay discarded on the floor where she had stepped out of it. As her mother entered the room, closing the door heavily behind her, Ming dropped to the edge of the bed, the two women staring intently at one another.

"I wasn't doing anything wrong," Ming finally muttered for the second time.

"It was wrong, Ming. It was wrong because you were going out of your way to keep it secret. If you didn't think there was anything wrong with your behavior then why did you feel you needed to be secretive about it?"

"Because you know how Daddy is. He doesn't want me with Dixon at all so I knew he'd throw a fit because I wanted to be alone with him."

"Ming, you and Dixon have only been dating for a few weeks. He picks you up, takes you out, and the two of you are alone and your father knows it, deals with it, and gives his approval. Don't try to make excuses about you two sneaking over here to be alone in this house, damn near naked, when you know neither your father or I would have approved of that."

"We just wanted to swim in the pool and hang out. That's all."

Roshawn heaved a deep sigh. "I think we need to schedule an appointment for you to see a gynecologist."

"I don't need—"

"You need to make sure you know your options and you're protected," Roshawn said, interrupting her.

"But, I—"

Roshawn's gaze was cutting, the girl's words dropping to barely a whisper before she could finish her statement.

"I wasn't born yesterday, Ming. I was eighteen once, too. Eighteen and in love with the most incredible boy and by the time I was nineteen we had you. So, please, don't think I'm so naive that I would even remotely believe that you and

Dixon aren't having sex. If you weren't, you wouldn't have needed to sneak over here to be alone."

Ming hung her head, a tear falling against her cheek. "I'm sorry," she said. "I didn't mean to disappoint you and I wasn't going to deny that Dix and I are having sex. But I've already been to see a doctor. I know what my options are."

Roshawn nodded. "Ming, you're eighteen years old now. There are some decisions you need to make for yourself no matter what your father or I might feel about it. But, you know how we feel. And, you know what we've taught you. Yes, I am very disappointed. And, I don't know that you're responsible enough to be sexually active. If you were, then you wouldn't be acting like such a child. You wouldn't be lying to me and your dad. And you wouldn't be sneaking around. But that doesn't matter, because you made the decision to do what you've done and now you have to deal with the repercussions. Did you at least use some form of birth control?"

The young woman nodded her head. "Yes, Mom. I'm on the pill *and* we used a condom."

"I'm sure the doctor told you nothing is a hundred percent fail-safe. Have you even considered what could happen? What you would do if you became pregnant? Have you thought about STDs?"

"Mom, Dix loves me and I love him. We'd get through it."

"Yeah, I'm sure you could get through anything if you had to, Ming. But why put yourself in that position at all?"

Ming swiped at the tears that watered her cheeks. "Please, don't hate me."

Roshawn shook her head as she wrapped her arms around her child's shoulders and hugged her tightly. "Don't be ridiculous. I love you, Ming. I only want the best for you. And you know perfectly well that I would never hate you. But I really need you to use your head and be smart about the decisions you make for yourself."

"Are you going to tell Daddy?"

"No, I'm not."

Ming smiled slightly. "Thank you."

"Don't thank me yet. I'm not going to tell him because you are. If you think you're mature enough to be having sex and sneaking around to do it, then you're mature enough to tell your father that you've been caught."

Ming dropped back against the mattress. Roshawn came to her feet, staring down at her. "You have a choice. You can call him now and ask him to come over to discuss this, or we can go there. But either way, it's a conversation you're going to have with your father."

Back in the family room the two men were still sitting on opposite sides of the room. Dixon's head hung heavily in his hands as he imagined the absolute worst that could possibly befall him before he'd be able to make it back to his dorm room. Angel was still sitting casually watching him as if he had swallowed his own canary and was only waiting to see in which direction the feathers were bound to fly. As Roshawn stepped back into the room both looked toward her, one smiling sweetly, the other's expression molded out of hard, cold fear.

"Chen and Allison should be here in about ten minutes," she said, cutting her eye at Dixon as she stepped into Angel's outstretched arms.

"Miss Bradsher, please—" Dixon started before being interrupted.

Roshawn held up her palm. "Save it, Dix. I'm sure Ming's father is going to want to hear whatever it is you have to say."

The boy's body sagged, his crestfallen expression moving Roshawn to give him a slight smile.

"Relax. I promise he won't kill you. If that were going to happen you'd be dead already. But since you and Ming seem to think you're grown, you're going to have to have an adult conversation about what you two were doing here. And we do know exactly what you two were doing."

The boy's cheeks reddened, embarrassment sweeping through him. Angel could feel the young man's pain and he shook his head ever so slowly.

"Why don't you and I go take a quick walk," he said, rising to his feet. He turned to Roshawn, kissing her cheek as he winked an eye. "We'll be right back."

Roshawn nodded, her gaze moving from Dixon to Ming who'd finally found her way back to the room.

"Come on, Ming," she said, heading in the direction of the kitchen. "You can help me make a pot of coffee."

Dixon stood up and followed behind Angel. Outside, the man stopped at the edge of the pool, the sight of it bringing a wave of memories over him and he grinned broadly. As Dixon stepped up beside him, he tempered his emotions, shifting his attention back to the matters at hand.

"I didn't mean to get Ming in any trouble, sir. I swear I didn't," the young man said, his tone pleading.

Angel nodded. "A man's daughter is his most cherished possession. A daughter is like fragile glass and fathers put them on pedestals to keep them safe from any harm. Ming's father is not going to be happy that you have put his child in harm's way."

"I wouldn't ever do anything to hurt Ming. I swear I wouldn't. I love Ming."

"Maybe so, but you are very young and Ming is even

younger. Her parents want only the best for her and what you've done doesn't show them that you respect that."

Dixon heaved a deep sigh. "What do I do?"

"Tell the truth. They will respect you for being honest with them. You sneaking Ming around and having her tell them lies and do things they don't want her doing says that you don't respect them. They can't trust you. You will have to prove yourself to them. If you love Ming then you will show them that respect by following the rules they have for her."

Dixon nodded, taking a deep breath. "They're not going to let me see her again, are they?"

Angel shrugged, his broad shoulders tipping skyward. "I do not know. But if that's what they ask of you, then you need to honor that. If you are any kind of man you will respect what they ask of you."

The boy shook his head.

"And if you don't," Angel said slowly, his tone firm as he turned to face Dixon, "and Ming gets hurt, I won't be very happy about that. You do not want to see me if I'm not happy. If you hurt Ming, I will have to hurt you. Do you understand me?" Angel asked, his dark eyes narrowed into thin slits.

Dixon nodded, his own eyes widening.

Ming stood staring out at them from the kitchen window as Roshawn pushed the start button on the automatic coffeemaker.

"Dix looks sick," she said, looking to her mother and then back outside. "What is Angel saying to him?"

"Probably what your father is going to say to him."

Ming shook her head as she turned back to face her mother. Roshawn leaned back against the kitchen counter, her arms crossed over her chest.

"How was your trip?" Ming suddenly asked. "Are you and Angel a couple now?"

Roshawn smiled. "My trip was perfect. Angel is a great guy."

"Are you in love?"

The older woman nodded. "It feels very much like love. Angel is a very special man and I enjoy him being in my life."

Ming moved to give her mother a hug. "I'm glad. I like him a lot. Are you getting married?"

"I don't know about all that now. We'll just have to wait and see what happens."

The two women were still holding one another when the front doorbell rang. Roshawn could feel the girl begin to shake in her arms. She tightened her embrace. "You'll get through this, Ming. But you have to act like an adult if you want your father to treat you like one."

Ming nodded. "I understand. Would it be okay if I spoke to Dixon for a minute before we have to face Daddy, please?"

Roshawn nodded. "Sure, why don't you ask Angel to come inside. We'll call the two of you back in a minute or two," she said as she moved toward the front of the house. At the front door Chen stood anxiously, Allison standing at his side. His mood was less than pleased as he rushed inside.

"What's going on? Ming sounded upset."

At that moment, Angel came through the back entrance. "John, hello," he said softly.

The man stood stunned for only a brief second before he extended his hand in greeting. "Angel, it's good to see you. You've met my wife, Allison, haven't you?"

Angel nodded. "Mrs. Chen, it's very nice to see you again."

"You as well," the woman responded softly. "And please, call me Allison."

Chen turned back to Roshawn. "What's going on? When did you get back from your trip?"

"Just an hour or so ago. When Angel and I got here we found Ming alone with Dixon."

"With Dixon? She was supposed to be at the Children's Center working this afternoon."

"We need to talk with the two of them, Chen, and I need you to stay calm."

Chen bristled. "Calm about what? Please, don't tell me she's pregnant, Roshawn."

Roshawn sighed. "Not that I'm aware of, but then there's always a possibility it could happen. She says she's protecting herself, but you never know."

Chen groaned, shaking his head, ire rising in his eyes as he stared at his ex-wife. "She's sleeping with him?"

"You'll have to ask her that, Chen. She says they're in love. You were that age once and in love, remember?"

"I remember that we had a toddler before your twenty-first birthday. I don't want that for Ming, Roshawn."

"Don't raise your voice at me, Chen," Roshawn said, her tone warning that she was not in the mood to fight with him. "I don't want that for her either, but she's eighteen now and we can't watch her every second of every day and expect that she isn't going to become intimate with a boy she cares about. But we need to keep talking to her so that she knows we're here for her. She needs to know that she can trust us to be supportive of her no matter what."

"I'm not supporting this, Roshawn. She's not going to see that boy again."

"That's intelligent, Chen. Remember what happened when your father and my father insisted we not see each other? We got married."

The man skewed his face, tossing up his hands as he raged in Cantonese. Allison's eyes widened, making her appear even more fragile and scared than normal. Roshawn just shook her head at him as she turned back to the kitchen. Angel reached out to squeeze her arm, entwining his fingers between hers as she pulled him along behind her. In the kitchen, the two took a seat at the heavy oak table, no one saying a word as Chen and Allison joined them.

Chen sat in silence, staring intently at his ex-wife, his paternal spirit shattered by the reality that his baby girl was no longer a baby. Although he'd always known this moment would one day come, he had never expected it this soon and before he'd had the opportunity to walk her down the aisle. As if reading his mind, Roshawn could sense the depth of his disappointment and she reached out to draw her palm down the length of his arm. Chen nodded, the duo seeming to have a silent conversation that Allison and Angel were not privy to.

"So, where is she?" Chen finally asked, his tone just a hint calmer.

"She and Dix are out by the pool."

Angel interjected. "This is a family matter. I should probably leave you all alone. I can send the kids in on my way out."

Before Roshawn could respond, Ming answered for her. "No, Angel, you should stay. You're a part of my family now. My mother wants you here and so do I."

They all turned toward where the girl stood side by side with Dixon, the young couple holding hands in the doorway. As Ming smiled in the man's direction, Angel nodded, reaching to grasp Roshawn's hand in his own. For a brief moment, Roshawn imagined that to Dixon, the four adults must have looked like a delegation from the United Nations sitting around the table staring at the two of them.

Ming greeted her father in Cantonese, leaning to kiss his

cheek before she and her boyfriend pulled two more chairs up to the table and sat down. The young woman took a deep breath, glanced quickly toward her mother who smiled her support, then turned to face her father. His expression was stone, his displeasure pouring from his eyes.

"Daddy, I lied to you. I didn't work at the center today. I spent the day here with Dix. Mom caught us together when she came home."

"We're sorry, Mr. Chen. We didn't mean to deceive you. We just wanted to spend some time together alone," Dix said, his voice quivering with nervousness.

Chen bit down against his bottom lip. Allison's hand rested against his leg and she squeezed his thigh gently, the quiet gesture of support stalling his desire to yell and yell loudly.

"Daddy, Dix and I have become very close. He's very special to me."

"How close is close, Ming?" He focused his gaze on Dixon. "Are you having sex with my daughter?"

The duo exchanged a quick glance before Ming responded. "I think I'm old enough to make my own decisions about who I do or don't have sex with, Daddy. But you should know that I love Dix."

The man shook his head, his eyes closed as his body shook. As he opened them, refocusing his gaze back on his daughter, his stare was glassy, misted over by the warmth of saline forming behind his eyelids. "I don't appreciate you lying to me, Ming. Not at all. I trusted you. And I don't like that you did it because Dix made you."

Roshawn rolled her eyes and the man glared at her.

"Dix didn't make me do anything," Ming asserted. "Whatever I've done, I did because I wanted to or thought I had to."

"Mr. Chen, Ms. Bradsher, I love Ming. I love Ming very much. We were wrong, but we only did what we did because we thought you would think we were getting too serious too soon. We weren't thinking. We made a mistake."

"You are too young for this, Ming. Way too young," Chen said, ignoring the boy's statement.

"You and Mommy were young and you two knew you were in love."

Chen couldn't help but look to Roshawn.

"Ming, you and I have had a number of conversations about that. Yes, Chen and I loved each other but the fact that we were so young was one of the reasons our marriage didn't last," she said.

"But your love did."

Her parents locked eyes for a second time, then Roshawn's gaze moved from Allison to Angel and back again. She sighed. "Ming, our love lasted because it was in your best interest. Your father and I remained friends because we loved you and loving you kept us connected. But how he and I loved each other wasn't enough to sustain a relationship the way you're thinking it will. That kind of love comes with maturity and experience. Your father has that now with Allison, and I—" she paused, turning to meet Angel's eyes "—I've finally found that with Angel."

The room grew quiet for a brief moment. Angel leaned to kiss Roshawn's cheek and on the other side of the table, Allison smiled with relief, her palm dropping down against Chen's thigh.

"None of us want you to make any mistakes that you might regret later on," Allison said, looking from Ming to Roshawn and back. "We all love you, Ming, and we want you to be safe and happy more than anything else."

Roshawn smiled and nodded her agreement, the two women exchanging a quick look between them.

"I don't think being with Dix is a mistake. I know how much I love him. And we've talked about this. We both want to finish school before we make any decisions about our future."

"What if you get pregnant, Ming? What then?" Chen asked, his voice rising slightly.

"Then we'll deal with it, sir. Together. I would never let Ming deal with something like that alone," Dix said.

"But I'm not going to get pregnant. I'm not ready for that. I know this is a lot to ask, Daddy, but I need you to trust me. Please? I promise I won't disappoint you or Mommy again."

The room grew quiet as the adults sat staring from one to the other. In the distance the drip, drip, drip of a leaky faucet seemed to be magnified. The sound vibrated loudly in beat with the lull of the refrigerator and the ticking of the clock that rested against the wall.

"You will not have any privileges for the next month for lying, Ming. None."

"Yes, sir."

"And, Dix, you are going to have to regain my trust. I don't appreciate you sneaking around with my daughter the way you have."

"I understand, Mr. Chen."

Chen nodded. "Ming, show your friend to the door and say goodbye. Then take yourself home. Allison and I will be right behind you."

Ming nodded. "Yes, Daddy."

They watched as the two said their goodbyes, Dix moving to shake Angel's hand and then Chen's, who eyed the boy with pure disdain. Ming hugged her mother tightly, then moved to wrap her arms around her father. Chen held her tight for only a moment before releasing his hold, reaching to wipe the moisture from his eyes before it fell. No one spoke until they were both out of earshot, the front door closing firmly behind them.

"I hate this," Chen finally muttered. "I really hate this."

Angel nodded his understanding. "They grow up too fast."

The man smiled, looking from Angel to Roshawn and back, appreciating the obvious bond between them.

Roshawn shook her head. "We were just as bad, Chen. If our parents had half a clue what we were doing when we went to Spain they would have killed us both. And we probably would have kept it a secret too if we hadn't gotten pregnant."

Chen nodded, his eyes meeting Angel's briefly before he dropped them to the floor.

Angel smiled. "I was fifteen. My father caught us in the fields, my girlfriend and I. He was not happy. Not happy at all. She was much older than I was. Almost twenty-four. Her family sent her away and I never saw her again."

Allison chuckled. "I was a little older than that and my mother found my birth control pills hidden in my sock drawer. She went ballistic. It was horrible."

Roshawn rose from the table, grabbing four coffee mugs from the cabinet and filling each with the hot brew that she had made earlier. Sitting back down the group talked for a while longer, reminiscing, planning, sharing, and getting to know one another before Chen and Allison moved to head for home.

Chen hugged his ex-wife as she stood at the front door wishing them both a good night. "I don't know how much more my heart can handle, Roshawn," he said, his eyes searching hers.

Roshawn smiled. "Your heart will be fine. Ming's a good girl. She'll be okay."

Shaking his head Chen tossed her a wry smile, grabbed Allison's hand and sauntered slowly toward the car. She and Angel stood arm in arm as they watched the couple pull out of the driveway and drive down the street, disappearing out of view.

Angel kissed her forehead. "I should be going," he said. "My father is probably wondering what has happened to me."

"You know you can always stay. I really don't want you to leave."

The man grinned. "I don't know if I would get any rest if I stayed. You could get me in deep trouble."

Roshawn pressed her body tightly against his. "Now would I do that?" she said facetiously as she kissed his mouth.

Angel chuckled. "Yes, you would." He hugged her, molding his arms tightly around her.

"Thank you," she said as she brushed her cheek to his. "Thank you for being here."

He nodded. "Thank your daughter. She made me feel very welcomed."

"That's my baby girl." She kissed him one last time. "Drive safe and call me once you get settled."

Minutes later Roshawn had locked and secured each door, her body finally feeling the effects of jet lag and the difference between time zones. She was too tired to call Seattle, she thought, making note to do so first thing when she woke the next morning. As she entered the master bedroom, switching on the lights in the room, the disheveled bed was the first thing that caught her attention. Shaking her fists, Roshawn screamed at the top of her lungs. "Ming Louise Chen, I'm going to kill you!"

Chapter 19

The two men sat comfortably in the lobby of the hotel, occupying two upholstered chairs that adorned a back corner. Both were sipping on large mugs of coffee spiced with Kahlúa and rum.

Israel was shaking his head, his concerned expression belying his good mood. "I'm sure they will do what's best for the child," he said. "That is such a difficult age. Your children think you know everything there is to know in this world and they know nothing. I remember it well."

Angel smiled, having heard the same dissertation from his father more times than he cared to count over the years. He took another sip of his drink.

"So, what do you and Roshawn plan to do now, *hijo?*" the man asked, his good mood swinging into high gear.

"We've not made any plans yet, *Papí*, but soon. This is still very new to both of us. We have much more to learn about each other."

"You love each other. That is all that is important. It will be as I said it will be and I will be holding my grandson before I die."

Angel laughed. "Then it is well that you will be with us for a very long time, *Papí.*"

His father grinned broadly. "Don't wait too long. I am an old man. God may call me home to be with your mother when we least expect it. I can only hope that you and Roshawn will be married well before then."

Angel shook his head from side to side. "She is an incredible woman, *Papí.* There is nothing meek or mild about Roshawn. She is all fire. A man could get burned easily with that one."

"A man who does not have her heart may get burned. You have her heart. What you need to remember, *hijo,* is that Roshawn is not a woman you can dictate to. She has her own mind and she will speak with her own voice. Not yours. She is like your mother that way. She will keep you challenged. You will have to be an honorable man to hold tight to a woman like that. A very honorable man, indeed."

The younger man nodded his understanding. The two sat quietly for just a minute more as both thought about the women they loved and loved hard. Israel smiled as he stared toward his son, the boy a mirror image of his mother. His mother would be proud of him and she would be proud that he had found the likes of Roshawn to give his heart to. He reached into his shirt and unlatched the clasp of the large gold chain that hung around his thick neck. An intricately carved gold band hung from the length of it and he shook the ring loose and into his hand.

"What are you doing with Mommy's ring, *Papí?*" Angel asked, watching as his father replaced the chain around his neck sans the ring, the jewelry still floating against his palm.

"I have been waiting for the right time to pass this down to you. I am happy now that this is the right time." The old man beamed, his joy radiating through every line in his face. "Your mother wore this ring for me and my mother wore it for my father. It is only fitting that the woman you love should wear it for you. One day I hope that your son will know love and you will pass it down to him. This is as it should be."

Israel leaned to press the ring into his son's palm, wrapping his own hands tightly around his child's. "This ring has been many times blessed. Many times." He smiled and leaned back against his chair, satisfaction brimming at the edges of his eyes.

Angel fingered the precious trinket against his large fingers, slowly nodding his head up and down. He locked eyes with his father, the two holding the stare as they reflected on the past and the promising future that lay in wait for them. As he secured the ring in the breast pocket of his suit jacket he smiled his thanks, knowing that there were no words which could ever convey his gratitude. Thanks would come when the ring rested on Roshawn's finger and he could lay his own child into his father's arms.

The two chatted for another hour before Angel knew he needed to get to bed to rest up for the game the following day. As they made their way to the elevator, a family of three caught his eye, the father holding tight to an infant, the mother holding on to her husband's hand. Angel smiled, gladly signing an autograph as he envisioned himself in that position one day, Roshawn and their child at his side.

* * *

Although she was laughing, Roshawn really wasn't finding any humor in the situation. "I tell you, Jeneva, I am so ready to snatch a knot in that child's—"

"Now, now," Jeneva chimed into the receiver, cutting her off. "I can remember you and Chen getting buck wild in your mother's bed once or twice and don't say you didn't."

Roshawn shook her head. "I swear, Jay, I'm getting too old for this nonsense," she said sighing heavily.

Her friend laughed. "And you're thinking about having another one? You don't know tired yet. It was easy when we were in our twenties, and Ming and Quincy were babies, but take my word for it, being almost forty with a toddler ain't no picnic. And, I speak from experience. Alexa is wearing me out big-time."

"Well, you just wait. She'll be fifteen soon and then I can say I told you so."

"I still can't believe you told him you'd have his baby."

"I told him I would *think* about it. You know I always thought about having more kids. Now that Ming's all grown up, I can't help but think about it more seriously. I can't help wondering whether or not I'd be even a better mother now that I'm all grown up myself."

Jeneva smiled. "Yeah, I think when I was pregnant with Alexa I was thinking a lot of that myself. But there's no denying, Roshawn, you and I did a great job with our kids. We've got good children."

Her friend grinned. "That we do. And I really think I would love to have another child. What I'm not so sure about is if I'm interested in being married again."

Jeneva shook her head into the receiver. "Ouch! Why not?"

"I don't know. Marriage requires so much of yourself and I've been enjoying my freedom for so long, I don't know if I'm interested in giving that up to any man."

"Who says you have to give anything up, Roshawn? You're just sharing yourself in a whole other way. Make it about what you're getting in return, not what you might be losing. Besides, we both know that married or not you will never allow any man to confine your spirit. And I don't care who he is or how much love you have for him."

"Well, if I do, I'm still not giving up my name. My father blessed me with this name and I plan to keep it. And I can tell you right now it's going to be a fight with Angel just like it was a fight with Chen."

Jeneva laughed. "I wouldn't stress over it. You've won the battle before, I'm sure you'll win the battle again."

Roshawn nodded. "So," she asked, changing the subject. "What's Bridget up to? I tried to call her, but she wasn't answering any of her lines."

"I haven't talked with her much myself lately. There's something major going down with that law firm she works for. Every time I hear from her she's working late, working early, or just plain working. I don't think she's had ten minutes to herself since you left."

"And, how's that brother-in-law of yours? Those two hook up yet?"

Jeneva chuckled. "You know they haven't! But Darwin's good. He's in Los Angeles this week meeting with some folks about doing a television cooking show. This is his third meeting so it may actually pan out. He's very excited."

"Very nice! Please, tell him I said hello the next time you speak to him and wish him good luck for me."

"I will. Look, I've got to run. The baby just woke up crying. You take care of yourself, girlfriend. And, we can't wait to meet this man of yours."

"Soon. Very soon. I love you, Jay. Kiss Mac, Quincy and the baby for me."

"I will. Hug my girl and tell her I said to call her aunt Jeneva some time soon."

Roshawn rolled over and hung up the receiver, falling back against the pillows. She inhaled the scent of her freshly washed sheets, still seething over Ming's indiscretion. They would definitely be continuing their discussion the minute she saw her child again, she thought to herself. The telephone ringing pulled at her attention.

"Hello?"

"*Holá!* How did you sleep?"

"Good morning. And I would have slept better had you stayed."

"I was thinking the very same thing myself when I woke up this morning. I was thinking how much I missed you."

Roshawn smiled and she could feel Angel smiling back. "So, what are your plans for the day?"

"I'm headed to the stadium now. We have a game this evening. Will you be there?"

"I wouldn't miss it. You're going to hit me a home run, remember?"

The man chuckled. "I do, and I will. Then we can do dinner?"

"I'd love to."

"Good. I will call you later in the day."

"Please. And hug your father for me. Tell him I said hello."

The man nodded as if she could see him. "I will tell him."

After hanging up the telephone, Roshawn lifted her body from its resting spot and headed toward the shower. She had had a long day and, with any luck, an even longer night was ahead of her.

Chapter 20

Roshawn dropped down into the chair in front of Chen's desk. He sat staring out into space, a cold cup of coffee perched on the desktop in front of him. Before sitting down, Roshawn had replaced it with a fresh cup, two sugars and no cream, just the way he liked it.

"How did the evening go with your daughter?" she asked, eyeing him curiously.

He nodded, tossing her a quick smile. "We did a good deal of talking. Our daughter isn't a child anymore, Roshawn. She's quite a young lady. And she's just like her mother—spirited, determined and headstrong with a mind of her own."

Roshawn smiled. "Then we raised her well. But you already knew that."

"Remember when she was five years old and we took her to China to see my folks? I remember those eyes of hers, how she looked at the world with such wonder and awe. Everything was new and shiny and exciting and that made it new for us as well. There's nothing like seeing the world through your child's eyes for the first time."

The man paused briefly as he drifted back in time. He took a deep inhale of air, blowing it out slowly before he continued. "Don't you wish we could freeze those precious moments and keep them that age forever?"

"We freeze the memories, Chen. Those we can hold on to. The children we have to let go of so they can continue to experience the wonder and awe of their lives."

The man shook his head as he sighed. "Yes, I know, but I don't like it."

She gave him another caressing smile. "So, why don't you and Allison have more children?"

His gaze rested on her face, his own expression suddenly reflective. "We've talked about it, but I don't know if I can love any other child as much as I love Ming."

Roshawn shook her head. "Your heart is big enough for a million children, Chen. And what about Allison? Doesn't she want kids?"

Chen clasped his hands together in front of him. "Allison does what I want. She will be happy no matter what."

Roshawn rolled her eyes, the dark orbs spinning to the sky with obvious annoyance. "You really are a piece of work, John Chen. I cannot believe that after all these years you are still as sexist and as arrogant as you are. What makes you think just because you want it that Allison is happy about it? Why would you refuse to allow her to have her own thoughts and emotions?" she chided.

Chen shrugged. "It just is what it is, Roshawn."

"Well, keep it up and it's going to be another round in divorce court for you."

The man stared, contemplating her statement, his head waving in denial against his shoulders. He sighed. "Okay, first my daughter and now you. I can't take much more. Let's change the subject. How are things with you and Angel? You both looked pretty cozy together last night."

Roshawn grinned as she came to her feet. "Let's just say he's made me very happy," she responded, clearly amused.

"As happy as I made you, Roshawn?"

Roshawn laughed. Loudly. The sound vibrated through the room. She eased over to the door, turning to stare back at him. She ignored the question. "I have a lot of work to catch up on, boss. Can I get you another cup of coffee?"

"No. But you can answer my question."

Her head waved from side to side, the large, double hoop earrings adorning her lobes, clinking lightly. "Let's just say Angel makes me just as happy as Allison has made you."

Chen laughed with her. "Well, then I think you and I have finally found where we belong."

Roshawn nodded, her energy shining brightly from her eyes. "Now that, John Chen, couldn't be more true!"

With the morning behind her, Roshawn was anxious to be finished with the afternoon. She had two homes to preview before the first ball was thrown out at that evening's game and she wanted to head home first to change her clothes. Angel had managed to call her twice to say hello, to see how she was doing, and to tell her that he loved her. Remembering the conversations made her smile and she was grinning foolishly when a delivery man from United Florists stepped into the room, a vase of twelve red roses adorned with a large red bow, clasped between his two hands.

"Excuse me. I have a delivery for Roshawn Bradsher?" he said, nodding in her direction.

"I'm Roshawn."

He placed the floral container on the desktop then reached into the pocket of a white smock for a small clipboard. "I just need you to sign here, please," he said gesturing with his index finger to one line on the printed document. "Then we can bring the rest up."

"What rest?" she asked as she scribbled her name quickly, staring at him with a curious eye.

The young man grinned. "We have ten dozen red roses to deliver. I'll be right back," he said as he spun out of the room as quickly as he'd come into it.

Chen stood paused in the doorway, watching the interaction. "Did I hear him right? Did he say *ten dozen?*"

Roshawn cut her eye in his direction and shrugged. She reached for the gift card that was perched precariously in the center of the flora, the sweet aroma rising like steam to tease her nostrils. Reading it quickly, she smiled, her expression all-telling as she cast another gaze toward Chen.

"I guess I don't need to ask who they're from," he said with a light chuckle.

Minutes later, the delivery person and two other men strolled single file into the office, each carrying the most beautiful bouquets that Roshawn had ever seen. After a second and then a third trip, every empty spot was laden with a crystal vase, flowers spilling over every square inch of the room. The scent was breathtaking, the view spectacular, and Roshawn couldn't help but grin and grin broadly as everyone within gossiping distance peeked a head in to inquire about them.

At half past four, Nina came bursting through the office

door. Spinning her body around to take in the view, she laughed excitedly. "So, the rumors are true. You nailed the crown prince."

Roshawn laughed. "I did not *nail* him."

"Whatever. I heard that you went away with him this weekend and you didn't even call me when you got back to give me the details."

"What details?"

"Details like the man sent you your own private rose garden? Details like that smile on your face is so wide that he must have been packing a bat the size of...of...a bat?"

"You're a fool."

Nina dropped down into a chair. "So, how was it? Is he as beautiful naked as he is with his clothes on? Give a friend something to work with. I'm desperate."

"Why are you desperate?"

The woman shrugged and rolled her eyes. "Patrick's been cut off until further notice. The man's a lying, cheating snake and I'm about to sever him where it hurts the most. His wallet."

Roshawn shook her head. "What happened this time?"

"Nothing. I just don't like his attitude and I am so tired of all the women who keep hanging on to him like he's a hook in a meat market. I'm just frustrated and he refuses to understand."

"That man loves you and you keep giving him grief over nothing."

"You just wait. I'm sure the first time Angel pushes you aside to deal with one of his *fans,* you'll have plenty of your own grief to be giving him. So, what color are we wearing in the wedding?"

Roshawn laughed again. "What wedding? The man and I are just getting to know one another."

The other woman rolled her eyes. "I'm sure you know everything that's important. He sends good gifts, he's cute, he's rich, and unless I'm misreading your good mood, he's got great moves in the boudoir. Marry him quick before someone starts whispering prenuptial in his ears."

Roshawn laughed. "He can have a prenuptial agreement. I'm not interested in his money."

"I didn't say you had to be interested in it. But you should at least make sure you get half, just in case it doesn't work out. I know I'll be getting my fifty cents and then some."

"You're being cynical. I'm more of an optimist, I think. I don't need half. I have my own."

"But half of his could be your own and it sure wouldn't hurt you none."

Chen's entry interrupted the conversation. "Nina, hello. How are you?"

She shifted in her seat to sit straighter. "I'm doing very well, John. How are you?"

The man nodded. "Good. I'm good. Thank you for asking." He turned to Roshawn. "Are you and your rose garden leaving us soon?"

Roshawn smiled. "I'll be out of here in about ten minutes. And I'm only taking half of my rose garden home."

"Well, let me know when you're ready. I can help you and Nina take them down to your car."

She nodded as he disappeared into his office, closing the door behind him.

"So," Nina said, sinking back down in her seat. "What's on your agenda?"

Roshawn glanced down to her watch. "I have an appointment in thirty minutes, then I need to swing by the house to change into something comfortable before I head over to the ballpark. Are you going to the game?"

"Of course. Patrick won't know how mad I am if I don't show up."

Her friend shook her head. "Leave that man alone. He loves you and you do love him."

Nina grinned. "I know. That's why I'm enjoying every minute of making him squirm."

As the real estate woman navigated her Jaguar convertible from downtown Phoenix into the valley, Roshawn was only slightly disappointed that the first home they'd viewed had not been what she'd thought Angel and his father would want. Having a good sense of what the family was looking for, she was determined to find the exact piece of property that would meet their needs and thus far, none of the homes she'd seen had panned out.

Interestingly, she thought as she stared out the passenger side of the vehicle, the afternoon sun beaming down over her shoulders as they rode with the top down, with the last home she had not only thought about Angel and his father, but also herself. She had invisioned herself in the space with them, at Angel's side, doing and being for him the way she imagined he would want a wife to be. The memories of their time in Santo Domingo had fueled the fantasies and Roshawn had known instantly what type of home she would want for herself and for Angel if they were able to live harmoniously as two halves of a whole.

The woman at her side was chattering nonstop, first at Roshawn, then on her cell phone, and then back at Roshawn. "You are going to love this next home. It hasn't been on the market long and I can tell you, darling, it's not going to last long. It's a true beauty. The owners are extremely motivated so Mr. Rios would be able to close quickly."

"How quickly is quickly?" Roshawn asked, tossing a glance in the woman's direction.

"Very quickly. Obviously, there should be a home inspection, and of course, your attorney will need time to ensure the title is clear for transfer, but I imagine, that he could easily close within thirty days. Forty-five max, especially since Mr. Rios doesn't have to bother with a mortgage contingency. Cash moves things quite quickly!" she exclaimed, her excitement at the prospect of a cash sale and her sizeable commission gleaming from her eyes. The woman excused herself to answer her ringing cell phone.

Roshawn nodded, turning her focus back to thoughts of her and Angel living together as a family. The possibility was engaging and overwhelming as Roshawn played out every possible scenario of their being together in her head. Minutes later, the agent turned into a private community of four hilltop homes, pointing at the house that lay ahead of them.

Roshawn knew before she stepped one foot into the home that she would raise their child there. She would love her Angel there, see her daughter married in the gardens that lay outside, welcome her friends and family were they ever to visit, mourn her losses there, and live out as many of her days within the confines of its walls as she possibly could. It would be the place she would call home. Because with no uncertainty, as the real estate agent pulled past the private gate up the winding, tree-lined drive that led to the residence, Roshawn knew it was where she and Angel were meant to live and love each other beyond reason. The sheer magnitude of that fact hit her so hard that it took every ounce of her stamina to stall the wave of emotion that shot through her and keep the floodwaters of her tears from falling like much needed rain.

Located within the shadow of Camelback Mountain, the Tuscan-style architecture exuded an old world charm that was reminiscent of the grand architecture of the Dominican Republic. She had no doubts that Angel and his father would be instantly drawn to the stunning views of the rugged desert mountains and sparkling city lights that shimmered off in the distance.

As she stepped through the doorway, her mouth dropped open in awe. It was more than even she could have imagined, she thought as she rushed from room to room, completely ignoring the woman who raced behind her, expelling her sales pitch with each breath as she struggled to maintain a plastered grin across her pale face. Eventually, it dawned on her that Roshawn was far from interested in anything she had to say and so she let the woman wander alone, exploring at her own pace, while she herself retreated back outside to negotiate another sure deal on her cell phone.

Roshawn was enamoured with the beautiful stonework and the hand-carved cabinetry with its impeccable craftsmanship and attention to the most infinite detail that lent a timeless elegance to the home. She kneeled to brush her palm against the gorgeous travertine flooring that extended throughout the public areas of the home, and then again over the hand-hewn red oak floors that decorated the family room, library and office space. The entertaining areas were grand-scale and included a wet bar, wine room and outdoor kitchen with an adjacent alfresco sports bar and nearly two thousand square feet of covered patios.

She stood fantasizing about the possibilities the amazing

infinity-edge pool with its cascading waterfall would afford them. She could only imagine for the moment what she and Angel could do in that pool and as she did she found herself breathing heavily with wanting. Shaking the images from her mind she moved on to the theater-style media room and the enormous chef's kitchen with Viking appliances that she could see herself and Israel both fighting to commandeer. Two separate wings afforded more than enough privacy for father and son, each boasting individual master suites, with lavish baths and magnificent his and her walk-in closets, plus private office space that Roshawn could have easily seen transformed into a nursery. A third wing housed three additional bedrooms, a third office area and exercise room. From start to finish the property was a complete work of art. And even with the magnitude of its substantial size, it exuded a warmth and comfort like no other she'd seen before it.

As she stepped back outside the agent ended her call, her grin returning to full bloom. "What did you think? Don't you just love it? This house is a definite showpiece."

Roshawn nodded. "I think he'll be very pleased."

"How soon do you think you can get him here to look at it? I'm available any time."

"I'd like to bring Mr. Rios by later this evening. He's playing a game in an hour but I'm sure he and his father would be available afterwards."

The woman nodded. "Darling, I'll tell you what. No one else is scheduled to show the house until later this week. Take the keys, bring them by at your convenience, and then call me so we can get the paperwork started. And please, extend my congratulations to Mr. Rios."

Roshawn smiled her gratitude, bemused by the woman's assumptions as the thin redhead dropped the keys into her hand, spinning back in the direction of her car. As they made their exit down the length of driveway, Roshawn couldn't help but turn back one last time for one more lingering look at the house she instinctively knew would eventually be her new home.

After making four quick stops and returning to the house to prepare for the evening, Roshawn hurried to change out of her Diane Von Furstenberg dress and then raced back to the stadium for the game. She was anxious to see Angel, so much so that she made use of John Chen's position to gain entry through the players' entrance and into the rear elevators to meet him outside the locker room doors. She waited anxiously for the team to exit, making their way through the tunnel, into the dugout, and up onto the pristine field.

Angel could not have missed her standing there if he had wanted to. She leaned easily against the wall, her hands pushed into the pockets of her hip-hugging jeans and the blue silk halter top shimmering against her dark complexion. Her head was newly shaven, her makeup meticulous and she exuded an aura of staunch confidence, sensual elegance and raw sexuality.

Not only did Angel notice her, but so did the other players who stared with blatant appreciation. Angel was slightly taken aback when one or two catcalled for her attention and he made a mental note to put them all in check the first chance he had. He wasn't about to have any other man show his woman an ounce of disrespect.

He moved quickly to her side and kissed her boldly. "What are you doing here?"

"I just wanted to say thank-you for the beautiful roses and wish you a good game."

Before he could respond the team's manager was calling his name. "Rios, let's go! We've got a game to play!"

Roshawn kissed him quickly. "I love you. Go hit my home run. I'll be right here waiting for you after the game," she smiled.

"Rios! Now!"

Angel gave her a quick wink as he rushed in the direction of the chiding voice. Up in the bleachers, Israel was holding a seat for her, his Titans baseball cap marking the reserved spot. As she approached him, he jumped up to embrace her, hugging her tightly before they both sat down, that cap comfortably back on his head.

"Holá, Papí," Roshawn said, greeting him warmly. "How are you?"

"I am a very happy man. My son has found love and now I shall have a daughter, a granddaughter, and very soon, a grandson."

Roshawn laughed, saying nothing as she shook her head. The old man laughed with her, joy shining in his eyes. He reached for her hand and squeezed her fingers.

"So, what did you think of Santo Domingo?" the old man asked, his gaze shifting between the two teams warming up on the field.

"I loved it. I had a wonderful time with Angel. Your sister was so welcoming and you do have an incredible home."

The man beamed as he patted her knee, his eyes still locked on the activity below. Roshawn watched him for a few minutes as his gaze skated back and forth, his attention focused on Angel who stood in center field catching and throwing the ball back and forth with his teammates as they warmed up. She smiled as she allowed him his time, his mind clearly lost on following every minute of activity surrounding the game. Her name being called made her turn to look up in the bleachers and she tossed her hand up in greeting as Nina waved excitedly, settling herself down next to her old pal Cedric.

Israel cleared his throat, heaving a deep sigh as the team ran off the field into the dugout, the announcer preparing them for the start of the game. Within minutes, the Titans and their opponents were lined up on the field for the national anthem. On this night the song was being sung by one of the choirs from the local high school. As they all stood at attention, hands and hats resting over hearts, Israel sang with them, respect for the waving red, white and blue flag gracing his expression.

As the song ended, he reached for her hand and squeezed her fingers. "Angel must have a good night tonight. He must do well," he said, his tone almost pleading.

Roshawn squeezed back, reaching to wrap an arm around the old man's shoulders. "He will do just fine. His mind is focused and he promised me a home run."

Israel laughed. "He promised me one also."

She grinned. "Then I guess that means he's going to get two good hits tonight, *Papí*."

Israel beamed. "I guess that does," he said excitedly as the first ball was finally pitched and the beginning of the game commenced.

Patrick made his way to Angel's side, the two men staring out to the field from the dugout. The game had not started well, both pitchers shutting out the first three innings. As the Titans took their fourth inning turn at bat, the trend seemed to be continuing as the first two batters struck out at home plate. As the third batter eased up into the batter's box, both men couldn't help but wish for a better outcome.

"So, you feeling good tonight, Angel?" Patrick asked.

The man nodded. "I'm feeling very good." He tossed the man a quick look and smile before refocusing on what was happening on the field. The umpire had called a time out as the two opposing coaches met him midfield for a brief pow-wow.

"How are you and Roshawn doing?" Patrick ventured to ask.

Angel grinned and nodded his head, not bothering to comment further. Patrick grinned with him as he gave him a tap on the shoulder. Returning their attention to the game, both watched as the batter hit a high fastball, sending the first hit of the night over the right fielder's head. Both cheered as the man made it easily to first base and poised himself ready to head to second. The following batter took his first strike as Angel readied himself to bat next. With two outs, one man on base, and a second possible hit coming, Angel wanted to be prepared. He palmed the gold cross and his mother's wedding band, which hung from a heavy gold chain around his neck. Saying a quick prayer, he pulled the crucifix to his lips then tucked the jewelry down into his jersey to lay securely against his chest. On his third swing the batter clipped the ball just hard enough to send it sailing toward the shortstop. The ball took a hard hop on the grass surface, rolling out of the man's reach and enabled the Titans' two runners to make it safely to first and second base. The crowd cheered with anticipation as Angel stepped up to the plate, swinging his bat back and forth over his shoulders.

Both Roshawn and Israel leaned forward in their seats, their hands clenched in prayer before them. Both were eyeing Angel anxiously, silently wishing him success as they watched the first pitch sail by him, the umpire calling it a ball.

"Ball two!" the man chimed at the second pitch. Angel

stepped back out of the box and gave the pitcher an annoyed look.

Roshawn muttered under her breath. "It's too early to start playing games, boys. Pitch the ball and let the man hit." She jumped to her feet and yelled at the top of her lungs. "Pitch the ball!"

"Ball three!"

She tossed up her hands, ire gracing her face. She would be furious if they walked Angel on purpose, blatantly denying him the opportunity to put the bat on the ball. A second time-out was called as a coach walked to the pitcher's mound to have a conversation with his pitcher.

Roshawn continued to rant. "I can't believe this. They're scared. That's why they're not pitching to him."

A man behind her joined in. "They're not pitching because that fool *can't* pitch. He was a real waste of their budget. They could have hired me for all the good he is!" The woman beside him laughed at his intensity as he continued to rant along with Roshawn.

"Let's play ball!" someone else screamed at the top of their lungs.

Angel eased back into batting position, his eyes locking with the pitcher's. The man sneered and Angel laughed, challenging him as he winked an eye in the player's direction. Angel saw it the minute the man released his hold on the ball. The pitch was as near perfect as any he'd ever seen. He watched it as it left the tips of the pitcher's fingers, sailing sweetly in his direction. He shifted, dipped his left shoulder ever so slightly and swung. The sound of the wooden bat splintering was music to Angel's ears as he watched the ball sail back in the other direction, flying straight down the center of the field and over the back fence. The subsequent rush of water from the cannons announced what everyone else had already known. The Titans had the lead, three runs to zero, thanks to the home-run hit of one Angel Rios. As Angel rounded the bases, the audience cheered and Roshawn and Israel both danced in their seats.

"That one was mine, *niña!*" Israel chimed, clapping his hands.

Roshawn laughed. "I beg your pardon. That one was mine!"

As Angel touched home plate, his team there to greet him, his smile embodied the intensity of his emotions. He acknowledged his fans as he jogged off the field, waving his gratitude. His gaze scanned the seats where his father and his woman stood supporting him. He gave a quick nod in their direction, wishing he could jump into the stands to embrace them both. As he took a seat on the bench, players still tapping him against the back and congratulating him, Angel struggled not to let his emotions get the best of him, moisture rising behind his eyelids as relief flooded through his person. He nodded, pleased with himself, his confidence resurfacing with a vengeance. Angel Rios was back and once again he was a force that would have to be reckoned with.

Chapter 21

Roshawn stood alone as she waited for Angel to finish in the locker room. Israel had feigned exhaustion, wanting to give the two of them time alone. Although Roshawn had begged him to stay, to join them for dinner and a tour of the house she hoped would be their home, he had declined, securing a ride with Nina. Before his departure he had visited the locker room to congratulate his son, pride gleaming over his expression for all to witness. Emotion had rained down his face as he had hugged his son, then Roshawn, as he made his way out the door. His joy had been so endearing that Roshawn had found it almost impossible to fight back her own tears. By the time Angel made his way to her side, the moment had passed and her bright smile had returned, greeting him warmly as he pulled her into his arms.

"So, how did I do?" Angel asked, his arm wrapped around her waist as they headed for the exit.

Roshawn shrugged, rolling her eyes skyward. "I guess you did okay."

He laughed. "Just okay? That's all I get?"

She grinned. "You did great!"

He shook his head and laughed with her, the two of them enjoying the moment of light bantering. "So, where would you like to eat?"

"I made plans for us already. I have a surprise for you."

Eyebrows raised, Angel looked at her curiously. "A surprise?"

She smiled coyly. "A good surprise."

"I like surprises," he said as they stepped out into the warm evening air.

A crowd of fans were gathered in wait, all cheering as Angel stepped out into the light. He smiled in greeting, tossing a hand up to wave as he led the way toward the car, pulling Roshawn behind him.

"Don't you want to sign autographs?" Roshawn asked, as she pulled the car keys from his hand and headed to the driver's side of the vehicle.

Angel shook his head no. "Not tonight. I just want to get away from the noise and be alone with you."

Roshawn unlocked the doors to the SUV and relocked them as they got inside.

"Where's your car?" he asked, looking around the parking deck.

"Nina took it. She drove your dad back to my house for the evening. Patrick is picking her up there and you can pick Israel up when you drop me off."

He nodded. "So where are we off to?"

She grinned as she started the ignition and pulled out of the space. "It wouldn't be a surprise if I told you, now would it?"

He sighed, waving again as they pulled past the spectators and cameras that still stood staring their way.

As Roshawn pulled into traffic she looked in his direction. Angel's head was bobbing easily in time to the music on the radio and he looked relaxed. She inhaled deeply, relishing the fresh scent of the soap and body spray that he'd just bathed in. When he reached his arm across the back of the driver's seat and lightly brushed his fingers against the back of her neck, the moment felt natural and comfortable and Roshawn could just imagine what longevity could do for their relationship. She smiled as she realized he was staring at her. She cast another quick gaze toward him and he smiled back.

"What are you thinking?" she asked, her gaze flickering from the rearview mirror, to the road, to Angel, and back to the road.

"I was thinking about how beautiful you are. You are like a precious gemstone—rare, and delicate, and unique. I will have to handle you very carefully. I would not want anything to ever happen to you."

"Mmmm," Roshawn purred softly. "Do you use that line on all the women?"'

He chuckled. "No. Only on my woman." He leaned back in his seat, still staring at her, his gaze detailing every inch of her profile.

"Stop staring," Roshawn said, the heat of his gaze inciting an erotic warmth throughout her body. "You're going to look the color right off a me if you keep that up."

Angel laughed loudly. "I surely would not want to do that but I'm just addicted to how spectacular you are."

Roshawn pointed to her tote bag on the floor beneath his feet. "There's a blindfold in my purse. You need to put it on. We can talk about how spectacular I am later on."

"Why do I need a blindfold?"

"Don't ask questions. Just do what I tell you to do," she said smugly.

The black eye cover lay right on top of her personal items and Angel pulled it into his hand.

"Put it on," Roshawn implored.

Covering his eyes, Angel could feel a nervous energy suddenly swell within him. "I'm not so sure about this," he said, reaching to pull it back off.

"Don't you take that off yet," Roshawn scolded as she made a sharp right turn that had him sliding in his seat. The warmth of her palm pressed against his arm, stalled his reluctance and he heaved a deep sigh.

"This had better be good," he said.

"This is going to be better than good," Roshawn said, the car speeding up just slightly. "In fact, this will make those two home runs and you winning that ball game seem like a trip to the dentist."

Angel shifted his body, trying to relax as the car surged forward. He felt the steel carriage beneath him as it turned left and then right, Roshawn driving it only a short distance farther before coming to a complete stop.

"Don't move and don't touch that blindfold," Roshawn commanded. Her voice was low as she leaned close to his ear, her breath warm against the line of his lobe. Angel was suddenly more anxious than he'd been that first time he and Roshawn had been together in his bed. She kissed his cheek, then exited the vehicle. Angel listened intently as she seemed to be rummaging for something, then the driver's door slammed closed and all went silent.

Angel cocked his head to the side, trying to get a sense of his surroundings but all he could hear was the faint rustle of the wind blowing lazily about. Just as he was tempted to pull the covering from his eyes the passenger door opened and Roshawn grabbed him gently by the arm.

"Don't you dare," she said, her tone scolding.

"Don't what, Roshawn? I was not doing anything."

"You were thinking about uncovering your eyes."

"How did you know?"

"I can read your mind as well as I can read your heart," she said, her lips brushing against his cheek a second time.

Guiding him out of the vehicle and around the front of the car, Roshawn positioned him where she wanted him. She moved to stand behind him, her hands resting gently against his hips. "Welcome home," Roshawn said, her own excitement shimmering in her voice. Releasing the black scarf from around his head, Roshawn waited anxiously as he allowed his eyes to adjust to the light.

She had parked just far enough back that the house stood imposingly before him. She'd turned on all the lights and the home glowed against a darkening background as the day's sun was drifting off behind the range of mountains in the distance. Angel gasped, spun around to stare at her, then turned back to look at the house.

"Roshawn!" He gasped, taking a few steps toward the front door and then stopping. He turned back again, extending his hand in her direction. She grinned widely, her head bobbing up and down as she sensed him feeling the same rush of emotions that had consumed her when she'd first come up the driveway. As he wrapped her fingers beneath his own he pulled her to him, hugging her tightly as he kissed her mouth.

"Let's go inside," Roshawn said as she pulled him up the front steps and through the front door. Once inside, she guided him from room to room, staying out of his way as he slowly explored the home's interior. Every so often she would point out the details she thought would engage his interest as they had engaged her own. From the expression on his face, she knew that Angel was just as enamored as she had been.

The master bedroom was the last stop on the tour and Roshawn could feel herself being consumed by her excitement as he approached her final surprise. She grabbed his hand and moved to stand before him, pressing her body tightly to his.

"Angel, I love you," she said as she kissed him lightly. "And when I saw this house I knew instantly that it was meant to be our home."

Angel smiled, his head nodding his agreement. "It's wonderful, Roshawn. It's exactly what I was looking for."

"Well, I have one more surprise for you," she said as she guided him forward, the two of them stepping inside the large room.

Angel looked about the empty space, confusion gracing his face. "What…?"

She pressed her index finger to his lips to silence him as she pushed him toward the adjoining space behind the closed door. Allowing him to lead the way, Roshawn paused as he slowly opened the room's door.

A bassinet sat room center, the white basket and base skirted behind a dainty white fabric skirt with baby-blue gingham detail. A small, cocoa-brown teddy bear dressed in a Titans sweatshirt peered out from the center of the infant bed, a bottle of champagne and two glasses sitting behind it. As Angel stepped closer a tear ran down his cheek, dripping to the floor beneath his feet.

Roshawn whispered. "I think we should paint a mural on

this large wall. Maybe a ball field and an image of his daddy
hitting a home run. I think a sports-themed room would be
very nice for our son."

Angel nodded, the words still caught deep in his heart.

Roshawn continued to speak, reaching for the champagne
and popping the cork. She passed the glasses to Angel to hold
as she poured. "I knew the minute I saw this space that it
would be perfect for a nursery. And I knew," she said as she
stared into his eyes, "that I wanted to give you a son to lay
in this nursery every night. I wanted that with you, Angel."

Angel kissed her, his excitement pulling at her lips as his
skated eagerly across her mouth. "I love you, Roshawn!" he
exclaimed, joy spilling into the room. "And I am so happy
that you will be the mother of my children!"

"Children?" Roshawn exclaimed, her eyebrows raised in
surprise.

Angel laughed. "I convinced you to give me a son. More
children will be easier to convince you of once we have the
first one."

Roshawn laughed with him. "I wouldn't be so sure of all
that."

The man beamed. "I am as sure as I know how much I love
you that you and I will make beautiful babies and we will be
a fine family. And if it is not to be," he said, blushing slightly,
"then we will have great love trying to make those babies."

Roshawn took a sip of her champagne. "Now, that trying
part is exactly what I'm talking about."

The evening had gotten away from them as they'd sat on
the floor, leaning against the cradle, making plans about
their future. The champagne had been replaced with slices
of pastrami, rye bread, Swiss cheese and assorted condi-
ments that Roshawn had packed neatly away in the kitch-

en's refrigerator. They'd eaten, clearing away the mess as quickly as they had made it and then they'd called the listing agent to put in a formal offer to purchase the property. Both were excited about heading to her office the following morning to do the paperwork that would make the house their home.

Hours later as they eased into Roshawn's house, the television was playing softly in the family room. Israel lay sound asleep against the oversize sofa, his legs extended comfortably, a chenille throw pulled up over his shoulders.

Roshawn smiled as she whispered in Angel's direction. "You should stay. He looks so peaceful."

Angel shook his head. "You wouldn't mind?"

"Of course not. It's too late to disturb him. He can sleep here or if you want to wake him, the guest room is ready."

"What about Ming?"

"She won't be here until the weekend. I promise, no one will come barging in to disturb him, or us."

Angel smiled. He shook his father lightly. *"Papí?"*

The man barely stirred as he rolled, turning his back to his son and snoring loudly.

Roshawn giggled. "Leave him alone. He's out like a light." She extended her hand. "You get to sleep with me," she said coyly.

Angel smiled. "Why do I get the impression that we won't be getting much sleep?"

Her smile widened. "Because if we're having children, then you need to practice," she said whispering loudly.

Angel chuckled, pressing his palm over his mouth to stifle his laugh. Both paused to see if the noise had disturbed Israel, and when the man didn't move, they eased out of the space and toward the rear of the home. Once inside Roshawn's bedroom, the bedroom door closed and locked behind them, Angel laughed out loud, pulling her into the curve of his arms as he wrapped the length of them around her body.

He held her close, savoring the sensation of her touch as she gently caressed his back and shoulders. Although he didn't say so out loud, there was one more thing that needed to happen and if anyone had looked close enough they would have seen the wheels spinning plans in his brain.

The next morning the aroma of hot coffee and frying bacon from the kitchen awakened them. Roshawn lay curled within Angel's arms, her eyes closed as her nose switched eagerly. The scent of baking bread caused a pain of hunger to suddenly rumble through her midsection and Angel's palm beat hers to her stomach, his fingers kneading her flesh gently.

"He's taken over your kitchen," Angel said softly, tightening the arm around her. "Can you smell it?"

She nodded against his chest, her face brushing the area over his breastbone. "It smells really good," she said, shifting one leg over his. "Do you think he'll serve it to us in bed?"

Angel laughed. "Probably not. *Papí* believes family should eat together at the table."

Both took another deep inhale. At that moment, Israel knocked on the bedroom door, calling out to them from the other side. "Breakfast is ready, *niños!* Come and eat or you both will be late. It's almost eight o'clock."

"*Sí, Papí!* We're getting up now," Angel called, stretching upward as Roshawn threw her legs off the side of the bed.

He rubbed her bare back, gently caressing the soft flesh. "What time do you have to be in your office?"

Roshawn shrugged. "I should be there by nine, but Chen

won't mind if I'm a few minutes late. But you and I have to meet the real estate agent at eleven and we need to be there on time. What time do you have to be at the field?"

Angel reached to scratch the inside of his thigh. "Not until this afternoon. We don't play until seven tonight."

Roshawn nodded, tossing him a quick smile. She took another deep breath. "I don't know what your father is cooking but it smells really good," she said. "I need to hurry up and get dressed."

He watched as Roshawn lifted her body from the bed and headed into the bathroom. As she disappeared from his sight, his mind once again drifted to the idea that had consumed him most of the night, billowing through his dreams and every wakened moment. He had much to accomplish before the day was over and he knew that he wouldn't be able to pull off his surprise alone. As he contemplated who he needed to call and all that needed to be done, he found his excitement steadily growing. A few minutes later the sound of the shower beckoned to him and he rose from his resting spot to join her, anxious to get the day started.

Angel was dressed and out in the kitchen before Roshawn had even begun to apply what little makeup she wore daily. By the time she was ready, making her way to the dining area to join the two men, she realized that she didn't have much time at all, the clock ticking quickly toward nine. In the kitchen the duo was huddled in deep conversation, whispering hurriedly. Both stopped abruptly as Roshawn stepped into the room, her gaze shifting from one to the other. She instantly sensed that they had been talking about her and she could not go without making comment.

"Good morning, *Papí*," Roshawn said, moving to kiss the man's cheek. "Breakfast smells wonderful!"

"Good morning, *hija*. How are you this morning?"

Roshawn nodded slowly. Her eyes played a game of tennis between the two of them. "Very well, thank you," she answered as she took a seat on one of the counter stools.

The man passed her a cup of hot coffee and a plate of food, the aroma of cheese omelets with salsa sauce, buttered toast and strips of crisp bacon simmering against the porcelain.

"So," Roshawn said casually, "what were you two just talking about?"

Angel cut a quick eye toward his father, who took an easy sip of hot fluid from his own mug.

"Angel was just telling me all about the home that you have found. I am excited to see it."

Roshawn smiled, her gaze resting on Angel's face. The man was obviously nervous and her awareness of such made her ever more curious. She pulled a fork full of egg mixture to her mouth, savoring the flavors. "This is very good, *Papí*. Isn't it, Angel?"

The man nodded, his eyes still dancing to avoid hers. "Yes," he said, his voice cracking ever so slightly. He cleared his throat before continuing. "The food is very good."

Roshawn nodded slowly, mirth rising in her stare. She locked eyes with Israel who was grinning broadly.

"I think an old man must confess, *chica*. Angel and I were talking about you before."

"*Papí—!*" Angel started before being interrupted. His father held up his hand to keep him from commenting further.

Roshawn looked from one to the other, still enjoying her meal and the entertainment.

"Yes, *chica*, we were talking about you. I was telling my son what a blessing you are to his life. He is a lucky man to love such an incredible woman. Isn't that right, *hijo?*"

Angel tossed Roshawn a quick look as his head bobbed up and down. Roshawn chuckled softly as she dropped her fork to her empty plate.

"You two sneaky devils are up to something and don't think I won't find out what it is," she said as she rose from her seat.

Israel laughed again as Angel sat looking as if he'd been caught red-handed.

"No, Roshawn, you're wrong," he said, his tone imploring. "We're not up to anything."

"Sure you're not," she said as she shifted through a kitchen drawer, pulling a key and key ring from the clutter. Crossing to his side she pressed the key into Angel's palm. "You and *Papí* clean up this mess. I have to go to work."

"That's woman's work," Angel said jokingly.

She laughed. "If you say so, but for now it's yours, unless you want to come clean and tell me what you're up to?"

Angel laughed with her as his father joined in. "*Papí,* you wash and I'll dry," he finally said after catching his breath.

Israel shook his head as he headed toward the family room. "No, *hijo*. I cooked. You wash *and* you dry."

Roshawn kissed Angel's cheek. "You two fight it out on your own. I have to get to work. Pick me up at ten-thirty," she said as she headed for the door. "I love you. Bye, *Papí*."

Angel sighed. "The things a man will do for love," he said as he picked up the dirty dishes and piled them in the sink. "The things a man will do."

John Chen was on the telephone when Roshawn came into the office, dropping her bags in front of the reception desk and her body onto a chair in front of his desk. He held up his finger, motioning for her to give him a minute to complete his call, his expression becoming anxious. His tone shifted, suddenly on guard as he responded politely.

"I understand. Yes, certainly." He paused as he listened to the caller on the other end.

"Whatever I can do to help, please, just let me know."

Pause.

"Of course."

Pause.

"I will be sure to ask her when I get home."

Pause.

"I know she will. I also have two other names that you might want to include."

Pause.

"That's right. I know they'd be delighted, as well."

Pause.

"I'm sorry, I actually have someone in my office and I'll need to call you back so we can discuss it further. You do understand?"

Pause.

"Great. That sounds like a plan. Give my regards to—" Chen suddenly caught himself, stopping in midsentence as his gaze fell on Roshawn then shifted quickly away. "Goodbye," he said as he hung up the telephone. He smiled in her direction. "Good morning."

"Who was that on the phone?" Roshawn asked, taking note of his obvious discomfort.

Chen shrugged. "Just a lead on a potential prospect. No one you'd know."

Roshawn nodded her head slowly. "How's my daughter?" she asked, changing the subject.

"Frustrated. She's missing that Dixon boy."

"I remember that feeling. It'll pass."

"I should have grounded her for the year."

Roshawn laughed. "Chen, she's eighteen. You're doing well that she's even paying you an ounce of attention. You need to work on letting go. It's time you let your daughter spread her wings."

"It's not her wings I'm worried about her spreading," he said grimly. "I wish I could put her in a chastity belt."

Roshawn shook her head. "You're impossible."

He chuckled. "So, what's up with you? Anything going on that you want to share?"

Roshawn tossed him a curious gaze. "Why would you ask that?"

"No reason. I just thought maybe with you and Rios being an item now that you might have some news to share with me."

"Well, if I do, you'll be the first to know."

He grinned, reaching for a file folder on his desk and shuffling through its contents. Roshawn continued to eye him with reservations, sensing he'd swallowed a secret she was not privy to.

He looked up, his eyebrows raised. "What?"

"Nothing."

"You sure?"

"Positive." Roshawn came to her feet and moved toward the door. She turned back to face him. "Oh, I found Angel and his father a home. They'll be meeting with the agent this morning to formalize his offer."

Chen nodded. "That's great. How soon do you think they'll be able to move in?"

"Probably by the middle of next month if all goes well. And I guess I should tell you that I won't be going back to Seattle."

Chen smiled, his expression unchanging. "That's good news. That's very good news."

Roshawn smiled back, making note that he wasn't the least bit surprised. "Don't you want to know how long I'll be staying in your house?"

He shrugged. "No. I figured at least until the middle of next month, but I wasn't worried."

Roshawn laughed. "I know that was Angel on the phone. And I know you're in on whatever he's up to."

Chen's gaze fell back to the folder. "I don't know what you're talking about. I have a meeting in a few minutes. I need to review these papers before I leave."

Roshawn stood staring at him as he tried to avoid her gaze. She could almost see the rise of anxious perspiration that was beading against his skin.

"Go away, Roshawn."

"Tell me."

"I don't know anything to tell."

"Liar."

"Yes, I am. Now get out of my office before I fire you."

Roshawn laughed. "You tell him that I will find out. Sooner or later one of you is going to slip and I'm going to know what you're up to."

"Let it go, Roshawn. I swear, it's all good but you need to just let it go."

"Now, John Chen, I know that you know me better than that. I'm just getting started. You and Israel and Angel better watch yourselves. I think you guys forgot who you're messing with."

Chen laughed, his head waving from side to side. "Now I'm really scared."

Chapter 22

Almost a month and a half had passed and Roshawn didn't have a clue what Angel had been planning, if anything at all. In fact, with all that had been going on she'd barely had time to even give the prospect of his plotting a second thought.

The purchase of their new home had gone smoothly, the two of them able to close on the house faster than they'd anticipated. A quick trip to the state of Washington had reunited her with her best friends, both offering unlimited support as Roshawn had packed what remained of her life in Seattle and had put her own home on the market.

There had been no opportunity to introduce them to Angel. His baseball schedule had him playing back-to-back games with few days left to do anything but rest. Wherein Roshawn should have known something was amiss when neither of her gal pals seemed concerned about not meeting him, her mind had been too preoccupied with too many other thoughts to give it any reflection at all.

Between them, Roshawn and Israel, with the help of an interior designer Angel had insisted on hiring, had navigated furnishing their new space, both amused and relieved that their tastes were so similar. Although Roshawn still had not officially taken up residence in the new house, she was only days away from doing so and her excitement about such ran in tandem with her anxiety over the ramifications.

Ming stood watching her mother as Roshawn toyed with fabric and paint samples, unable to make up her mind about which colors would and would not fill the space that would be Ming's room whenever she came to stay. She shook her head as Roshawn muttered under her breath.

"Mom, why are you having such a time with this? I already told you what I wanted."

"But are you sure, Ming? We didn't even consider the blue-and-green combination."

"I'm sure. Why are you so out of sorts?"

Roshawn tossed her child a look, the question knocking her off sides for just a brief minute. She dropped down to the new mattress that had been rested against the new bed that Ming had selected. "I am starting to obsess a bit, aren't I?"

"A bit? I've never seen you like this." Ming took the seat beside her, pulling the samples from her mother's hands and tossing them behind her.

"I guess I'm just worried that things won't be perfect for Angel."

"Angel doesn't care. He only wants you and *Abuelo* happy. And why haven't you moved in yet? I think he and Daddy are starting to wonder what the problem is."

"There is no problem. I just wanted to wait until things were more settled here. I'll move in a week or so."

"More like a few days or so. Daddy and Allison have rented the house to some flight attendant friend of Allison's."

"He what?"

"He told me to tell you and to ask when he can arrange to give them the keys. He didn't think it would be an issue since you do have a home to move into."

Roshawn said nothing, mulling over her daughter's comments. She and Chen worked side by side daily and the man hadn't wanted to confront her about her living arrangements. Just wait until she got her hands around his neck, she thought to herself. Ming reached for her hand and held it.

"What's the matter, Mommy?"

"Sharing your life with a man is a big commitment, Ming. This thing with Angel just happened so fast and even though it seems perfect, we both know that nothing ever is. I'm just looking for the pitfalls and trying to make sure that nothing can get screwed up without my knowing it."

"Don't you love him? Because I know he loves you. Angel loves you a lot."

She nodded, a rich smile filling her face. "I love Angel very much. But I loved your father once too and it was great right up until the moment we both took those vows, made it official and moved in together. Then things fell apart. Angel and your father both have that same conservative, controlling nature. I just don't want what happened with me and Chen to happen to Angel and me. I'm guess I'm just scared that I won't be able to handle it as well the second time around."

Ming nodded, wrapping her arms around her mother's shoulders. "Get over it. Angel's not Daddy and you are not that same young girl. You know better now and you've learned from your experiences. You'll do just fine."

Roshawn gave her child an incredulous look. "Aren't you something with the advice!"

Ming grinned, her face beaming. "I learned from the best."

Taking a deep breath, Roshawn stood back on her feet. She reached for Ming's hand and pulled her up beside her. "Why don't you and I go get our nails done?"

"Sounds like a good idea to me. Besides, I want to talk to you about Dixon. I don't know if I can make tomorrow's game. Dix and I want to go away for the weekend."

"Away? Away where?"

"The Grand Canyon. We plan on driving from Phoenix to Sedona to see the red rocks. From there we'll drive to Flagstaff and then the town of Williams. And then on Saturday we'll pick up the train into the Grand Canyon, spend the night and come back on Sunday."

"Have you told your father yet?"

Ming nodded. "He said it would be okay."

"He said *okay?* We're talking about John Chen, aren't we?"

Ming shrugged. "He just said that we needed to show some responsibility and then he gave Dix a long lecture."

"Well, wonders never cease to amaze me."

"You don't mind, do you? I know this will be Angel's first home game in two weeks and you were hoping we could all be here, but this is the only chance Dix and I will have before classes start."

Roshawn sighed. "Of course I don't mind. There will be plenty of other home games. And just because I was planning a family dinner doesn't mean you have to be there," she said sarcastically. She rolled her eyes and then laughed, Ming laughing with her.

"Besides," Ming added as the two women made their way out of the room. "It'll be Angel's first night back. I doubt you two will miss me being around anyway."

The quick jaunt to the nail salon had been exactly what Roshawn had needed. She and Ming had laughed and giggled about everything and about nothing, both enjoying their mother-daughter moment. After a quick lunch, Roshawn had dropped off Ming back at her father's home. After checking in with Chen to see if she was needed for anything in the office she had the afternoon free and she was actually looking forward to having some time to herself to do absolutely nothing.

As she puttered around the house, shifting furniture and knickknacks, Roshawn couldn't help but think about why she was delaying packing and moving the two suitcases she'd arrived in Phoenix with from one side of town to the other. She was scared, and although she loved Angel with everything in her and enjoyed every minute they'd spent together, she didn't want to risk seeing the relationship end if things weren't what they seemed once the doors were closed behind them. She chuckled, knowing that she was also being ridiculous. Angel had promised her a lifetime of love and she had no doubts that he would do whatever it took to ensure he kept that promise.

Picking up the telephone she dialed Chen to discuss her move, letting him know that she would be out and in her own home by the weekend. She also let him know she didn't appreciate him sending the news of her eviction through their daughter.

Chen laughed. "I would have told you myself, but your moods have been all over the place lately."

"So, you were just scared."

"Yes, and I'm not ashamed to admit it," he said with a deep chuckle.

As she hung up the line, looking around the space that she would share with Angel, she knew that it was well past time for her to make that move. Taking a deep inhale of breath and blowing it out slowly, she released all her anxiety and fear, tossing caution to the wind that she would truly be happy as long as she and Angel were standing side by side.

Taking a quick glance at her watch, Roshawn picked the receiver back up and dialed. She tried with little luck to reach Nina. The woman wasn't picking up on any of her phone lines and it had been three days since the two had last spoken. As the line rang on the other end, Roshawn wasn't sure if she should worry or not, and then Patrick answered the call, his breathing heavy as if he'd had to race to pick up the line.

"Hello?"

"Patrick? Hi, it's me, Roshawn."

"Hey, Roshawn. How are you, darlin'?"

"I'm great. When did you get back?"

"Just this second. They got us out on an earlier flight. I'm sure Angel will be walking through the door in a minute himself."

"Great games you guys played. That was a nice hit you got against Los Angeles."

"Thanks, darlin'. You lookin' for Nina?"

"Is she home?"

The man shook his head into the receiver. "No. I'm tryin' to track her down myself. She's got some friends visitin' here with her for a few days so they've been running all over Phoenix trying to get into trouble."

"Oh. I guess that's why I haven't heard from her. Well, just tell her to call me when she gets some time."

"I will. You take care now."

"Bye, Patrick." As Roshawn hung up the line she found it odd that Nina hadn't said anything to her about entertaining company. The two had become close and each was usually privy to the other's plans. As she thought about it, she realized that she'd missed Nina's last call earlier in the week. The two had been playing phone tag ever since. Roshawn imagined that Nina just hadn't had an opportunity yet to catch her up on what was going on in her life.

She picked up the receiver and dialed Seattle. Minutes later she was even more dejected as both Jeneva and Bridget hadn't been around to pick up her call. Before she had time to bemoan the fact, Angel's voice rang out from the front foyer.

"Roshawn? Are you here?"

She raced down the hallway in his direction, her excitement at his arrival pushing everything else out of her thoughts.

"Angel! Patrick said you guys had just gotten back. I wasn't expecting you until tomorrow."

"I thought I could surprise you," he said, kissing her warmly. "Patrick spoiled it."

"I missed you," Roshawn muttered, her mouth dancing against his. "I missed you very much."

He grinned. "I missed you, too. Where's *Papí?* Is he here?"

Roshawn shook her head. "He and your interior designer have gone furniture shopping."

"Does that mean you and I are alone?" Angel asked, his voice dropping to a seductive whisper.

Roshawn nodded, a rush of wanting inciting her to breathe heavily. "Very alone."

Angel kissed her again, spreading her lips with his tongue.

As he entered the sweet, lush cavity, he could feel her tremble with anticipation, her excitement fueling his. Angel lifted her up into his arms, carrying her easily toward their master bedroom. Roshawn grinned, kicking her feet in the air as he rushed through the entrance and dropped her heavily against the padded mattress.

Kicking off his shoes, Angel pulled at the buckle to his pants, pushing them past his hips to the floor. Roshawn suddenly burst into laughter as he posed superhero-style, his hands on his hips and his chest protruding forward. A pair of white briefs with red hearts hugged his pelvis. He spun around, leaning over to show the wording across his buttocks, Roshawn's Honey, printed in bright red ink across the fabric that covered his butt cheeks.

Roshawn couldn't remember the last time she had laughed so hard. Tears spilled from the corners of her eyes, rolling down her cheeks. Her stomach hurt from trying to catch her breath and the entire time Angel stood alternating his poses as he winked and blew kisses at her.

"You're a fool!" she finally managed to gush, reaching out her arms to pull him against her.

"I'm a fool in love," he answered as he kissed her, painting wet, mushy kisses against her forehead, eyelids, cheeks, nose and mouth.

"Where did you get that thing?"

"That's my secret," he said. "And I bought you a pair, too. They say, Angel's Chica. We can wear them together. You can put yours on now if you'd like."

Roshawn shook her head. She pushed her hands past the elastic of his briefs, easing them down over his hips. "What I would like," she said coyly, "is to get you out of yours. We can wear them together another time."

"I think we can do that," the man said with a wide grin, and then he gasped, loudly, as Roshawn stroked his manhood. "Oh, yes," he said, his voice dropping to a loud whisper, "I think this is much better for us to do."

The couple lay side by side, Angel's nude body curved around Roshawn's like a warm blanket. The sun was still shining brightly through the wall of windows into their bedroom. Although they both knew Israel had returned an hour or so earlier, neither had made any effort to move from the warmth and security they'd wrapped around themselves.

Roshawn pulled Angel's arm tighter around her waist, clasping his fingers between her own. She purred softly, arching her body like a lazy cat as she caressed him with her backside, her buttocks grinding gently against his crotch. She hummed in pleasure as Angel rested his palm over one breast gently caressing and teasing the orange-size mound of tissue.

He leaned to kiss her ear, gently brushing his lips along the line of her profile. Her body was so sensitive to his touch that with each stroke and every touch, she could feel herself wanting to scream out in pleasure, to succumb to the rise of heat growing within her. Angel could sense the depth of her desire, the wealth of it as large as his and so he continued to tease and play with her body, wanting her to feel as intensely as he did.

"Every time I make love to you I think it couldn't get any better and then we make love again and it is just so incredible," he said as he hugged her tightly, trying to meld every inch of his flesh to hers.

Roshawn smiled, her eyes closed as she allowed her breathing to fall into sync with his, the rise and fall of his

broad chest brushing against her back. In that very moment
she wouldn't remember ever feeling as complete, as whole,
as satisfied, or as content as she did right then wrapped in
Angel's arms.

"Have I told you lately how much I love you, Angel?"

The man smiled. "How much?"

"More than I could even begin to put into words."

"For always?"

"For ever and ever."

"We have so many things to plan, Roshawn."

"Like what?"

"Our wedding, the honeymoon, our babies…"

Roshawn chuckled. "You haven't even asked me to marry
you yet and you're talking about a honeymoon." She laughed
again, brushing the bottoms of her feet against the front of his
legs.

"You're right. I haven't done that yet, have I?"

"No, you haven't. All you have asked of me is if I would
have your son."

"But that was very important for a man to know."

"I'm sure it was."

"And I asked you to move in with me."

"No, you didn't. I just told you that I would be moving in
with you whether you liked it or not. I mean, if I'm planning
on giving birth to your son it seemed only right."

Angel nodded, kissing her cheek. "That's a good point."

"I usually make very good points."

"And I like that about you. I like that very much." He
paused as if in deep reflection, drumming his fingers against
her arm.

"Something you want to say," Roshawn asked, her tone
teasing.

"I was just thinking that we really should talk about that marriage thing, huh? We really can't have a honeymoon if we don't have a wedding first," he said with a smug grin across his face.

"We won't be having that baby until then, either."

"No?"

"No!"

"So, maybe you should ask me to marry you, Roshawn?" She laughed. "Or you could ask me."

"I could do that. That would probably be a good thing at some point."

"At some point," Roshawn answered.

Angel rolled above her, easing her on to her back. Leaning on his forearms he stared down at her, joy growing like wildfire over every inch of his expression. "Right now though," he said, his body pushing gently against her nakedness, "right now I think we should make love one more time."

Roshawn pressed her palms against his chest. "Really?"

He nodded. "We must practice making our babies so that when you ask me and I marry you, we'll know how to do it right." He pressed his mouth to her mouth, his lips teasing and caressing hers. Roshawn's voice caught in her throat as a rush of electricity fired through her body, setting an explosion off in each of her nerve endings.

"Practice is good," she finally muttered.

He nodded, his tongue dancing a slow glide from her mouth, down the length of her neck and toward the cleavage between her breasts. "Yes," he whispered, "practice is very good."

Chapter 23

The next morning Angel woke up on edge, nervous energy consuming his spirit. Roshawn noted his discomfort, commenting on it after the man had rushed out the door for the ballpark.

"*Papí,* what's bothering Angel?" she asked as the two sat enjoying their morning coffee.

The old man shook his head. "I don't think there is anything that is upsetting him. He is very happy. I'm sure he is just nervous about the game tonight."

"But he's been playing so well. Why should he be nervous?"

"His beautiful woman will be there and she has not been there in a long while. I'm sure he just wants to do well to impress you," the man said nonchalantly. Israel took another sip of his coffee. "You should not worry, *niña.* Angel is just fine."

Roshawn nodded, jumping to her feet as she finished the last drop of morning brew from the bottom of her cup. "I need to run," she said as she reached for her purse. "I want to stop by to get the rest of my things from Chen's house before I go into the office."

"Do you need help, *niña?*"

She shook her head. "No, there really isn't much there. Nothing I can't handle alone."

"Then I will see you later at the game, yes?"

"Of course. Would you like me to come pick you up, *Papí?*"

"No. I will get there fine," he said with a wide grin.

She pulled her fingers through his hair. "We need to give you a trim, *Papí.* I can cut it when we get home tonight."

The man flapped a hand in her direction. "Not to worry. I am sure you will be much too busy."

She smiled. "I'm never too busy for you, *Papí.*" Roshawn kissed his cheek goodbye then headed out the front door.

As soon as the car pulled out the driveway and disappeared out of sight, Israel picked up the telephone and dialed. "*Hijo,* she is gone to the office now."

On the other end, Angel grinned, winking at the four women who stood at his side. "*Gracias, Papí.* We will be ready. You know what you have to do."

Israel laughed with glee. "She will be very surprised. Very surprised indeed!"

Roshawn was starting to get annoyed. She had less than an hour until game time and Chen seemed intent on working her last nerve. As she printed the last spreadsheet of data that he'd insisted on having before they could leave for the day, she began to pack up her desk for the night. When he called her name for the umpteenth time, gesturing for her attention, it took everything in her not to go kicking and screaming to see what it was he wanted.

Chen was hanging up the telephone as she stepped into

his office, dropping the spreadsheet onto his desk. "You do realize what time it is, don't you, Chen?"

"I'm sorry, Roshawn. I know it's late but you never know when these things will come up."

Roshawn heaved a deep sigh. "Well, is there anything else that needs to be done before I leave?"

Chen paused, stammering slightly as he spoke. "Well…as a matter of fact…"

Roshawn rolled her eyes, her jaw tightening, as she bit down against her bottom lip.

"I…um…well…I need to ask you for a big favor, Roshawn." He eyed her tentatively. Roshawn dropped down to the leather seat, crossing her legs first and then her arms against her chest.

Chen continued. "That was our media and promotions person on the phone. You know how the organization plays games with fans before each game and how they get the kids and the parents involved with the team and Baxter the Bobcat during the seventh-inning stretch?"

She nodded, her expression indicating that she really wasn't interested.

"Well, they're shorthanded for tonight's game. They called to see if I knew anyone who'd be able to help and I immediately thought about you."

"For tonight's game?"

"Yes. It not much work. You'll be right down on the field and in the dugout so you can see Angel."

Her gaze was cautious. "I don't know, Chen…."

"Please, Roshawn. I need you this one time. Do it for me. But I need an right answer right now. If you'll do it then we need to get you over there."

Roshawn shrugged. "I guess so. And only because I'm going to be there anyway."

Chen grinned. "Great. I appreciate this. Let's go. We'll take my car and you can get yours later." He rose to his feet.

"I'll meet you at the elevators," she said, moving ahead of him. "I just need to run to the ladies' room."

"Thanks again, Roshawn. You're a lifesaver." He watched as she grabbed her belongings and headed out the office and down the hallway. Reaching for the telephone he dialed quickly and waited for it to be answered on the other end. "Hi, Ming. Tell Rios everything is right on schedule. Your mom and I are headed that way right now."

Minutes later Chen guided Roshawn through the security gates to the basement offices beneath the stadium. A heavyset man dressed in a pinstriped suit that was two sizes too small for him greeted them in the employee area. As he pumped her arm up and down, it was obvious that he was feeling stressed about something.

"Am I glad to meet you!" he exclaimed. "I can't tell you how much I appreciate your help, Ms. Bradsher. I'm Chuck, the promotions manager."

Roshawn smiled weakly. "Hi, Chuck. It's my pleasure. So, what do you need me to do?"

The man rushed to one of the employee lockers, pulling a brown fur animal suit and headpiece from the cabinet. As he held it up, Roshawn's eyes widened, her exasperated expression not lost on either man. She turned to face Chen who was smiling stupidly in her direction, his hands held up as if in surrender.

"I didn't know, I swear, Roshawn."

"It's only for a short while, Ms. Bradsher. You've seen our Baby Bobcat character before. The young lady who usually plays it is out with a sprained back and we can't find anyone else in the organization small enough to fit in the suit. You'd be perfect."

"I am not wearing that rat suit, Chen. I cannot believe…"

"I'll pay you, Roshawn. Do it for me," Chen said, his goofy smile still plastered across his face.

"How much?"

"Fifty dollars?"

She paused, cutting her eyes from the suit to him and back. "Make it a hundred."

"One hundred? Really, Roshawn…"

She turned and headed toward the door, glaring as she brushed past him.

"Okay! Okay! One hundred dollars."

The other man laughed. "For one hundred dollars I'd squeeze into it if I could."

At that moment, the Baxter character made his way into the room, the young man who donned the costume carrying the massive head in his hands. "Hi, there! Are you playing my baby sister tonight?" He extended a pawed hand. "I'm Jimmy. Jimmy Donovan."

Roshawn eyed the extended appendage, ignoring it as Jimmy dropped his arm back down to his side. She jabbed her tote bag into Chen's chest. "Here. Hold this," she said as she reached for the costume.

Both he and Jimmy continued to grin widely as she stepped into the outfit, adjusting it around her petite frame. Chuck rambled as she studied the headpiece, shaking her head in disbelief.

"All you have to do is jump around beside Jimmy here and wave. Lots of waving. Either myself or my assistant Karen will be with the two of you at all times. The heads are a little heavy and sometimes you get a kid or two who wants to tug on your tail and it'll be hard for you to turn around. We'll be there to fend them off."

Jimmy interjected. "It's really not the kids you have to worry about. The adults will give you more of a problem most times."

"Oh, great," Roshawn said, her tone devoid of any enthusiasm. "How long do I have to wear this thing?"

"Just until we're finished with the fan activities after the seventh inning. We'll run the bases once or twice and during the fourth and fifth innings we're in the Peter Piper Den taking photos with the kids."

She glared at Chen for a second time. "Seventh inning?"

He smiled and shrugged, inching his way slowly toward the door. "I'll be up top. You're going to do just fine, Roshawn. I can't believe what a great sport you are. I'll catch up with you later. *Wo ai ni!*" Chen waved and rushed out the door before she could fix her mouth to tell him exactly what she thought.

Jimmy laughed. "It really isn't so bad. We usually have a great time."

Roshawn cut an eye at him. "I just bet you do," she said facetiously.

Chuck smiled sweetly. "And just remember, Ms. Bradsher, we have only one rule that cannot be broken. You can never remove your head while you're in any of the public areas. It would traumatize the young kids to see Baby Bobcat beheaded. So you can only take the head off if you're in one of the closed employee areas. And don't ever, for any reason, speak. Wave, nod, shake your head, gesture with your hands, but no talking is allowed whatsoever."

Roshawn tossed him a wry smile. "Just great."

Ten minutes later, Roshawn the Baby Bobcat and her big

brother Baxter were both heading through the employee tunnel to the field. Chuck was trailing close behind them. As they stepped out onto the green grass, Baxter leading the way, Roshawn couldn't believe she was headed to the pitcher's mound dressed like a brown matted rodent. The crowd cheered and Chuck whispered behind her.

"Wave, Roshawn. Lots of waving. And jump. Baby Bobcat does a lot of jumping."

Laughter rang loudly from one of the luxury team suites on the upper concourse. Ming shook her head as the group gathered pointed in Roshawn's direction. "Mom's going to kill you all when she finds out," the young girl said.

Her aunt Bridget giggled. "She's going to kill you, too, Ming. You know she's going to be mad you didn't tell her."

Jeneva joined in, baby Alexa glued to her hip and clapping her hands excitedly. "I can just hear her now. She may not speak to any of us ever again."

Nina grinned. "I have to get plenty of pictures. This is absolutely priceless."

Ming moved to her father's side, Allison settled in the plush seat in front of him. "And I can't believe you, Daddy. I didn't know you could be so devious."

"Don't take this the wrong way, Ming. I'm only doing this as a favor to Angel to make your mother happy," he said as he wrapped an arm around her shoulders.

Bridget laughed. "Don't let your father fool you, baby girl. He and your mother use to get into a lot of trouble doing things they had no business doing, in places they had no business being. And it wasn't always your mother's idea."

Ming laughed as Chen blushed profusely, swatting a large hand at Bridget's head. "Don't you pay your aunt

Bridget any attention, Ming. She doesn't have a clue what she's talking about."

Jeneva laughed. "But I sure do," she said, passing Alexa into her father's arms.

Mac shook his head, moving to take a seat beside Israel. "Mr. Rios, these women are a wild bunch. We men are never safe when we're around them."

Israel smiled. "I'm going to like these women. I'm going to like them very much, I think."

Mac grinned as Jeneva, Bridget and Nina all moved to Israel's side to hug and kiss his cheeks.

Nina giggled. "You boys really need to take some pointers from a man with such good taste."

Back on the field Roshawn and Baxter were still dancing about. Angel stood watching from the dugout as Patrick moved to join him.

"She's going to kill you, you know."

Angel nodded, trying to stifle the laughter that threatened to spill over. "I know. But this makes us even for that hot-sauce trick. And look at her, she is having a good time."

Patrick laughed. "I bet when she gets out of that costume you're going to see just what a good time she was havin'. Just make sure she isn't too close to any of these bats. I'd sure hate to see you get hurt."

With minutes, till the start of the game, Roshawn was ecstatic when Chuck motioned for her to follow him off the field. Shaking the length of her bobcat tail one last time, Roshawn sprinted off the field, waving both hands as she disappeared from view. Back in the tunnel, Chuck congratulated her.

"Good job, Ms. Bradsher. You're a natural at this."

"It's kind of hot in this thing."

Jimmy chimed in. "It takes some getting used to. If you need a break though, just let us know."

She shrugged. "No, I'll be okay I guess. What now?"

"You'll just walk the stadium, stop at the food court to shake hands with the kids, just some fun stuff. Are you up to it?"

Roshawn nodded, the oversize mask blinding her view and then snapping her neck back. "I guess. Whatever it takes to get this over with."

Angel had gotten a home run his last hit and as the end of the seventh inning approached, a twinge of nervousness was settling in his midsection. The coach came to tap him on the back, the other players extending their congratulations and well wishes. As the Titans secured their last out, indicating the start of the short break, he broke out into a cold sweat. Patrick stood at his elbow, cheering words of encouragement as the team's mascots appeared back on the field and the stadium announcer sounded out over the PA system.

"For all you Titan fans we're only going to take a quick break for some brief announcements. If you need to take a break, the food and beverages are flowing from out food stands and we're sure there is something there for everybody.

"Now it's time for our seventh inning Race the Bobcat game and this time we've got some special visitors with us who think they can beat that bobcat around the bases. Come on out, gang!"

Roshawn heaved a deep sigh as Chuck continued to chorus like a broken record behind her. "Wave, baby. That's it. Jump, jump, jump! Give 'em another wave!" He leaned in close to her. "Okay, you get the first lap. They'll bring a few kids on the field, Baxter will help them bat a ball one of the players will pitch and then when the kid takes off running, you just pretend to run after them. Of course, you'll let them win. Any questions?"

Behind the mask, Roshawn rolled her eyes. "No, Chuck. I think I can handle this."

"That a girl!" he chimed cheerily, before adding, "and remember, no talking!"

She turned as the lucky fans stepped past the dugout security who guided them out onto the field. Inside her mask her mouth fell open as Jeneva stepped toward them, baby Alexa toddling at her side as Jeneva's son Quincy trailed behind them. Two other youngsters also raced onto the field excitedly.

Roshawn was ready to bust as Chuck set them all in position. A boy named Tyler and his twin sister Kim got to go first. Roshawn couldn't even begin to wrap her mind around what was going on as she trotted slowly behind Kim first and then Tyler. Before she realized it, Baxter had helped Alexa take her swing and she and her big brother were both circling second base toward third. Roshawn trotted behind them, pretending to fall to the ground from exhaustion as the two kids touched home plate. Quincy held his sister protectively as Alexa laughed and clapped with glee.

Roshawn eased her way to Jeneva's side and whispered loudly. "What are you doing here?"

Her friend chuckled. "Shhh. You're not supposed to talk. Don't scare my baby."

The announcer continued to incite the crowd with his banter and cheers and laughter rang around the stadium. "Are you ready for our next game!" he shouted. "Let's play Bounce the Bobcat!" he said and Roshawn groaned loudly.

Jeneva and her family were escorted to the sideline and

when Roshawn glanced over to them, Angel was standing by their side, his arms crossed over his chest, and a Cheshire-cat grin spread across his face.

The next game involved the participants donning padded bubble suits to do battle with the bobcat mascot Sumo wrestler style. As Bridget slowly made her way to the cushioned mat, the padded suit impeding her gait, Roshawn knew that she had been had and had good. Angel had gotten the best of her right under her nose and she hadn't been able to decipher one clue that could have forewarned her. Over on the sideline, Nina, Mac and Israel had joined the others.

"Okay," Chuck called. "We just do this to give the kids a laugh. Pretend to wrestle. Let the fan toss you off the mat and then you're finished. And remember, no talking!"

Roshawn nodded as she and Bridget stepped to opposite sides of the large circled area that had been marked out for them. She shook her bobcat finger at her friend, her head waving from side to side. Bridget laughed.

"Come and get me, baby. Think you know everything, heifer. Not!"

Ten minutes later, the game was over and as Roshawn moved to follow behind Bridget toward her family, Chuck grabbed her arm.

"I'm sorry, Ms. Bradsher. We have one more thing you have to do." He pointed to the pitcher's mound as Baxter spun her back in the other direction, guiding her by the hand to stand midfield. The announcer's voice pulled at her attention.

"Ladies and gentlemen, if I can direct your attention to the activity on the field and the screens, please. We have one last event before we resume play and we hope you'll all join us in a special celebration." An image of them standing there flashed full-screen across the Jumbotron.

Roshawn watched as Baxter pointed toward the largest screen directly behind them, a digital message slowly evolving over the surface.

Tears swelled in Roshawn's eyes as she read the words posted for the whole world to see. ANGEL RIOS LOVES ROSHAWN BRADSHER. BABY BOBCAT, WILL YOU MARRY ME?

Without her realizing it Angel had made his way to her side and he tapped her lightly on the shoulder. Spinning around she watched as he dropped on one knee, a large diamond ring extended in his hand. She tossed a quick glance back to the sidelines where Ming, Dix, Chen and Allison had joined the rest of them.

Angel laughed. "See, I can be devilish, too, beautiful lady."

Roshawn couldn't help but laugh with him.

Angel suddenly turned serious. "I would never have imagined falling so deeply in love with any woman as I have fallen with you, Roshawn. You have become my entire world. I cannot imagine myself waking up or falling asleep without you by my side. I never knew that it was possible to have someone love me as much as you have shown me your love. I don't ever want to lose that or you. Will you marry me, Roshawn, and be the mother of my children? Will you let me love you always? *Por favor?*"

Laughing and crying, Roshawn nodded her head, the bobcat headpiece waving up and down, and the entire stadium erupted in a loud cheer. Angel jumped to his feet and hugged her, wrapping his arms around her and the costume, and beside them, Baxter clasped both paws above his head, waving them in victory. Fireworks flashed across the screen and "Here Comes The Bride" was playing loudly over the speakers as their friends and family cheered in celebration.

Minutes later, Roshawn stood room center sans the bobcat suit. Angel kissed her, his mouth like velvet against hers. "I love you so much," he said as he gave a quick hug.

Roshawn nodded, the sweet lift of her smile all the response he needed, love shimmering flecks of light and gold from her eyes. "You need to get back," she said, gesturing toward the dugout below. "They're about to get the game started again."

With his arms still around her he turned to their friends and family. "Thank you, all," he said softly. "I couldn't have done this without you."

Israel nodded his agreement, Ming hugging him with one arm as she hugged Dixon with the other. As they watched Angel sprint back out to the game, Jeneva and Bridget moved to Roshawn's side to give her a deep embrace. Jeneva wiped at the tears that filled her friend's eyes.

"You guys do know I'm going to have to get you for this, don't you?"

Bridget giggled. "We love you too, heifer."

Jeneva nodded, her gaze resting on each face in the room. "You know, girls, I really like how our little family is growing."

At that moment a rush of noise filtered loudly from the stands below. They all turned to see Angel as he stepped out one last time, waving as his fans cheered their well wishes. He stopped to blow one last kiss in Roshawn's direction before disappearing into the dugout. The announcer's voice rang out over the intercom. "Wasn't that just spectacular, folks? I think we've got us some love in the lineup, all you Titans fans! Let's give Angel Rios another round of applause, why don't you!" The crowd cheered once again as the announcer continued. "Congratulations, slugger, now that's what we call a real grand-slam hit. Okay, Tucson, let's play us some baseball!"

Dear Reader,

Once again, I am thrilled to tell you how much I've enjoyed doing this and how truly blessed I feel to have been shown so much love and support. Your expressions of encouragement and praise have been a resounding source of inspiration and there aren't enough words to tell you what that has meant to me.

Love in the Lineup was truly a fun and engaging story to write. I wanted to make you smile and laugh and feel good when reading it, so I pray that you enjoy the experience as much as I did. I hope that I've left you satisfied, and nourished by the adventure, and feeling that true love is a possibility for us all.

Again, thank you so much for your support, and please, visit me at my Web site and continue to send me your comments.

With much love,

Deborah Fletcher Mello
www.deborahmello.com

FORGED OF STEELE

The sizzling miniseries from
USA TODAY bestselling author

BRENDA JACKSON

*Sebastian Steele's takeover of
Erin Mason's fledgling company
topples when Erin takes over
Sebastian's heart*

NIGHT HEAT

AVAILABLE SEPTEMBER 2006
FROM KIMANI™ ROMANCE

Love's Ultimate Destination

AVAILABLE JANUARY 2007
BEYOND TEMPTATION

Available at your favorite retail outlet.

Visit Kimani Romance at www.kimanipress.com.

KRBJNH

Leila Owens didn't know
how to love herself let alone
an abandoned baby
but Garret Grayson knew
how to love them both.

She's My Baby

Adrianne Byrd

(Kimani Romance #10)

AVAILABLE SEPTEMBER 2006

FROM KIMANI™ ROMANCE

Love's Ultimate Destination

Available at your favorite retail outlet.

Visit Kimani Romance at www.kimanipress.com.

KRABSMB

Single mom Haley Sanders's
heart was DOA.

Only the gorgeous
Dr. Pierce Masterson could
bring it back to life.

Sweet Surrender

Michelle Monkou

(Kimani Romance #11)

AVAILABLE SEPTEMBER 2006
FROM KIMANI™ ROMANCE

Love's Ultimate Destination

Available at your favorite retail outlet.

Visit Kimani Romance at www.kimanipress.com.

KRMMSS

He found *trouble* in paradise.

Mason Sinclair's visit to Barbados
was supposed to be about uncovering
family mysteries not the mysteries of
Lianne Thomas's heart.

EMBRACING
THE MOONLIGHT
(Kimani Romance #12)

Wayne Jordan

AVAILABLE SEPTEMBER 2006
FROM KIMANI™ ROMANCE
Love's Ultimate Destination

Available at your favorite retail outlet.

Visit Kimani Romance at www.kimanipress.com.

KRWJETM